Stench

Mike Johnson

Stench

Press

Published by 99% Press,
an imprint of Lasavia Publishing Ltd.
Auckland, New Zealand
www.lasaviapublishing.com

Copyright © Mike Johnson, 2021
Cover design © Jennifer Rackham, 2021

This book is copyright. Apart from any fair dealing for the purpose of private study, research, criticism or reviews, as permitted under the Copyright Act, no part may be reproduced by any process without the permission of the publishers.

ISBN: 978-1-99-115192-6

For Zoe Penhaligan, without whom this story would not have been completed; Paul Mountfort, for the title; Carol Shortis, for manuscript reading and feedback; Phillip Mann, for his enthusiasm; Anna Rogers for her dedication and care and my wonderful family for their love and forebearance.

Contents

Foreword	9
Trapdoor	11
Rachel	35
Crowbar	63
Mitch	95
Prisoner	127
Mask	147
Baby	165
Hikitarua	191

Foreword

Mike Johnson's *Stench* is definitively located in genre: it is a teen-flick horror movie set in small town New Zealand with an implicit acknowledgement of the works of Ronald Hugh Morrieson, although Johnson's Hikitarua is somewhere on the Canterbury Plains, not in the North Island. There is another, crucial difference: the horror in Hikitarua is metaphysical, not, as in Morrieson's fictions, a consequence of scandalous human misbehaviour. A group of bored teenagers in a summer irritated by incessant nor-westerlies breaks into an old hospital and prises open a trapdoor from which the malodorous stench of the title emanates – with catastrophic results.

Cinematic as the book is, it would nevertheless be difficult if not impossible to film, simply because the central mystery, the malignity lurking inside the trapdoor, is expressed odoriferously, not visually. There have been experiments with odorama, so called, in the cinema; but I doubt that anyone would want to release this stench from their scratch-cards, even (or especially) in the dark.

Stench's narrative invention, like that of Tarzan Presley, is what carries the book. The grisly tale is told by Baby, a big lunk of a girl who is, everyone assumes, intellectually disabled. She is in the special class at school, has trouble with language – her sentences, primitive as they are, tend to come out in reverse word order – and lives partly in a fantasy world. She is, perhaps, a kind of autiste; given a privileged view of what her mind is like, we quickly realise she has a degree of psychological insight denied the normals she moves among. Not that these normals are particularly normal. Like a degenerate Famous Five, without Timmy the dog, they are bent in various ways by their histories, their desires and most of all by their hopeless vulnerability both to each other and to the evil force abroad in the hospital. Because Baby lives half in a shadow world already, she can see the dysfunction of her brother and his friends as well as the shapeless malevolence living in the trapdoor – if living is the right word.

Stench is conventionally plotted and resolved: not a criticism, since genre requires in the main that you keep to the rules. Its innovations – the olfactory monster, the autistic narrator – are sufficient to keep our interest; and the insights of Baby into the behaviour and misbehaviour of her friends, along with her observation of others in the town, including her parents, teachers at the school and the local cops, are the matter of the book. She accurately and wittily describes the progress of the shared delusion of her cohorts, and especially her older brother Adrian, in a way that will massage the fears, and possibly increase the insight, of parents of teenagers everywhere. The gruesome horror of the ending, with its vision of a hell in which the buried secrets of the town exact awful retribution upon its somnolent residents, is followed, after the escape and rescue of the heroine, by a sinister twist in the very last word of the book: a consummate performance.

Martin Edmond, originally written as a review for *The New Zealand Review of Books*, 2004

Trapdoor

After they closed down the hospital, before selling it off to the bulldozers, a few of us broke in at night through a loose window at the back and ran around the corridors in the dim light playing ghosts and dead people.

That part was fun.

It was what came afterwards that changed everything.

Josie was the first to notice the hospital. We'd been past it a thousand times but never seen it. We weren't really coming from anywhere or going anywhere, just hanging out somewhere in between. You can do a lot of that in Hikitarua where there's nowhere to come from or go to but the usual old places like school and the milk bar or the service station where the big tankers pull in.

The hospital, its front yard covered in weeds, its main door nailed shut, wasn't worth looking at and didn't invite you to stare. Someone had shut up its face and that made you look the other way.

Josie had been glancing over her shoulder to see if her brother Maro was following and was looking for a way of giving him the slip. The hospital driveway offered a short cut through to the back street. We'd been idling along, not doing much, except Adrian trying to shoulder Josie off the footpath and Josie looking out all the time for Maro. Carpenter trudged along behind them and I followed behind him.

There was nothing special about the day. The nor-west arch was already hard glazed in the late afternoon sky; everything that was dry waited for night, and a touch of cool. There was the faint aftertaste of petrol in the air and I knew that one of the big tankers must be refueling in the station upwind of us. They came at night when there wasn't too much through traffic around.

Josie skipped ahead and led the way down the side of the hospital, deep in the shadow of the fence that paralleled it. She expected everyone to follow, which we did, Adrian close behind eager not to be upstaged.

As I left the street for the shade of the driveway I thought I caught a glimpse of someone following us, too small or too quick to let me get a good look. I didn't pick Maro as our mysterious tail because it was hard for him not to be big, clumsy and upfront.

Once she got near the end of the building, Josie stopped, turned and looked at the place. Not much of building, just long and two-storeyed with a roof painted rust red and plastered green walls. There were rusting grills over the upstairs windows.

'Let's take a closer look,' she said.

Adrian immediately adopted a pose of anticipated boredom. This was clever of him, for Josie often did the same thing. On the other hand, everybody in Hikitarua anticipates boredom most of the time and we're not often disappointed.

It was Carpenter, who loved poking into things, who found the window. He crept down the side of the building, testing the latches as he went, peering through the glass to the dusty darkness inside. Doors and windows were either locked or boarded-up, giving the building a blank-faced appearance, like someone trying to look out through closed eyelids.

'Who'd want t' lock up a silly old building like this anyway?' Josie said, as if she wasn't the least bit interested any more, but her eyes were roving all over the hospital, testing it against some idea that had hatched in her brain. Her thin, vulnerable face looked suddenly brave and cunning.

For myself, I didn't like the look of the place, and I wished that Rachel were with us. I felt safer with Rachel around; she didn't change all the time like Josie, and didn't seemed to care that I was the big little moron of the gang, Adrian's despised sister and the youngest at fourteen. Rachel understood feelings without having to be told, deep and silent, whereas Josie's brain was too busy buzzing to notice them. Josie loved to talk; she hated silence; the moment there was a space to think in, she'd be filling it up with verbal candy-floss.

'It's just a stupid old broken-down empty hospital,' she said, peering intently into the windows. 'Nobody comes here, that's the thing. I was probably born here. Bugger that.'

Ignoring her clatter, I put my ear to the wall and listened. It felt as if the building had nothing inside, no walls, no floor, no ceiling, just a big empty Nothing. No sound came from within, and that was strange. Every place, every building, every shaped thing, had its spirit and every spirit had its voice. The dawn chorus of spirits could be deafening. Even the petrol pump down at the Hikitarua service station had a cranky old throat that complained every time it was put into operation. I'd heard our Formica table at home hold a single dull note forever, and the roses in Mrs. Inna's garden sounded deep gongs. Her dog, Softy the rottweiler, could hear them too because he barked at them. Our revolving washing line cried out for its ancestors when it was swung about.

This building had no voice, no song, and that was impossible.

I wanted to say something but didn't want to face the same old wall of sneers and jeers from dear brother Adrian, who never let me forget that I was there on sufferance, his sufferance, and if I didn't keep in line, he wouldn't let me tag along. He'd shut me out of everything. I'd be cut off from everybody, even Rachel.

I talk backwards when I talk to Adrian because my nervous tongue moves the wrong way. If Rachel were here, I thought, she'd back me up; even against Josie she can say the words that stumble on my tongue as if she were reading them off the top of my mind.

In the meantime Carpenter found what he was looking for around the back, which was handy because no one could see from the street.

A window in a glove of shadow. A little unimportant window in the shade of a back porch, hardly worthy of notice. The latch was broken and a covering board was loose, as if someone had got tired of the job of nailing it up. You could tell it was loose because that covering board was hanging at an angle, making an arrow, pointing towards the broken latch like a signal.

It was an easy matter of tugging it free, but Carpenter stepped back from that. Having brought us this far, he would take us no further. He'd let someone else make the decision to break in, but he kept looking at the window and looking back to Adrian with clear expectation. Carpenter was game so long as everyone else was game first.

'Let's see if we can get in,' Josie said.

'They call it breaking and entering,' Carpenter announced. He didn't talk so much as spout off. He was getting nervous all of a sudden. He was in dread fear of getting involved with the police, and what his father would say if he found out.

At this point Adrian got interested. Here was a chance to prove to Josie how cool he was, and what a hero he could be. When Carpenter mentioned breaking and entering Adrian snorted as if he knew all about that sort of stuff. No sweat. All in a night's work.

'You can be sent to prison for that,' Carpenter said. 'Well, you would but I wouldn't because I'm still fifteen.' Carpenter didn't want to get to sixteen; then he'd have to face going to prison, or having sex.

By way of an answer, Adrian spat into his palms and looked across at Josie to see if she were watching. There was no point in being a hero if the right person wasn't watching.

Josie didn't care either way. She was bored and would have gone home if she didn't think Maro might be waiting for her there. She gave the impression that she was hanging out with us because she had nothing better to do, nowhere better to go.

'I wish Rachel hadn't gone away,' she said mournfully, as if Rachel was the be all and end all of everything. She made it sound as though Rachel had gone away forever, not just a day. She liked to have someone other than Adrian to boss around, but I liked Rachel because she was kind to me, and listened. Sometimes she knew things other people didn't know, or could do things other people couldn't do, and Josie didn't realize that. She thought that Rachel was all meek and mild and didn't see her other side. At the same time it was hard for me to hear my own feelings coming from Josie's lips.

'Me and da boyz are gunna do some bashin.' Adrian said, stepping into the role of his Warhammer miniatures hero, Orc Commander Gorebag Ironclaw. Once he started doing it he could keep it up for hours: the simple brutality of the Orcs was an endless source of amusement and admiration for him.

With a muscular tug Gorebag pulled the board free. The window, its glass broken and jagged, swung open of its own accord as if we were being invited in, and let out a black breath.

Carpenter again hung back. He was happy to let Adrian take the lead again. He would scurry hard behind.

The four of us looked at the open window.

We were like expectant moths looking at a dark flame. The evening was hot and sweet with exhaustion, the way it feels at the end of a day of nor-west winds. A fattened moon stood on its end with a star on top; the sky behind still had a faint glaze, as if it had just come out of the kiln.

Everything looked ordinary and commonplace. This was Hikitarua, our home town. We knew the shape of the sky and the taste of the air. We knew the way the houses sat on their lawns and the pine trees bordered the playing fields of the domain. Nothing could happen here but heat in the air and the intermittent arrival of petrol trucks. People lived and died and when they were sick they went to hospital, except now there was no hospital.

'It's only a dull old empty building,' Josie said. And when she said it you could see it that way. Just a boring old two-storeyed building, deserted shadows and emptiness; the open window was a black hole gaping at us like a missing tooth.

A sweet decaying taste filtered out.

I tasted it before I smelled it. It made me want to spit, so I spat. I didn't have a word for it.

'Don't be a pig,' Adrian said to me, in his version of being my big brother and being responsible for me, his idea of a good time at my expense.

'P'raps we'll find something interesting,' Carpenter said. 'Like test tubes or petri dishes.' He put on a superior look because he figured none of us would remember what a petri dish was. I grinned but I tried to hide it because I always grinned at the wrong places, and that made me look like the idiot they all thought I was. Except Adrian. He knew about me. He was never fooled by all that stuff about me being in a special class at the high school. He was envious. He saw it as a way I had devised of getting out of doing a whole lot of senseless toil, but he didn't see further than that.

'Yeah!' Adrian said to Carpenter's suggestion in his tough voice, as if there was someone around to beat up. He couldn't let the opportunity to show off in front of Josie go by. His love for her made him hurt; her power over him made him furious. That's why he was in hero mode, approaching the gaping window with a swagger. Gorebag Ironclaw rides again. The last we saw of him were his feet, kicking as they disappeared into the black hole; I didn't check to see whether Josie was impressed: I was trying to see what had swallowed up my brother.

Carpenter followed hard behind.

I was next because I'd rather be with Adrian than alone with Josie. I didn't like it when she got all unpredictable, and not having an audience didn't bother her, not when it came to being nasty to people.

In this case she was nice. She looked all small and lonely in front of the dark window. Her eyes had grown huge in her head, like a child looking at something she will never forget. She was dressed in jeans shorts, a white blouse and a thin linen jacket. She looked like Raggedy Anne who'd forgotten to get dressed properly in the morning. Although she was fifteen she could look ten. Rachel always seemed so much more mature than Josie, although only a year older. Rachel could handle herself with poise, like a woman - Josie could never manage that.

'This would be a perfect place to hide.' Josie said, biting the ends of her hair. Her voice lowered to a whisper, 'Hurry up, I want to make sure that Maro doesn't see us. He's a cunning bastard.'

I clambered through into a new kind of darkness. Not the sharp kind full of star shadows, but an impenetrable murk. I could hardly make out the bunched forms of Adrian and Carpenter before me, huddling in the memory of light from the window.

Josie made us wait for a few minutes before she came through. Carpenter wanted to press on and explore but Adrian wouldn't leave until Josie had come through.

We coughed and breathed and breathed and coughed; there was lot of dust and dead stuff in the air.

Josie came through cursing that her shorts would get smudged because she likes to have them massively clean, but her eyes were glowing with secret pleasure.

·

The first thing I noticed was the smell of sickness in the air, like something rotting, and the slimy feel of it on the walls, but nobody said anything. Already I'd tried to spit it out. If you could touch that smell it would be wet and sticky; if you could taste it you'd puke. I guess you'd expect a hospital to have such a stink hiding behind all the other smells, the antiseptic and the floor cleaner, rubber and peeling lino. Yet I was uneasy because I couldn't put my finger on what it was, couldn't say it smelled of this or that or the other. And I didn't like it. All the hairs on my arm and the back of neck stood up and my breasts shrank. I peered around, helpless, into what had once been a storeroom. There was the lingering mustiness of old cardboard and paper, but it wasn't that.

'Are you alright, Baby?' Adrian said. He was always afraid I'd get scared, and he always forgot how I hated being called Baby. Also I knew he was only asking me now because he was a bit scared himself.

There was a buzzing in my ears. I looked behind me and saw a mason fly trapped on the glass window, its wings trembling with dust and death.

'Right I'm all,' I said, getting my words muddled as usual. They mixed up with the darkness before me. I can usually get out little phrases like this no trouble; it's only when I come to link up longer ideas that I run into more difficulty with my throat.

'Of course you're all right,' he said, not looking at me.

'Right I'm all,' Josie mimicked, making a big deal out of my high, baby voice. 'How come you're so stupid, Baby?' At the same time she was looking at Adrian. What was the use of firing an arrow if it landed only on me? There was something fixed, almost feverish, in the way her eyes fastened onto him.

'Bugger off,' I said, which is as much as I could manage with a tongue that couldn't keep track of the shape of my thoughts.

'Leave her alone,' Adrian said to Josie, his voice full of tension. I couldn't understand where the tension came from until I had a good look at his face, in the half gloom, staring about wide-eyed. Like being deep inside a cave, it put pressure on him, made him want to sweat.

It was the smell that did it. Pervasive, insidious, this odour was haunted by deep time, deeper than disinfectant and cockroaches. It went right to the back of your nose. We were all very quiet. The place seemed to be waiting for a sound it could echo, or turn a little echo into a massive one. My arms went all prickly with goosebumps when I thought I saw a human figure lying in the doorway to the next room. There was the upraised lump of the chest and one outflung arm. Then I saw it was just the way the shadow from the door jamb and the soft light from the window lay together.

Josie giggled and I wondered it she'd seen it too.

Adrian was encouraged by her giggle. A silly little laugh that made him weak in the knees and absurdly proud all at the same time. 'Me an' da ladz are gunna do some bashin,' he said, and headed off towards the doorway. Josie giggled compliantly and Gorebag Ironclaw giggled too. It was a letdown but he couldn't help it; he was too hyped up with nervous energy, just like she was, to keep up a stone-faced Ironclaw cool.

With our fearless leader in front, we eased from the storeroom into the next room, which, by the look of it, had once been a kitchen. The bench was still in with the old sinks which nobody had bothered to remove, about eight of them. There was a hole where a stove had been ripped out. Carpenter told us that, pointing out where the gas pipes still came up the wall, crucial evidence.

We spoke in hushed whispers as if someone were sleeping in the next room. We soon got tired of the gas pipes and the sinks with locked cupboards beneath, and moved on into the main corridor.

I didn't like the corridor. It was too wide and long and had too many doors leading off it. Some were closed and some open just far enough to admit a slice of misleading light. At the very end there was a bigger door, some wooden triangles and a window with a red pane of glass in it, like a single bloodied eye.

The doors led to empty wards, and we started by moving from ward to ward, seeing what we could find, talking in quiet voices about what might have happened to all the sick people and the dead people and the babies. Especially the babies - a hospital always has plenty of babies, not just old people with tubes coming out of their noses. Josie harped on and on about the dead people and the babies.

Carpenter, who likes to be sensible, said the sick people had been moved to a bigger hospital further away where they could get looked after better, with more scientific facilities. He'd seen it on TV: grateful patients with brave looks on their faces being rolled on trolleys into bigger hospitals. One, a man with a sick heart, had given the thumbs up sign to the camera.

To annoy Carpenter probably, Josie said, 'They buried all the dead people and babies under the floor-boards, t' get rid of them. T' shut them up.' She flicked her lank blonde hair off her face the way she thought made her look cool.

'That's just stupid,' Carpenter said. He'd heard a lot of stupid things from Josie's mouth. Just crazy nonsense and babble that she'd come out with once she got started.

'That's all they ever want to do, isn't it? Shut them up, slap their faces, fuck them up one way or the other. They don't know about the revenge. The dead people and the dead babies are planning a big revenge…aren't they, Baby? See, Baby knows! Baby knows what's coming.'

'She doesn't know what you're talking about,' Carpenter said, silly enough to take her seriously. He looked up towards the far door, the main entrance. We all looked up there, but none of us made any move, just as none of us were saying what was really on our minds.

It's too late already, I thought. Whatever it is, we are inside of it somehow, and we're not talking about what's happening to us because our voices are getting lost inside ourselves.

Josie was still going, 'I don't want to be sick. I'll never be sick as long as I live. I'll kill myself first. I'll never end up in a place like this, puking my guts out.'

'How come? Everybody gets sick eventually.' Carpenter said this as somberly as if it were the highest truth you could find anywhere. 'Even the Universe is going to run out of energy. The science teacher told us that. So how come you're never going t' get sick?'

Josie wasn't saying. She just smiled her tomboy smile. It wasn't aimed at Carpenter, though. The real target was Adrian, too cool to be seen to notice it, of course, or her demonstration of how easily she could deal with a worm like Carpenter, the little kid who always asked why and never knew when to stop. Carpenter didn't get many brilliant smiles like that because he had a fat round face and fat round glasses sitting on fat round nostrils. When he had a problem it looked like he was thinking through his nose. Mum said he had a face only a mother could love. I've never asked her how she knew that.

Adrian had hair long and dark to suit his moods, and made sure he wore some strands of it over the front of his face the way the geeks did in the magazines Josie looked at. His face might be thin and bony, but it was handsome, and his dark eyes looked through you to the other side. He could do that to me, his sister, so I guess he could do it to Josie. Only Carpenter was immune; to him, things like that were water off a duck's back.

'They wouldn't put anyone under the floorboards,' Carpenter said in his don't-be-silly voice, which was the only way he had of getting back at her for the smile he couldn't have. But the idea had caught hold of her. She wanted to promote it in the face of Carpenter's stubborn common sense. It was a way of getting back at him, and Adrian too.

'How would you know?' she said.

Carpenter looked like it would be too tiresome to try to tell her, so he hid behind his glasses and pretended to be thinking about something else.

'The sick people went home,' Adrian said, to settle the matter. 'I saw it on TV. That old lady in the wheelchair went to live with her daughter.' He was talking about Mrs Horton who was paralysed down one side.

I had to say something so I marshalled my thoughts and desperately lined up the words. The dead people went to heaven. That's all I wanted to tell them. The first three words came out in a rush. 'The dead people...' Then all I could think of was heaven and so I said it, with the last two words following foolishly out of place behind. '...heaven went to.'

'Who went where?' Adrian said, quick to cash in on my stumble tongue.

Everybody laughed. They couldn't see what I saw and I couldn't explain. It was the smell. It reminded me of roses after rain. It had a purple and red heart. It glowed inside when people died. It had no pain. Nobody would believe me anyway, because I was a retard, they thought. Josie didn't want me tagging along, I'd heard her say it outright to Adrian one time after school: 'Why don't you leave her at home? The fat retard.'

There are some words you can't escape.

Carpenter kept going as if I had never said anything. Adrian was right, he said, and why should people stay at hospital when they could go home? He cited Mrs Carson's mother, who'd broken her hip. His mum said that Mrs Carson was staying at home to look after her crippled mother, and couldn't go out to work.

I knew this was true, I heard Mum say. Lots of sick people did go home when they closed the hospital. I didn't say too much of this to the others; sometimes it suits me to have them think that I'm a bit of a dill-berry.

Adrian lost interest in the conversation. In fact while Carpenter was going on about Mrs Carson, he disappeared. Josie gave a short screech and Carpenter shut up straight away. There was an awkward, desperate little silence among the three of us as we looked around for him.

'No silly tricks now, Adrian.' Josie said nervously.

There was a cry from one of the rooms and we all rushed in that direction. Adrian had found the women's toilets, and on the wall, where once a wash basin had stood, was a dirty old mirror that no one had bothered to salvage. Adrian was staring at the mirror, at his own stricken face.

'What's the matter?' Josie clutched at his arm, ready to scream.

'Why should anything be the matter?' Adrian was all surliness.

'Because you yelled out.'

'No I didn't.' He said it in such a blatant way I knew he was lying. He did that sometimes when he couldn't think of any other way out: lied to your face when you'd just heard or seen him do something.

Josie knew about him too. 'You're full of shit. Grade A shit.' But the mirror had taken her fancy. She flounced up to it and pretended to powder her face. 'This is what Margot does, that's Dad's girlfriend, and she gets some perfume and lifts her neck up like a hen having a drink and dabs the perfume on right here, in this little soft part of the throat...' As she talked she turned her head about, first one way, then the other, following herself with her eyes.

'Let's get out of here,' said Adrian. 'It stinks of shit.' He was sweating hard and I wondered why. Something had just scared the hell out of him.

Carpenter was already making hastily for the door. Being in the women's made him uncomfortable; you'd have thought someone was going to tell him off or give him a detention or something.

In front of the mirror, Josie began waving her arms and talking about dead people again. Crazy, dirty talk with the mirror. 'I wish Maro was dead, then we could bring him here so he could be with the other dead people. There's always dead people at hospitals. They have a special room for them to be dead in called a mortuary. I've just remembered that word. When you're ready to be dead you go in there and they shut the door.'

She pulled a horrible face at herself.

Adrian grabbed her and pulled her towards the door. As soon as he touched her she went rigid. 'Get your hands off me!' she screeched.

Her voice burned and I had to cover my ears. As I did so, I saw myself in the mirror, hands over my head like big ear-muffs, eyes staring. There was a woolly, thunderous silence.

Then I saw the other face. It was right beside mine, only inches away, sharing my mirror space, staring at itself. Its features shifted and merged from one form to another - dog face, cat face, human face, alien face - in a frantic, headlong search for itself. Only its eyes remained the same, sheer and unwavering.

I took my hands away from my ears and the sounds of the others retreating came as if from far away. The face disappeared.

I rejoined the others in time to catch Josie's scream.

⸰

It was a real scream, not a giggly pretend one. It came from the back of her throat as the air rushed out of her lungs. She was kneeling on the strip of lino that ran to the front door, looking wildly around, chest heaving.

'I saw someone.' She pointed to the doorway of the ward opposite the women's. 'Someone looking at me.' A shape with the light behind it looming at the door, perhaps. None of us could see it. I saw a chip of moonlight glowing where a person's eye might be. I saw shadows lying quietly without pretence across the door jamb.

'If he's one of the dead people,' Adrian said sincerely, 'I'll piss right in his face.'

This boast made us all laugh. Except Josie who was shaking all over. 'Don't joke about it,' she said, pulling at her blonde hair as if she were swinging on church bell ropes. Shakily, she got to her feet.

Carpenter didn't hear her. He was busy trying to match Adrian's cool. 'And make them eat their own shit,' he said enthusiastically. The dead held no terrors for him.

Adrian was contemptuous of this. 'You can't make the dead do anything,' he said. He needed dead people around to prove how brave he was, and Josie needed them around to prove how scared she was. Already, she was moving closer to Adrian while he carried on as if he could front up to a whole cemetery of dead people for her sake.

To prove just how brave he really was, Adrian strode over to the door Josie was staring at and disappeared with great casualness into the ward beyond. All of us held our breath. A moment later the dead person came out and stood in the doorway, just like Josie said, except it wasn't a dead person, it was Adrian. Josie didn't scream this time but stared at him. There was terror on her face and something harder to work out that was twisting the corners of her mouth upward into a smile or a snarl, I couldn't tell the difference.

'I want your blooood,' Adrian said in a deep, husky voice.

Josie stared at the shadow with revolted fascination.

'It's only Adrian,' Carpenter said, as if none of us knew.

'Don't be stupid, Adrian,' That was Josie, trying hard to sound as if she knew what was going on.

Adrian laughed mockingly. He was sixteen going on nineteen, and could make his voice all deep and strange. He liked to pretend he was not himself. Now I thought of that face in the mirror; was it struggling to be Adrian's face?

'Don't do that, Adrian,' Josie said. She spoke severely, as if she were older, not a whole year younger than him.

None of this jabber and boasting sounded real to me. I heard voices, but they returned as echoes, sounds filling up the air. Something moved around us, through us, hollowing out our voices, emptying out our meanings. We could smell it but we didn't know what it was. It could listen to us and suck the meaning out of everything we said. Words were husks our mouths threw away. I was glad I had trouble talking because I didn't have to try.

We didn't know what it was or why, but standing in the hall among doors I got my goosebumps back. I kept thinking of old people with tubes up their noses, machines feeding smells into them. Horrible smells. Smells that had been scraped off the walls. And I caught the smell again; it left damp tracks across my skin. The ghost of a snail.

All of us felt it, it froze everything, it made the hospital seem like a big cathedral with shadows trailing off into a criss-cross of corners.

And the Adrian shadow in the doorway never moved.

Josie fell to her knees. She was reduced to craven blubbering. 'If you don't stop that, Adrian, I'll hate you for the rest of my life, I really will. I'll hate and hate and hate. You don't understand anything.'

At that moment, a dreary drone started up. It was the Hikitarua fire alarm. It started low and drew itself up into a single relentless, flat note. Volunteer firemen would be tumbling out of bed and heading for the town's red fire engine. I had a sudden yearning to know where the fire was and to see the leaping flames.

Carpenter tried to be sensible, and talked as the fire alarm droned towards a deeper, mournful silence. It was silly to be scared. After all, he said, the hospital was just an empty building, lots of empty rooms with empty windows. He appealed to our reason. He was right. There were only empty wards with empty wire beds that creaked if you pulled at them. Cupboards with nothing but rat shit. Greasy light switches. Toilets that still stank of piss. The dead people and the sick people and the babies were gone. All this was very true. His words brought us to our senses.

Adrian came out of the shadow of the doorway and was himself again. It was too boring to hang around in the same doorway for ever and ever, not moving. Josie covered herself by laughing. She'd hated having to plead with Adrian.

'Let's look upstairs,' he said with a crooked grin.

There were new realms to conquer.

▫

We all pooled our bravery, and there was some giggling and fussing. A gleam of triumph in Adrian's eyes as he looked around at everybody. 'This is our place for good,' he said. 'No one can touch us here.'

It suited him to think that.

'Until the bulldozers come,' said Carpenter.

'They won't come for ages,' Adrian maintained. 'I heard Dad talking about it. He said they'd be months mucking around with resource consents and things.'

Since nobody knew exactly what these were, no one said anything. Whatever, they sounded big and important enough to hold back the bulldozers.

Having disposed of this objection, our great leader, Adrian Gorebag Ironclaw, led the way upstairs with a slow, ponderous tread, as if he were leading a whole tribe of devotees. He was coming to like the hospital now; something in him answered to the place. He liked its murk and endless shadows; in here he could do anything he liked and there'd be no one to see him, to stop him.

Every step he took made the shadows look different, and cast his body into a different shade. At the top of the stairs there was another corridor, but no door at the far end, and no oval of coloured glass.

More doors led off to more empty wards. I slipped away from the others and went to a window. I wanted to see if there was a fire anywhere and, more than that, I wanted to see Hikitarua and reassure myself that it was still there. Sure enough, it was. Quiet under the street lamps. Love it or hate it, it was always there. I just had time to take in the familiar streets and the familiar calm, when I thought I heard something hit the roof. Light and swift, landing on all fours.

Something else cried out in the voice of the police siren, all wild and whippy down the road looking for the fire.

I returned to the others in time to catch Adrian's zombie act. He'd discovered a way to scare Josie, and it excited him. He was keen to exploit it, for it gave him pleasure to have her in his power. We had to sit at the top of the stairs and watch as he lay in front of us, closed his eyes, crossed his hands over his chest and pretended to be dead. That was reasonably boring. Then his eyes snapped open and he got out of his imaginary coffin, just like a Dracula movie, making a ghoulish sound. Carpenter laughed, but I didn't think it was so clever. Corpses don't usually smirk. Josie screamed, which is what Adrian wanted, and when she ran down the stairs, he set off in hot pursuit.

Carpenter ran after them, honking and braying, and I was left alone to the sound of voices floating up from below. They were staggering around, arms outstretched, eyes shut or wide-staring, bumping into one another and giving each other frights, careering through the wards, chasing and giving chase, shrieking and screaming like a pack of idiots, their screams echoing off the walls.

It was all just a big excuse for Adrian to hunt Josie, and get his hands on her.

I waited for a moment before descending, looking around me, wondering what I'd heard on the roof. In the dusty stillness nothing moved. The voices from below sounded distorted, elongated as if they were travelling through a long, bendy tube to get to me.

You don't fool me, I thought to whatever it was out there. I know you're there, I just don't know where you're hiding.

When I got to the landing on my way down, I found that the zombie party had degenerated. Below me, on the floor, Josie lay on her back struggling with Adrian, who was on top of her. Carpenter looked passably scary with his glasses off, his eyes bulging and his slobbery mouth open, tottering forward on zombie legs towards them. Then I saw that Adrian had his teeth in Josie's neck.

Mum sometimes called him a greedy little bastard.

▪

Adrian stopped only because I arrived. He rolled off Josie looking guilty and angry. There was a red mark on Josie's neck. She pushed him away with loathing.

'He tried to feel me up,' she announced.

'I did not.'

'Of course you did. You've got hands like weasels. Weasel fingers.'

'It's only a game.'

'Next time you try that little game I'll scratch your eyes out. Nobody touches me, right? I mean nobody. Nobody touches moi!'

She got up and brushed herself down and walked away, towards the front of the building where we had not yet explored. Her legs wobbled as if I were seeing them through moving waves, and I wanted to stop her, stop her walking any further, to keep away from that end of the corridor. I didn't know why, I just knew that danger lay there.

'Stop!' I cried. 'Stop, Josie!'

Josie kept walking.

'Look at Baby, she's scared,' Adrian said, delighted with the idea, happy to follow after Josie. He lifted his head and sniffed like an animal testing the wind.

'Come back, Adrian,' I was frightened for him, for what would happen to him.

'Why don't you go on home, Baby,' Josie said in an undertone. 'You don't belong here.'

Adrian hesitated. Everything hung in the balance, it could have gone either way. We might have turned and gone out into the pure starlight, never to pass into these shadows again. We might have got bored with the silly old hospital. Adrian might have wandered towards us, back along the lines of his life, drawn Josie back with him. He could have picked up where he left off. Instead, he had to live up to the drama of the moment. He couldn't allow himself to be humble for once.

Meanwhile Josie had stopped. There was something in her stillness that alerted me. She was standing just before the final alcove, before its curved arch. The oval piece of red glass in the window above glowed softly, like a luminous egg, touching Josie's head with a wan aura.

'There's something here,' she said quietly. 'I can smell it, but what is it?'

Adrian didn't sound that interested in the answer. He'd grown so cool nothing could touch him, his hair so slick it looked like a helmet, except for the few deranged strands.

It was the first time any of us had mentioned the smell. Adrian was the first to follow her, with me coming behind Carpenter. Somehow I was walking on the tips of my toes. I kept glancing through the open doors of the empty wards as if there was something I hadn't seen yet.

Josie hadn't moved. She turned on the same spot, round and round, eyes burning. 'It's the Stench,' she announced, and from that moment on it had a name. She had named it; it was hers. The Stench was different from other, ordinary smells, even nasty ones, because maybe it wasn't a smell at all but something else, something that used your nostrils as a passageway into your body. It was stronger here than anywhere else. Heavy and expectant. Our eyes watered and our nostrils pinched. We couldn't locate any source of it. It was all around us, everywhere and nowhere. Yet we were right on top of it. In the middle of it. I felt I was standing on a dark, disintegrating glass.

The Stench had fingers. Grubby, horrible fingers. It felt its way across our skin looking for a way in. It trickled into our lungs with the air we were breathing.

'It's around here somewhere, I know it is,' Josie said fervently, as if it was the most important thing in the world.

'I hope it's not toxic,' Carpenter said.

'What do you mean?' Adrian was in a mood to deny anything that upstaged him. He saw himself in a movie, and he was the hero. That meant he got to do all the brave things. He was our Commander in Chief, old Gorebag; we existed to glorify him and I was the only one who knew it because a sister can always know a brother.

'Sometimes they used to store things under the building, y' know, drums of things, chemicals and cleaning stuff,' Carpenter said.

'It doesn't smell like cleaning stuff,' said Adrian with great certainty. He was a Solomon, parting the true from the false with a sword.

'It's not like the stuff they use on the floors,' said Josie, quick to support Adrian for her own purposes. She knew when to push buttons, pull strings; Adrian was an open book to her.

'I was just giving an example,' Carpenter said, his usual pigheaded self. 'I wasn't saying that it actually was cleaning stuff. There's heaps of other toxic stuff. Like radioactive isotopes.'

Josie rocked a little on her heels and the globe of faint red light slipped down over her face like a bloodied tongue.

'What's radioactive isotopes?' Adrian said with deep scepticism.

'It's what they treat cancer patients with,' Carpenter said. 'When it's finished they have to throw it away in the garbage.'

'It's nothing like that,' Josie said insistently. 'It must be the dead people. Lots of old dead people and babies...'

Carpenter groaned. 'Not that again. I bet there's just some simple, ordinary explanation.'

Adrian was looking from one to the other. I could see his dilemma. He agreed with Carpenter, of course, but didn't want to get on the wrong side of Josie, not after the zombie business and the mark on her neck. The ice was thin enough as it was.

Enraged, Josie stamped her foot. 'You're fools!' she screamed. 'Fools!' I was inclined to agree with her, but didn't want to say so; Josie was on the edge of an abyss, she didn't need any further pushing. 'Anyway,' she continued coldly, 'you're not going to be of any help, I can tell. You'll never find it.'

'Find what?'

Instead of answering, Josie took a step back, allowing the faint coloured light from the window to fall on the floor. 'It's here,' she said in a whisper, sinking to her knees. The red glass crossed her face as she bent over. Her fist hammered on the faded lino. 'It's under here. That's where it's coming from.'

Adrian and Carpenter stared dumbly at the spot. Not even our fearless leader could find anything to say. There was a covering of old lino on the floor, which meant they couldn't see anything. There was some ancient pattern on the lino, worn so thin by countless feet you could hardly make it out, but whatever, it would have to be peeled back for us to see what lay beneath. That involved solving certain technical problems, like nails holding down the lino. Adrian stood looking at it, lost in thought. 'We could cut it,' he said at last, after great mental effort.

Carpenter was down on his hands and knees examining the edge of the lino. 'Some of these tacks are rusted in. There's some kinda gunk...'

'It's under here,' Josie repeated, as if she didn't quite believe it. 'It's really under here.'

Adrian nooded doubtfully.

'We'd need a Stanley knife,' Carpenter said at last, a gleam of interest coming into his eye.

'What are you talking about?' Josie shouted as if they were deaf. Her eyes were wide and staring, and a thin veil of sweat had come out on her forehead.

'To cut the lino,' Carpenter said with great patience. 'And see what's underneath.'

Josie stared at him rigidly. 'Just tear the lino up!'

They had a mission then, the three of them: some crusty old lino to conquer. It was easier said than done, but once they found a weak spot, and worked on it a while under Josie's frenzied directions, it began to lift.

Carpenter cursed their lack of the proper tools - a good crowbar would have fixed this job - but what they lacked in skill was made up for by Adrian's display of physical prowess, tearing at the lino with his bare hands, trying to pop the tacks that held it by brute force alone. This was partially successful, mainly because the material was old and brittle, and soon he and Carpenter and Josie were able to put their weight behind it and the lino came up like a scab lifting off a wound.

They stood there, panting and triumphant, the defeated lino flung back, staring at the old tongue-and-groove flooring, dusty and crusted with lino glue.

'We dealt to that fucker,' Adrian said.

Josie was already on her knees again, scuffling in the dust and crud searching for something. Once, forlornly, she looked up at the coloured window and I knew she was looking for its pale ghost on the floor. I was glad when she couldn't find it; every step was taking her deeper in, and she didn't know where it was leading.

With the lino peeled back, the Stench was more intense. Adrian had gone pale and I knew that the pressure was back on him again, that same queasiness he'd felt when he first stood in the storeroom under the window and looked around. He gave me a quick, claustrophobic glance.

Josie was scratching at the floor like a cat.

'Let's get going,' Adrian said, fighting his fear.

'Not yet,' Josie whined. 'You go if y' want to. I don't care.'

That made Adrian uncomfortable, but it didn't make him leave.

Suddenly Josie gave a scream. 'It's here! Here!' She scrabbled desperately at the floor.

Carpenter knelt to look.

She'd found it. It was well disguised with dust and hard to see in the flooring, but the outline was there. We all moved forward to stare at it.

A trapdoor.

And it stank.

We retreated to the kitchen, which became our base. It felt more comfortable to be here, where food had been prepared, and there were only two doors. The Stench wasn't as strong, and we could see our escape window like a pale lamp hanging in the wall through the storeroom door. I wondered if the mason fly was still alive.

'This is our place now,' Adrian said. 'We mustn't tell anyone about it.'

Josie nodded in emphatic agreement. 'And we'll lift the trapdoor. And see what's making that stink.'

'A crowbar would do it,' Carpenter said, his mind full of the technical aspects.

'And we mustn't tell anyone,' Adrian harped. He pinched Josie's arm, but he was looking at me, full of distrust. He was now truly regretting bringing me along.

'Rachel,' Josie said quickly. 'We have to tell Rachel. 'She can come with us next time. I've got to have Rachel. I've just got to.'

'Rachel of course,' Adrian said generously. 'But no one else.'

'Maybe Baby will blab,' Josie said, giving me a spiteful look. I didn't know what I'd done wrong, but you never did with Josie, and you never knew which way the wind blew until it was in your face.

Adrian laughed contemptuously. 'She can't get around her own tongue,' he said.

'Yes,' hissed Josie, 'but she's learning to write, I've seen her.'

'Don't worry. She just watches everything. She can't do much.' He threw me away with such carelessness you'd never have believed he was protecting me.

'Don't open it,' I said. I spoke without thinking and got the words around the right way. I couldn't hide my joy at this, and gave them all a great golden, beaming smile.

None of them noticed. It was just me being a grinning idiot again. If Rachel had been here she wouldn't, like the two boys, have fallen under Josie's power so easily.

'I don't know I want to come back,' Carpenter said. It was a hard thing for him to say, because it had no certainty in it. The other two pounced on him.

Instantly, Adrian said, 'Don't be silly. You must.'

'You're bringing the crowbar, remember?' Josie said, smiling.

'I didn't say I was bringing one. I said...'

'I thought you did. I could have sworn you did.'

'Me too,' Adrian chipped in. 'I have the same recollection.'

'I just said a crowbar would be the right tool for the job.'

'And so it is!' Josie said ecstatically. 'Your father...'

Carpenter grunted and went red in the face. His father had all kinds of tools - tools for everything, he'd often boasted.

But he'd have to steal it. Josie took his arm and leaned into his face. Carpenter clawed at his steamed-up glasses. 'Just for one night, Carpenter. He won't miss it for one night.' She wasn't ready to smile at him, not yet.

'But this is a horrible, smelly old place,' Carpenter said.

Josie didn't argue with that. 'But it's ours, no one else knows about it. We can come here whenever we like. It's private and secret.' She nodded violently. 'Private and secret,' she repeated, her mouth twisting up as if she had just tasted lemon.

Since Carpenter was silent, Adrian started in again. 'It's our own place. We can do whatever we want. No one can stop us.'

'That's right,' Josie said. 'No one in the world can stop us. And we can stay as long as we like and nobody could find us.' A fervent note entered her voice. I saw her look towards the door and the window beyond.

Carpenter mumbled something. He was avoiding the issue by kneeling down and fiddling with the catch on one of the locked cupboard doors.

'Why bother locking them?' he said to Adrian. 'I mean, they're going to knock it all down, aren't they?' His eyes roved around the room for some kind of tool to use.

Since one window faced the moon, it wasn't quite so dark. There was a square of blurred light on the old lino floor. In the middle of that Carpenter knelt, picking uselessly away at the cupboard doors with his fingernails. He'd run his fingers through his hair so many times it was sticking up in a natural mohawk.

'Well are you going to come tomorrow or not?' Josie demanded of Carpenter.

The Stench had caught up with us again, a faint unmistakable stickiness on the air. Carpenter was sweating, just as Adrian had been, but Adrian had recovered, and was in his cool, impervious mode. He had no sympathy for Carpenter.

'Of course he's coming,' Adrian said.

I'd had enough. The thought of the trapdoor haunted me, and the thought of Josie wanting so badly to lift it haunted me even more. Adrian would play along, believing he was the king-pin. Carpenter would be persuaded, because he didn't have any other friends.

I wanted to get out. I had to get out. I got up and blundered into the storeroom like a blind person. I banged open the window, which was easy for me because I'm big.

The others weren't far behind.

◘

We all breathed easier once we were back outside the building, under the stars; it was the same gentle night. There was a hugeness to the sky and the spread of the stars that drew me in and made me a part of it. The Milky Way was laid out in a spinning array, taking part in the great, fervent mystery of the universe far away from Hikitarua and an abandoned hospital.

I felt as if I had just climbed out of a box.

Adrian put the board back across the window and told us yet again to all keep quiet about it, otherwise all the kids in Hikitarua would be in on it and it wouldn't be special any more.

'You're coming, aren't you.' Josie said to Carpenter, as if it were an accomplished fact.

'I guess so.'

Josie stayed on the attack. 'And where are you going to get a crowbar?' she demanded, as if this were a lesson he had to learn off by heart.

'From my father's workshop.' He cringed before her.

'He's just going t' give it to you, is he?' Josie's contempt flashed. She lifted her shoulders in mute despair.

'I'm going t' steal it.' His glasses flashed in the starlight.

Josie rolled her eyes at Adrian, 'Oooh, he's going to steal his father's crowbar!'

'Ahhhhh,' said Adrian, but his mind wasn't really on the job.

As we split up and went home, I looked back and saw that Josie was the last to leave. She stood in the tall, uncut grass, with her thin linen jacket flapping around her, staring at the hospital with a fixed gaze.

The moon came up over the edge of the roof and touched everything with ice.

Rachel

Adrian and I winged it back home as if we were two ghosts making good an escape from hell, and the moon came with us, racing between ripped bits of cloud to keep up with us.

The route home took us along the top of a retaining wall built on the banks of the Hikitarua River. This was mostly quiet and trickling, with a bed ten times too wide for the flow, but in the spring it swelled up, filling with icy water from the mountains, rolling stones down through its depths and covering shallow lupin banks. The wall, too low to have stopped any serious flooding, still offered the only view over the town until you climbed a tree.

Adrian didn't wait for me, and soon he was way ahead, a tiny demented figure fleeing along the wall, stumbling and jumping, the moon chasing after him. I kept running, not because I thought I'd catch up to him, but because I was afraid to slow down to a walk. Afraid of the big empty silence of the small town. It was better to hear something, like the sound of my bare feet on the hard ground, or my quick breath. I didn't want to think about the trapdoor; I wanted to cry, but it's hard when you're running and you don't want to trip over.

Soon I saw the motionless figure of Adrian ahead of me, squatting, looking out over the town. From the wall you could see everything

Hikitarua had to offer – everything from the all-night petrol station to the Milky Way. That's what they called the milk bar in Hikitarua, the Milky Way. It had coloured lights strung outside until ten o'clock to pull in the truckies. You could get fries, coffees and sandwiches. Otherwise there was nothing but a pub around the corner and a few streets and houses leading off from the main road.

In the distance, the Southern Alps, silky with snow, flanked the western sky. Hikitarua was quiet this time of evening, any time of evening actually; barely blinking – just a bit of through traffic, a car or two nosing into the pub. A man walking his shadow home. The milk bar light flickering.

That's about it, but I didn't care too much. I didn't care either about what they said about me, how I was retarded and everything, and how the teachers couldn't teach me to write. They knew nothing of what passed through me; they didn't know that the sounds coming from my mouth were notes from a song beyond their ears, one I heard from the City of Gates. When I opened my mouth to speak, a few notes of this song would emerge. Each was a bridge to the next, and I could sense the song itself in its entirety. Nobody knew anything about these things and I couldn't tell them, but I was reminded of them as the Stench was whipped away from my nostrils by the dry, sullen wind.

I turned to Adrian to say something about the hospital but he was too deep in heroic thought to notice me. He stood on top of the wall and looked out at the town, as I was doing, but I don't think he saw anything. Not that it mattered; there was nothing to see that he hadn't seen a million times before. He was like a cowboy who could jump on his horse but never leave town. He was like a genie inside a town-sized bottle, longing to be let loose on the world.

I was about to say something anyway, even if just to annoy him, when I caught a lingering whiff of the Stench, a tiny piece of the hospital stuck up my nose. It was just a taste, then it was gone. It was still there, then, on me, around me, in my clothes, playing hide and seek with my nose.

'We'll have to knock that street light out,' Adrian said abruptly. 'The one opposite the hospital.' I couldn't see that it did any harm; in fact it helped provide a little bit of light in the gloom of the building.

He rubbed his hands together like a fly cleaning itself. 'I think we're making a mistake bringing Rachel into it,' he said. Of course, he wanted Josie all to himself, but I wondered if he meant it. He liked Rachel too, although he didn't know how to approach her. A person like Rachel is way beyond Adrian's grubby reach.

'Nice Rachel,' I said, sounding particularly moronic, because nice is the first word I think of when I think about Rachel. The way it came out, it sounded like I was talking to a dog.

'Yeah, yeah,' he said. He was still looking out over Hikitarua as if it were the most fascinating place in the world, the Taj Mahal or something. 'Josie doesn't want t' be the only girl.'

I didn't count of course, in his mind. I was just Baby, his goofy sister, a necessary pest, tagging along with him saying silly things and making a nuisance of myself.

'Lonely Josie,' I said.

'Yeah, yeah,' he spoke as if nobody could ever say anything new. He wasn't too bad a person, my brother. It's just that he thought only of himself and the things he wanted. He wasn't afraid of the Stench in the way I was; he was just full of thoughts about how he could use it for his own advantage.

'And frightened,' I said. He gave me a hard look.

'What do you mean?'

Right at that moment when he really wanted to hear what I had to say, the words scattered like sheep before a tractor. What I meant to say was all tied up with Josie's straining face, her fingers scrabbling at the trapdoor's edge, the electric crackle in her voice.

'Josie is the world,' I said, and though I might have got the order right, the meaning was all to hell. One day I'd get it right and all the moments of language would arrive together.

'Bugger you, Baby,' Adrian said with a laugh and began to run. Then he stopped and came back and biffed me on the shoulder to show that there were no hard feelings. It was a good thing I had big shoulders. He was in his expansive mode. 'You're okay, Baby, you keep trying. Anyway, you're the bravest person I know.'

That was a silly thing to say, but I let it pass. I watched the sea wind tugging at his dark hair and tried to hide my blush.

Adrian laughed. 'Lets run!' he cried. He knew I couldn't run well because I'm quite big and clumsy, but I can do a fair imitation - a run for his money, as Dad would say. As we pounded along, the clouds opened and let the moon pull free. It was only a few days off full and looking fat and misshapen. Shadows raced across the wall in front of us. From one of the streets that backed onto the wall, we heard a man singing drunkenly as he walked home:

Irene goodnight, Irene goodnight
Goodnight Irene, goodnight Irene
I'll see you in my dreams...

Adrian and I stopped, panting, and grinned at each other. Old Gills McPickle, as Dad called him, you can set your clock by him. At 8 p.m. sharp he left the Hikitarua public bar and walked home, singing to Irene. He'd been known to leave half a glass on the bar, not wanting to miss his cue, according to Dad. 'His wife's name's not even Irene,' Dad said to Mum, grinning. We picked up the grin straight away and began passing it around among our friends. It became the rage to smile with one side of your mouth; that's how easily any silly thing can catch on in Hikitarua.

Sometimes Dad would begin a joke, 'There was an Englishman, an Irishman and Gills McPickle,' and everybody would laugh.

He didn't even have to finish the joke.

We came off the wall together, instinctively slowing down as we neared home. When we got to the gate, Adrian hardly had to pause as he swung around and hissed in my ear. 'We're being watched.'

I slung a quick glance around the blinkered streets, remembering the feeling I'd had at the beginning, when we'd first slipped into the shadow of the hospital, and the thump on the roof later.

Already. It had started already. There was no such thing as a secret in Hikitarua.

I glanced across at the Rabbitts' house. They have a particularly nosy daughter, a snotty-face nose at that. Her blinds were drawn: drawn blinds were Hikitarua's idea of respectability. Then I noticed a crack of light appear at one of the windows. That would be Serendipity Rabbitt spying on us if she could, wanting to know our business. I poked my tongue out at her, just to let her know.

As we approached the front door, Adrian put his arm around my shoulder. 'You're all right, Baby,' he said, in a voice that always melted me. No matter what the bastard had done to me, I always felt proud when he talked to me like that, proud to be that particular bastard's sister.

Mum and Dad were standing together at the stove where Mum was making omelettes. I love Mum's omelettes, which Dad says are the best in the world. It's the way she can mix in slices of tomato and chopped parsley and still keep the omelette light and fluffy; Dad calls it Mum's magic mixture. It's all bits of red and green floating in a jelly of yellow and white served up on a warm plate.

There was a trace of black pepper and frying butter in the air. Familiar smells.

Dad was smiling, which means he had got work at the Plant that day. He was giving Mum playful pats on the bum. He only did that when there was money in his pocket. I'm lucky because I have a smiling Dad who makes light of things, even in the dark.

Adrian and I crowded in to peer at the food. Adrian didn't like omelettes, so Mum was grilling some chops for him. That was dedication, because Mum was tired; I can hardly remember Mum when she wasn't tired. Maybe I could tell her about the Stench and the trapdoor and the horror that lay beneath. I could always get through to Mum, no matter how dyslexic my tongue.

'I can smell something off,' Mum said. She was batting Dad's hand away and trying to smile, but she had grey bags under her eyes. She was like a candle, burning low and bright.

'It's the bloody kids,' Dad said, 'They don't take a bloody shower in a month of bloody Sundays.'

Adrian and I cringed away. Dad looked half serious.

'Whatever, Dad,' Adrian said.

'That'd be right,' Mum said, sliding her fish slice under the mixture. Flipping an omelette is a great skill, and I wanted to see it - all that lovely gooey hanging egg - but Mum shooed us away.

'Go and have a shower, kids,' she said.

'They smell like a bloody sheep dip,' Dad said. 'They're as bad as dogs. Y' know that dogs will eat their own vomit. That's what they smell like.'

'I think you'd better get out of the kitchen too,' Mum said.

Dad leapt into the fridge, grabbed a bloody beer and skedaddled.

I had a hot shower anyway, although I had trouble adjusting the hot water spray. Cranky at the best of times, I couldn't seem to get it right. As if my skin was going hot and cold just to fool me. The pipes shuddered as I spun the lever.

I knew I couldn't get rid of the Stench, just wash it down the drain. In fact I stood under the shower with the water pouring over my head and down over my body without feeling a thing. The water did not touch my body; I'd grown an invisible skin over my real skin, an invisible skin that kept the healing water from flushing out the pores, sealing the Stench in. I was a carrier. It went deep inside my cells. It hid from soap and oozed with my sweat.

Since I was not allowed words, I sang a song to water under the shower that was only of syllables. I didn't know what it was, but I could put my arms out and swing around in rhyme with the song. The melody of my limbs belonged to water; the Stench couldn't touch them. The melody of the water belonged to my voice. That was my only way forward. I let my voice rip to the sky. It wasn't right, I cried in my song, it wasn't right to stand under a shower and not receive the blessing of water.

I sang until the shower went cold.

I shoved all my clothes to the bottom of the laundry basket.

I rubbed myself down until the towel wore thin.

I talked to myself until I glowed.

I put on fresh clothes so that I felt like someone else.

I'd just started to get dressed when I looked up and saw Adrian. He was standing at the door watching me.

'You'll never get rid of it,' he said.

Adrian got undressed and shoved his clothes to the bottom of the basket too. I got them all out, my clothes and his, and put them in the washing machine.

As Adrian got into the shower I noticed how pale and taut his skin was. It was easy to see him as a big bully type, but he wasn't. He didn't have that much weight to throw around. He was thin and bony and his skin sensitive; naked, you could see how vulnerable he looked.

I turned my back on him and faced the mirror with all the usual shock. I couldn't look for too long. I was fat and pink, like an albino; I was like a teddy bear with a bow tied around my neck. Look at my eyelids hard enough and you could see the blood circulating through my veins darker than the surrounding flesh, which was more translucent than pink. In a hard sun, you could see right through to my bones. My hair was not so much blonde as white, like an old person's; I'd been mistaken for an old person sometimes, in the wrong light.

This was Baby, the big little moron, the one who never got it right.

'You've used all the hot water,' Adrian said.

⸰

As soon as I got to the bedroom, which I share with Adrian, half a room each, I went directly to my chest of drawers and took out the heirlooms, my special pieces, fragments of history. They are ordinary things. I keep them in a carved box that must have come from India for there is an elephant chiseled onto the lid. The first item, and the biggest, is a book called Bobby and the Bumpkin, which is the first book I read, when I was about three. The bumpkin was a little dog-like creature that could change itself into the likeness of a burnt stick to avoid discovery. It had two attendant spirits, Wumps and Woggie, flying creatures, and it could talk to them, but only backwards. 'Apples want I!' It would command. According to Mum, that was when I started getting my words around the wrong way when I spoke. Then there was a photograph of my Great-great-grandfather staring at the camera apparently trying to empty his face of any expression, as if the lens were going to judge him. He had a large honest-looking beard and wide-apart eyes, but his lips, under the moustache, were full and pouting. There was a brass thimble that came from my great-great-grandmother, wife of the honest beard, and I imagined how many times it must have flashed in her fingers. What would she be thinking of as she sewed and sewed and sewed, the thimble flickering against the needle?

Holding the cool brass in my closed fist, and looking the photograph of my ancestor, it was easy to remember who I was and where I had come from. You had to beware of losing track of events in Hikitarua, which was somehow timeless because it had been abandoned by history. Even the seasons had lost track of themselves as the years grew warmer, the water dried up and fire hazard signs went to maximum. Any kid with a box of matches was a walking bomb. Hikitarua lived in fear of its own drying pasturelands.

It was easier, too, to believe that nothing extraordinary had happened at the hospital. A bunch of young teenagers had broken into a smelly old building bleeding dry rot, and had run around going nutty. What else was there to do around here? Sit in the milk bar? With the thimble in my hand, the whole thing became like a bad dream, far from the everyday reality of the world. I ran the events in the hospital back through my mind and saw them as perfectly ordinary; nobody from around here at least would have been very much surprised by them. And the Stench? Wasn't I making too much of it, turning it into something big and special, just as Adrian was trying to turn himself into the big hero? Gorebag Ironclaw Meets The Stench. It would all be over, fait accompli, before you stopped laughing. The Stench was only what we were pretending it to be. Me as much as anyone else.

I talk as if I stood apart but how could I stand apart? My brother was at stake, the Stench was in my nostrils. Rachel was just an idea, a hope, a pipe dream. The trapdoor waited with its mouth half open.

When Adrian came in he carried on as if everything was perfectly ordinary. Just another night out in Hikitarua with the gang, doing a little creative breaking and entering. Mum's the word now.

He spent a moment with his miniatures, a little army of Orcs locked in a dusty, forgotten battle with some stubborn Dwarves. In his less heroic days, when he'd just been an ordinary boy, he'd spent hours cutting and painting up these little beasts. There was Gorebag Ironclaw himself, sword upraised ready to strike. 'It's time t' give the stunties a good lookin' to,' was what he'd be saying to his sidekick, Gorefang Rotgut.

Sitting to one side were the little bottles of paint with the fine brushes which lay neatly on top of them. Next to the bottles lay his paring knife, used for cutting and pasting bits of plastic bodies to make up different warriors. It was short but very sharp, with a thin blade.

He picked up the knife up and studied it as if it were the most profound object in the world. He had that look he got on his face when he was just busting to tell me something, when the urge to boast got too much for him.

He stood by his bed for a time before replacing the knife and getting in, head lowered. He wasn't praying, that's all I knew.

'I got my hands on her titties,' he said proudly. It wasn't hard to see why he was so keen to get back to the hospital the next night, and why we all had to keep it secret.

I had the thimble clutched in my hand beneath the pillow.

That night in my dream I am standing inside the hospital, looking out the window to the sun-hardened sky. The sky is like a trapdoor, tight shut. Mountains can't move it. Rachel is there; her hands smell like honeysuckle and I kiss them for the dew on her fingers, which tastes as sweet as her fingers smell. She doesn't smile exactly, but holds her lips as if they had been kissed by eternity.

Inside the hospital, up near the front alcove, I find the floor has turned to sand, not hard packed, but shaped into waves. In front of me, the patch of coloured light from the alcove window floats. As I watch, it begins to pulse the way a jellyfish pulses. It rises into the air, still pulsing, hovers, rotating, leaning this way and that in search of a direction. Then I see Rachel standing nearby, her arms stretched out towards it with a look of great concentration, her dark curly hair lifting from around her face as if by a wind. Without all that hair her face looks small and vulnerable. Behind her, sand dunes turn into an endless beach. Suddenly I feel I've been made a fool of by the sea and the sky; the sky will open and we will all go up in the conflagration. Rabbits cook in their burrows. Pine trees explode. Rachel is protecting me but at great cost to herself. If I wake up quickly enough, I'll save her, never mind if the flames take me. No sacrifice is too great.

I sat up and the first thing I did was look across at Adrian's bed. He was sitting bolt upright, just as I was, looking across at me. We didn't say anything to each other. I don't think he saw me. He was still at the hospital.

'We'll nail it up,' he cried, and flopped back down, instantly snoring.

I didn't believe him.

Instead of going straight back to sleep I concentrated on the City of Gates, a place I visited which lay on a border between two twilights. Creatures inhabited it that couldn't be seen by mortal eye; even the eye of sleep could not discover them and only the notion of movement gave them away. Somewhere at the heart of this great city, which contained all the knowledge of the universe, there was a chamber, a stone and satin chamber I thought of it as, and in the chamber slept the Queen. I always imagined her asleep on a red rug, or stepping out of sunken pools, water glistening on her body. This was the Queen of the City of Gates, the inner jewel of the crown.

The city was not imaginary; it existed in some hidden corner of space, and we might see it only when flying between the sun and the moon, while going to sleep or waking up. Whenever I found it, I always seemed to come to rest at some distance, contemplating its beauty from afar. I called it the City of Gates because of its gates, hundreds of them all slanted at slightly different angles, facing different sectors of space.

It was better than any dream I could have made up.

⸻

The next morning around the breakfast table, Mum and Dad talked about the hospital while Adrian and I shut up and ate our porridge as good as the three bears, but you can be sure we listened to every word. When no one was watching I was able to sneak a little more brown sugar on my porridge.

Dad said there was going to be a meeting, and a man was going to come and explain why the hospital and its grounds would be sold and the building bulldozed. This was the same man who'd earlier come to explain why they had to close the hospital down in the first place.

Dad said he didn't have to go to a meeting to figure that out. Since the hospital was closed, why hold on to the building and the land? The assets, as he called them. The health authorities would sell it to a developer and we'd get some brave new development in Hikitarua. Some shops or something like that. Something to brighten the place up. Dad wasn't too sure.

He threw last nights empties into the rubbish.

'What's the use of more shops in Hikitarua?' Mum asked.

Dad didn't have an answer to that.

'It's an ugly building anyhow,' Dad said after a while. 'Musta been built in the fifties. That cacky green they used as an excuse for a paint job, shit …'

'Women had babies there,' Mum said, and looked at me because I'd been born there, but I wasn't a very good argument for the place.

Dad didn't have an answer to that either.

I sneaked a bit more sugar onto my porridge.

⸻

It was good to see the wider world of morning, as Adrian and I set out to walk to school through the bright, ordinary world of Hikitarua. We walked past sprinklers revolving around their lawns like the blades of a buried helicopter, past the roses lined up behind each other like obedient school children waiting to go into class in Mrs. Inna's garden (which she was watering with special water out of a bottle, her rottweiler, Softy, in watchful attendance - he wasn't barking at the roses this morning) past doors that led into ordinary houses and the smell of kitchens and beer, burnt toasties and buttered roast potatoes, past cars, bicycles with kids on them, and women with supermarket faces pushing prams to the sound of country music seeping from hidden speakers; everything tucked into everything else so neatly you couldn't see the cracks, and the whole thing tucked neatly into the horizon with its hills, its blue sky and forever sun.

Hikitarua, just another little Highway 5 town.

I half believed it. The sky was not a trapdoor; I'd made it all up out of fervency; there was no Stench. But I didn't believe that either. Hikitarua was a billboard town. There was nothing behind the image but another day under the sun for a cluster of corrugated iron roofs.

You'd expect to find the Stench in a place like this.

None of this ordinariness could be trusted. Hikitarua was a front. It only let me see what it wanted me too see, the rest was hidden. Hidden under the trapdoor in an abandoned hospital. Like the new paint job on old Hodge's house, which was only for the street, not the sides or the back, Hikitarua dressed itself up for your passing eye, not a good hard look. The town was only just there, hanging on to the surface, ready to slip away through the great crack in the world to nowhere land.

All it needed was a little push.

Beside me walked my brother Adrian, the very man to provide that little push, at least in his own mind. Adrian was deep in his hero trip and I couldn't get through to him.

'Listen,' he said, grabbing me by the shoulders. 'I don't think we should tell Rachel about the trapdoor. Let it be a surprise!'

'Surprise!' I said. He thought I was being retarded.

'Don't tell her, that's what I'm saying. You must say nothing to her about it.' The trapdoor is already using him, I thought. Using him to protect itself, from Rachel.

'Baby talk,' I said, ready to give him a go. 'The trap is sprung.' Again I rejoiced, for I had the word order right. The only minor problem was that the meaning itself was too out of left field, too lopsided, for Adrian to grasp. In his dreams he knew he should nail the trapdoor up, but only in his dreams; during the day he believed he would rule the world. As yet he hadn't sorted Rachel out, her role, her appointed place in his scheme of things. The mad Josie he thought he understood, but it was less easy to deceive himself when it came to Rachel.

We hadn't gone around too many corners when I had the feeling of being followed. I swung around and caught the culprit, Rabbitt herself, all ready with her grin of weak complicity, and wondered if it had been her following us last night. Rabbitt is not her first name, but everybody calls her that because her parent are Mr and Mrs Rabbitt, with the word written on the letterbox to make it even worse, and besides, no one was going to call her Serendipity.

Of course she wasn't following us now, just walking to school as we were. She just happened to be walking along behind us, which seemed to happen a lot. I had no doubt she was spying on us, me in particular; she had a fascination for me that made me squirm.

Rabbitt looked too young to go to school, and acted like it too, with her thumb in her mouth and her eyes all big like a baby's. For all her pint size, she must have been at least eight, way past the age where thumbs should be in mouths.

I gave her my don't-stalk-me look, but she pretended not to understand and gave me the wide-eyed-innocent in return.

Irritably, I dug Adrian in the ribs and showed him. He looked her over like a wolf bolting down its prey. With great maliciousness he said, 'Little Serendipity Rabbitt shouldn't play with the big kids.'

The Rabbit took her thumb out of her mouth.

'I'm not following you,' she said in her flat nasal voice filtered through many layers of mucus. She made it sound as if she were telling us she didn't understand us. 'I'm jutht walking here.'

'I'll break all your legs,' Adrian said, and the idea seemed to cheer him up, for a big grin came over his face.

By that time we were already through the town. I'd smiled at Rush Jimmy who ran the Milky Way, where they put ice cream into the milkshakes and served them in red and white cardboard Coke cups. I liked him because he had soft eyes. He kept his milk bar clean and gave me an extra scoop of ice cream in my milkshake. I'd turned my face away from Ernie Spright, who had a way of looking at you as if he already knew everything about you, especially the worst things. He never gave me anything but a fright.

Rabbitt trailed along behind, pretending not to be watching us.

Nearing the school gate and keeping an eye out for Rachel, I saw Josie's brother Maro biking past on his way round the block. He circled around when Josie went to school to see who she talked to. With his legs flogging the pedals on his mountain bike, he could do about three or four circuits, plugged into his Walkman, hard-core techno-punk slamming in his ears to keep him pumping, all the time keeping an eye out for his sister.

He gave Adrian a hard look as he pedalled past. He was on to Adrian alright.

I didn't see Josie but I saw Rachel, not up close, just a glimpse of her dark curls bouncing on her shoulders. I kept her in sight as long as I could but still did not see her face. I had to be content with her curls. In the meantime, Adrian linked up with Brad and Kahu and some of his other buddies. Brad and Adrian were giving the slender Kahu a hard time about something. I wished I knew what it was because I was sure it was something to do with Rachel. I watched him for a moment as he pretended to be with them, laughing coarsely at their jokes and sneering at everything that moved on two legs. This was Adrian in his element, a boy among boys, but he was only pretending. All the time he was thinking of nothing but the hospital, getting Josie there, getting his hands on her titties again.

It made me embarrassed to remember how I'd once liked Brad, and had wanted him to notice me; I was glad now that he hadn't. He'd turned out to be a big, coarse bully, the sort of boy who enjoys punching girl's arms in the corridors.

Then I saw Rachel walking along talking with Josie in a group of other kids. Josie and Rachel looked funny together, because Josie was tall and skinny and rough with brown skin and fair hair that bounced on top of her head when she walked, whereas Rachel was dark-haired and fair-skinned and had to look up and squint when she talked to Josie. I saw her looking up but I didn't see her face.

I knew they had to be talking about the hospital. Josie looked as she did when telling someone a secret, so furtive and close behind the hand that you might as well advertise to the whole world.

Everybody split to their classes. I went to the library where they needed me the most. I could hardly see my way. I was grieving for not having caught a glimpse of Rachel's face, or met her eye.

One look at me and she'd know.

Someone had to know. I didn't care what Adrian said. After all, what guarantee did he have that he'd turn out to be the hero anyway?

He might just stay the fool he was through it all.

◦

By the library door I ran into Carpenter, who was charging along, head down, not looking where he was going. For a moment he hardly recognised me.

'We're going to do it,' he said excitedly. 'We're going to mount a proper scientific expedition!' His eagerness made his face bulge.

Josie joined us, not looking in a hurry to go to class. She kept looking over her shoulder, as if she were only standing with us to get away from someone she didn't want to talk too.

'Did you get the crowbar?' she demanded of Carpenter. He didn't answer; he was breathing hard, his chest going in and out.

'What about Rachel?' Carpenter asked. He was holding himself back from saying something he was longing to say; triumph gleamed in his eyes.

'Who cares about Rachel?' Josie said savagely. 'Who cares what she does? I don't. Do you? Are you in love with her or something?'

'I thought she was coming.'

'Oh, she'll come all right, don't you worry about that.'

Just then our headmaster, Conk & Whiskers, went by on some important mission. He walked as if he navigated by means of his nose, which twitched as he went past, apparently reminding him of something, and he gave us a disapproving look. It was Josie he didn't like; I don't know why but it seemed as if he were out to get her, out to find fault wherever he could. She was the wrong person to cross his path if he was out hunting for someone to give a detention to.

Josie got a hard, set look on her face. 'He gives me the creeps,' she said, just loud enough for him to hear. And with a final tormented look, Josie was gone.

'I've got t' get t' class,' Carpenter mumbled, and held his coat across his chest as if the day were cold or he was hiding something.

More and more things were happening that I didn't properly understand.

⊡

I'd read all of the books in the library, some of them several times; this was a secret I kept from everybody, even the librarian. Nobody knew I was reading, right from the age of three, when I read Bobby and the Bumpkin, nobody knew. People thought I was just looking at the pictures because I turned the pages so fast. Nobody knew the difference. At home at night, when everything was boring, I could lie in bed, close my eyes, open the pages in my mind and read them at my own speed. I could see the pages laid out in front of me as if I were sitting in the library with the book in my hands.

What they did know, because the librarian had visible proof, was that I knew where the books went in the shelves after the kids had carelessly thrown them over the counter. No one noticed me: I just put the books back where they belonged and nothing was said, except the librarian offered me a biscuit from her morning tea ration with a smile on her face. It didn't matter to her whether I was reading or not; she never thought about it.

As I passed the shelves, the stories they held rushed out at me, some in rags and some in silken gowns. I liked the myths best, where gods visited people and talked to them and told them what to do. I was safe in the library and, except for the woman who tried to teach me to write, I was mostly left alone.

Not this morning, though. The remedial writing group came into the library because there was no other space. I was in that group, although already fourteen years old. My hands had the same trouble as my mouth when it came to making words. The only place I could speak freely was here, in my own mind. Nobody understood what a long way it was from my head to my hands. When I wrote it was my hands that did the writing and that was the problem. My words came out sloping all the wrong way and pointing back towards themselves.

The teacher, Mrs Manui, tried patiently to show me how to write. Some thought that because I couldn't make the letters I couldn't think, that I didn't know any words to think with. Mrs Manui was not quite like that because she'd seen me reading. Sometimes I tried to hide how much I read from her so she wouldn't bug me too much about the writing. She had a kindly, round face with a wart on one side of her nose, and her arms were big and kind and round too - and brown. She wore print dresses with bright patterns on them, and I didn't think she got paid very much for being with us specials, but she loved us and that made up for it. Perhaps she thought about us at night when she went to bed.

She tried to talk with me once, understanding that if people gave me the time, then I could talk. I felt an awful failure that time because I wasn't able to do it the way she wanted. My words kept wandering off in all directions so that my sentences got lost halfway through. I could only speak three or four words at once, and when the next lot came around they had something different to say. There was a gravity in most people's words that pulled them all in the same direction. With me, because I was a retard, my words had no gravity and therefore made no shapes, except inside my own thoughts when they all happen at once.

But Mrs Manui had a compassionate heart, and she wasn't so tough on me that she would stop me doodling on my pad while she read us a story. She loved stories and read them in her deep, rich voice, for she knew it would relax us and put us back in our bodies.

My neighbour, Donna, inched her chair away from mine, probably because of the Stench. Like a dream that won't go away even though day has come, it was hanging around me. A dream you carry around all day, blind to sweat and detergent, a dream of dusty corridors and restless trapdoors, wavering candles and gloom.

I was thinking of this when Mrs Manui began to read a story about six blind men who discovered an elephant for the first time. One blind man touched the elephant's legs and said it was a tree they'd found. Another touched its ears and said it was a palm leaf. Another touched its trunk and said it was a snake. On and on they went, getting it wrong while I fell half asleep at my desk, scratching with a pencil at a piece of paper.

I was just doodling while the story plodded by, killing time, when I realised I'd drawn Carpenter's face. He had the easiest face to draw because all you needed was a pumpkin with glasses on, but in this case I'd drawn him as a death's head with his eyes stuck right out and a big black tongue coming out of his mouth. It looked funny, but scary too.

I showed it to my neighbour, Donna, who giggled and put her hand up to her mouth as if I'd shown her a rude picture. I saw then that in a way it was a rude picture, and wanted to screw it up, but Donna had already handed it on around the class. It was only a matter of time before the teacher got hold of it. Mrs Manui was very understanding with us special class people, but she was very strict as well; if she saw the sketch, she'd be sure to say something about it.

Remarkably that didn't happen and I got the doodle back, somewhat the worse for wear. Someone had drawn a worm coming out of his eye. I smoothed it out on the desk with the palm of my hand. A moment later it began to crawl away. At first I thought it was the wind but the room was still and airless, and besides, no wind could make a piece of paper move that way, arching its back and pushing forward like a caterpillar.

Donna was watching it too. Donna has a super pretty face, all pale with light blue eyes and blonde hair. Her eyes were bulging now, watching the piece of paper move by itself. She looked at me with amazement.

When it reached the edge of the desk, we both watched it fall to the floor with a see-sawing motion. I looked up and saw Mrs Manui watching it too. She had stopped reading and was staring at me, a look of puzzlement on her kind face. Suddenly I felt like a traitor to her, and to all of them, to know something the way I did and not speak up about it. If you knew something and didn't say it, you were as guilty as the person who did it.

We hadn't even lifted it yet, and already whatever lay beneath the trapdoor was working its evil on us: Josie, Carpenter, Adrian and of course me - why should I escape?

Blushing, I screwed up the paper as hard as I could and shoved it into my desk.

The teacher went on reading the story.

The blind men started to argue and fight.

The library door slammed open and Josie came in, her face so pale you could see the bones working under her skin. Conk & Whiskers followed close behind.

'Get away from me!' Josie said with revulsion. 'You're molesting me.'

Conk & Whiskers stood inside the doorway. His body swayed backwards and forwards like a tall masted yacht in a contrary wind. 'You are on detention,' he announced pompously, apparently for Mrs Manui's benefit. 'After-school detention, I might add.'

'No, I'm not,' Josie said in a low voice, turning to face him. 'I'm not on any fucking detention.'

Mrs Manui stood up unobtrusively. I didn't notice at the time. I played the scene back to myself many times, and it was only after the third replay that I noticed it.

Conk & Whiskers came into the room, politely acknowledging the librarian and Mrs Manui.

'I wouldn't use that kind of language if I was you,' he said. 'It'll only make matters worse.'

Josie came at him, to meet him halfway. 'You can stick your detention up your arse,' she said. She looked across and saw me. Her lips twisted up. 'Have you learned to write yet, Baby?' she called in a cracked parody of a bright and cheerful voice.

Conk & Whiskers was out of his depth. He made a mute appeal to Mrs Manui, who held back, still assessing Josie. That can take a long time.

'We're talking about a suspension now, possible expulsion,' Conk & Whiskers said stiffly, holding himself up by the library counter. 'Your parents would not like that. Your father...' he let the word hang on the air.

I waited for Josie to laugh. She could always scream out a laugh in situations like this, trying to make everybody else look silly. I was wrong. There was just a moment when her eyes narrowed, then she went for him.

She lashed out at his face, screeching as if she were being murdered, scratching pieces of flesh under her fingernails where she could find it.

Mrs Manui was right beside her, arms around her waist, murmuring things. For a moment she drew away, as if repelled by a bad smell. Then by some magic, she pulled Josie free.

Josie shouted over to us, the cowed retard group, 'Fuck their suspension! I'm not coming back to this shithole anyway.'

I came out from the group and joined Mrs Manui. They knew we were all friends and hung around together. At the same time, I loved Josie then, because she wasn't pretending to be holding it all together the way everybody else was. She was going to pieces in front of us. And the trapdoor is not even opened yet, I thought.

'I don't trust you, Baby,' she said wildly, 'I don't trust you at all. You think too much. Don't try and hold me back or I'll scratch your fat lips off your fat face.'

Mrs Manui led her gently but firmly towards the door. Not even Josie could take any offence at her.

Conk & Whiskers followed after a dignified interval, during which he surveyed the artwork pasted around the walls as if that were why he had come into the library in the first place.

Then he left and we saw Josie with tears in her eyes and an angry look to her mouth as Conk & Whiskers marched her across the playground to his office. He looked very full of himself as he strode along behind her, his conk and his whiskers sticking straight out.

Afterwards I heard several stories. One was that she'd hit someone. Another that she'd grabbed a boy by his balls and squeezed. Another that she'd trashed someone's desk. Another that she'd pulled up her dress and exposed herself to a teacher.

The stories grew more weird and wonderful as they travelled. I believed everything and nothing.

At the lunchtime bell I was off like a rocket to find Adrian to tell him the news, secretly hoping to see Rachel first. For once the librarian could put away the books herself.

I caught a glimpse of him at the tuckshop line-up. He pretended not to notice; he was too busy acting tough with the kid next in line, his old bashing buddy Brad. Brad had a sneer instead of a smile which Adrian was all too fond of imitating. It involved curling his upper lip and narrowing his eyes. You can pick up a habit like that and find yourself doing it forever.

Brad always got that look on his face when he saw me. His narrowed eyes had a way of picking me to pieces as I walked along, as if he knew everything about me, about how I once looked up to him and admired him because he seemed shy and boisterous at the same time and could kick a football further than anyone else his age.

I didn't dare approach Adrian in case he made fun of me in front of Brad and the other boys - too many mean eyes to bear - so I drifted off to the lunch area where I saw Carpenter, inspecting his cucumber sandwich as if it were something that had appeared on his petri dish.

No joy here.

Later on, I thought I'd find Adrian hanging around with Brad and the boys but I was wrong. They were in a huddle by themselves without him. That gave me a good excuse to check out the girls' area, and there he was walking along without a care in the world, talking to Rachel.

Seeing the two of them together brought me up to a stop. For the first time it occurred to me that Adrian had a separate relationship with Rachel that had nothing to do with me or Josie - and it was something that I didn't understand. When I saw Adrian on the floor, on top of Josie with his hands all over her, I could understand it: there was no mystery in it, nothing unexpected. Adrian was predictable to that extent. Yet he walked along beside Rachel, so easy, laughing as if he could take care of the world; soft, even gentle, a mysterious delicacy entered Adrian's movements. Rachel seemed to understand him because she was smiling, and I caught my first glimpse of her face.

The light was on her. I could hardly look at her because I knew her features off by heart. The small face, the sensitive chin, the mouth like a rose. She was listening to Adrian but she wasn't necessarily believing him, which was wise. She held a smile inside her heart; it was the serene way her eyes looked up to the open sky. There were no trapdoors in her world. Not yet.

Suddenly shy of approaching them, I hesitated, and in that moment had to face Rabbitt, who was standing by the corner watching me, her thumb hovering near her plump lips.

I dithered and a cloud passed over the sun. Rachel's face vanished.

Rabbitt came over to me. The thumb was jammed in her mouth.

'You thtink,' she said. 'You should uthe thoap.'

I had to deal with that nuisance, and when I looked up, Adrian and Rachel had gone.

I spent the rest of the lunch-hour scouting around for Josie, or anyone. I checked out her usual haunts, even her smoking spots, but her face was not among the huddling smokers.

I saw Carpenter, though. He was still sitting alone eating his lunch and looking at some distant utopia. He seemed to be very pleased with himself.

At the very last minute I saw Adrian. The bell was already ringing for afternoon classes, and he was racing off somewhere. I saw a bunch of boys on his trail, who pulled up when they saw me. Kahu was among them, dark with anger. Brad was coming up behind. Adrian looked desperate. He stopped and smashed his fist down into his palm as if he were crushing some noxious insect. 'Have you seen Josie?' he said, his eyes wild, his pursuers closing in behind him.

'Detention-suspension,' I said, on a see-saw of language, praying he would stop and spend time with me. Yet he was off again, the same hell-hounds on his trail. He didn't get far. A moment later they were gathered in a half-circle around him, moving in on him in quite a serious way.

One of them was coming in low, so as to rip at his fly with clawed fingers, while another came in a bit higher, swinging for his chest. Another, a more cowardly character, was coming in under the protection of the second attacker, ready to kick viciously when the right flesh went down. It was always that sneaky guy at the end who did the most damage. It was Brad, he'd be type. It made me deeply ashamed to still wonder what it would be like to feel his fingers on my arm. It made me shudder to think about it.

Adrian himself was swinging around, ready to waste the lot of them, ready to play Gorebag Ironclaw to the very end. Then one of them saw me. It was Kahu. He came and waved his fist at me to warn me away.

I caught a glimpse of Adrian a little later. Usually he likes to have someone to show off to, even if it's only me - keeping me impressed is all part of it - but he just walked along giving people moody looks when they spoke to him, and dirty looks at me over his shoulder. When I saw him that way, so deep into one of his looks, I felt that if I lost him now, I'd lose him for good; he would disappear into one of his looks and never come out.

I ate my lunch on my way to class but somehow it didn't taste any good. I had sandwiches with Vegemite and cheese, and cheese and tomato with a piece of cold sausage that had white flecks of dried fat clinging to it. I couldn't bear to eat any of it and chucked it in the rubbish tin.

It stank.

When I got to the gate after school, Rachel was there alone. She was looking anxiously at the emerging stream of children and I didn't have to be told who she was looking for. My heart raced to see her although she was still some distance away. I stopped dead still, creating confusion and annoyance for those behind me, and some familiar abuse. My throat grew painful at the thought of all the things I had to tell her.

I had already had a good hard look at the detention room as I went past, heading for the gate after school. It wasn't exactly empty because Conk & Whiskers always managed to nail some evil-doers during his daily rounds, but Josie wasn't there. Not seeing her there gave me a chill.

I started to run forward to get to Rachel and tell her about Josie but tripped up over someone in front of me.

'Watch where y' goin', y' big moron,' someone said. A couple laughed but most didn't have the time.

I started to run. I was running but I wasn't getting anywhere. It was like a dream, and Rachel came no closer. The concrete was grey beneath my shoes. The bushes along the side of the school made spiky green shadows over my ankles. Rachel had seen someone; I wanted so much to get to her first but could not control the distance between us with my legs. I saw her raise her arms up into the air and signal. I lifted up my hand too, but I was in the middle of a river; I was getting carried further and further away from her with every moment.

It was Adrian she'd seen, slumping towards her with that crucified hunch he always assumed. His mouth was already opening. A gate to some future was closing. I was absurdly despairing, as if everything in the universe rested on one moment at a school gate in Hikitarua in the middle of nowhere.

Suddenly I was beside them. I'd been so close all the time. They were already in full flight of an argument.

'Josie would want y' to,' he said stubbornly. Adrian didn't look so good. He'd been roughed up a bit, rolled in the dust a few times and spat out the other end. A whole day had gone by and I hadn't caught up with what had happened to him at lunchtime. Now I figured the boys had beaten him up.

Rachel was unmoved. Her eyes were like opals dipped in the ocean. When she was happy you could see the ocean; when she was thoughtful the opal was nothing but dark. Her skin was lustrous and creamy pale, and the opal now gleamed, making her skin glow.

'Where's Josie?' she demanded, keeping her distance from the ramshackle Adrian.

In a silky voice, he said, 'I've been trying to tell you.'

'Gone,' I said, and felt the truth of it, the fact of her absence everywhere. 'Josie,' I said as an afterthought.

Rachel greeted me. She never forgot herself for a moment, how to be nice to people, polite, and acknowledge them when they arrive, no matter how anxious and driven the situation.

'Do you have news?' she said, looking me straight in the face, so serious, her lower lip swollen where she had been biting it.

'Josie is dead,' I said dramatically. It wasn't what I meant to say. To be made a fool out of; to be so close yet so far away.

'What does she mean?' Rachel demanded. She must have used lipstick that day, her lips were so red. Her hair was rich with hidden colours;

everything it touched came alive.

'Baby got spooked,' Adrian said with a tinge of brotherly contempt. 'It doesn't take much to spook her.'

'Fight,' I said, determined not to be silenced. 'Conk & Whiskers. Attack Josie and.'

Everything was hopelessly mixed up, but Rachel got it. She looked into my eyes and got it straight out of my head.

'I told you,' Adrian said, everything I was trying to say apparently proving his point.

'Josie's in trouble, isn't she?' Rachel said to me, ignoring Adrian.

I nodded gratefully. But Josie's trouble at school wasn't the point. When I closed my eyes I saw the trapdoor opening and Josie falling through it, mouth agape in a silent scream.

When I opened my eyes again some time must have passed because Adrian had pulled Rachel aside and was whispering urgently into her face, leaning towards her intimately. I heard Rachel say something but didn't recognise the sounds.

At that moment there was the sound of skidding bike tires, the grouch of brakes and there was Maro, fronting up to Adrian. Maro was eighteen, thick and hairy and not a great a fan of Adrian's. He wore these tight rugby shorts that showed his thighs, and he came on like some sort of athlete. He thought he was irresistible, but he was quite handsome anyway, without the conceit.

'Where's my sister?' he said to Adrian, getting off his bike and flipping it onto its stand. He needed both his arms hanging loose to look serious. His face was hanging pretty loose too.

Carpenter happened to arrive at the same time but nobody cared about that. He quickly pretended not to be there.

'I don't know,' Adrian whined. 'We were just talking about it.'

Maro grabbed hold of Adrian's arm and gave it a deadly squeeze. There was lots of muscle in that hairy arm. Adrian's face went pale. He didn't look so concerned about playing the hero right then, although it was an ideal opportunity for him.

'How would I know? She doesn't tell me everything.' Adrian gave a cowardly sneer.

Maro gave Rachel a hard look but didn't notice Carpenter. Carpenter had a way of hiding behind his glasses in situations like this; it made him look impossibly nerdish, or actually invisible.

Then Maro honed in on me. He came close enough for me to smell the sweat on his skin, and I could see it glistening on his forehead. It wasn't fear I could smell but something rich and salty. He was only just in balance; one touch and he would explode.

'I've heard things about you, Baby,' he said. 'That y' know things. That's what Josie says. She says you're not a retard at all. Maybe y' know where Josie is.'

'Leave me sister alone,' Adrian said, finding his voice. After all, Rachel was there to see it all, and that was better than having Josie even. Far better. He desperately wanted to impress Rachel; everybody did.

But Maro had already forgotten me. I was too odd and lumpy for him. It wouldn't be hard, looking at me, to think I was pretty goofy. Rachel was far better prey. 'You're her friend,' he said to her. 'She'd tell you if she'd tell anyone.'

'She told me nothing,' Rachel said, flaring. 'Why don't you go away! We don't know anything.' She spoke in a sharp voice that rang clear as a bell in the air. It was beautiful but of course it wasn't true. Maro fell back before it, grabbing the handles of his bike.

'I'll take out your face,' he said to Adrian.

Adrian gave the obligatory sneer.

'We want to find Josie too,' Rachel said, putting her hand on the handlebars and fronting up to Maro. 'Josie's my very best friend. I don't want to see her hurt.'

'Okay, okay,' Maro said, pulling the bike out of her grasp. 'But.' He stopped long enough to point at Adrian. 'He's lying. He's just a bloody liar anyway. It comes natural to him.'

And with that parting shot he rode off, front wheel lifting off the ground. Adrian gave his back the fingers.

Rachel took hold of Adrian's arm, right where Maro had squeezed it. 'She's at the hospital, isn't she?'

Adrian winced. 'That's why you've got to come.'

'I told Josie I wasn't interested. Some horrible old place.'

'You'd just as soon go to the milk bar and talk to Kahu,' Adrian said, as if that prospect were the end of the world.

'Or walk along the river,' Rachel said, not taking the bait, 'or go back t' my place and listen t' some sounds.'

'It doesn't matter,' Adrian said. 'She's there. She's depending on you.'

'How d' you know?'

'I seen her. I went back after lunch, after I seen Baby who told me about Conk & Whiskers. Josie's suspended from school.'

Rachel was deep in thought. Carpenter had lots to tell Adrian, but Adrian hushed him; there was no time now. Carpenter looked hurt. He didn't seem to understand what was going on around him. He scratched idly at his face where a pimple was coming up.

Rachel was setting off down the street, carrying herself proud and high, as she always did. Adrian set off after her, leaving Carpenter and me to lumber along behind. He quickly caught up with her and did a sideways skip along the footpath, trying to talk to her.

'Then you'll come?'

Rachel was deeply suspicious. She looked back at Carpenter and me and then to Adrian, but didn't stop walking.

'Why has she gone there?'

'To hide.'

Rachel stopped so sharply I bumped into her. 'There's something else wrong, isn't there?' she demanded.

She waited. Nothing happened. Kids moved around us. Cars came and went. The sky did nothing; it had that hard nor-west glaze you couldn't crack. There was a heavy dryness to the air, like you get on summer nights.

'I mean, you're all so strange. Josie going off. Carpenter looks like he's got a bar of chocolate up his bum. Baby's trying to tell me a story with her eyes. I wish she could talk. And you!' She rounded on Adrian. 'Maro was right. You are a liar!'

At that moment I happened to turn around and there was Rabbitt, skulking along behind. This time she had a Walkman hanging in her ear to match the thumb in her mouth. She wasn't too carried away by the music to notice that I'd seen her, however. She dropped back and tried to turn herself into a shadow.

'It's just a smelly old building,' Adrian said, skipping from one side of the pavement to the other. His voice had a peculiar pleading whine in it.

'I'm going t' walk home on my own now,' Rachel said with dignity. She knew how to cut loose when things were starting to drag.

'You know the time,' Adrian had recovered something of his own dignity. He made it sound as if he didn't care one way or the other. 'Bring something useful,' he added.

'The Secret bloody Seven,' Rachel said bitterly.

I laughed, but nobody, except maybe Rachel who flashed me a glance, knew what I was laughing at. I make this moronic honking sound when I laugh, which makes me sound ten times more stupid than I deserve.

Enid Blyton never thought about that.

◘

We walked home with Carpenter babbling into Adrian's ear and me walking a few paces behind, not listening, thinking about books in the library, and one in particular came to mind: Oliver Twist by Charles Dickens. There's a character called Sykes who is very nasty, and when I looked at Adrian, busy brushing away Carpenter's comments as if they were flies, I thought of Sykes and how Adrian could become like him. I wondered how you could do that without a special agony, I mean to be less, much less than what you could really be, without experiencing a pain so sharp it would bring you out of sleep screaming.

The sky was once more dominated by a huge nor-west arch. This band of high, stationary cloud framed the mountains and the orange glow of the setting sun behind them. The air was parched and acrid with a restless wind behind it. Everything it touched turned to tinder; dry rot ate into everything dead.

At some point Carpenter left, then Adrian was gone too and I felt deserted, betrayed by Adrian, and pretty stupid just walking along by myself. At the same time it wasn't hard to find him. I scouted around a few streets and picked up his trail on Old Train Road, which ran along the back of some houses by a watercourse. On the other side there was an old train station building that had been converted into a hay barn.

Somewhere along the line he'd hooked up with Brad. It made me sick to think of the things he and Brad would say to each other, especially about me. Brad thought I was pretty funny.

They were moving fast, chasing someone. When they stopped, I crept up on them behind the long grass on the side of the road. I lay flat with my head up like a cobra so I could see. Near one of my supporting hands, some ants were gutting the carcass of a beetle.

Adrian and Brad had Kahu bailed up, one on each side of him, and he was whining at them. Threatening and pleading, his face pale. He wasn't so strong, Kahu, and he was trying very hard to be brave.

It was Adrian who started it. He just started hitting, bashing and thumping Kahu. Brad was holding Kahu from behind, keeping his arms up behind his back, while Adrian kept hitting.

I thought it would stop after a few moments but Adrian went on and on until Brad let go and Kahu fell on the ground, rolling up into a ball. I thought that would have been the end of it, but Adrian started kicking then, putting the boot in wherever he thought he could do the most damage.

I don't know how long he would have gone on, but a few moments later both Adrian and Brad were startled by something I couldn't see. They looked fearfully up the street, then ran, leaving Kahu lying on the ground, groaning and crying.

I flattened myself down in the grass, lay still and waited. Behind the sound of Kahu moaning, the world was quiet. I could smell the Stench on the air faintly. A line of ants radiated from the dead beetle. A spider ran over my finger.

When I was sure they were gone, I scampered over to Kahu and lifted him off the dirt.

He put his arms around my neck.

'I want to kill them,' he said.

Finally turning into our home street, I felt no relief. A police car cruised by and our local policewoman, Mitch, looked out at me. Everybody called her Mitch, although it's a boy's name. She had lovely chestnut hair which, out of uniform, she wore long, and a small face with large clear amber eyes. I remember hearing Adrian and the boys saying that she was much too pretty to be a policewoman, yet her looks didn't fool anyone, at least for long, into thinking she was a soft touch. Far from it, she was the toughest of Hikitarua's three cops. At least, she was the smartest.

I wondered what she was doing in our part of town. Just cruising. The word would be out that Josie had run amok and vanished from school.

In its own, quiet fashion the search for Josie would be under way.

Crowbar

I didn't want to go. I sat in our bedroom, which is upstairs facing east, and looked out to the long, falling plains. The plains are like an extension of Hikitarua, but lying flat instead of upright.

I had a moment or two to think, Adrian having sulked off somewhere, and what I thought was that I didn't want to go. I could always refuse, leave Adrian and the others to their fate at the hospital; sit in the dark here at home and watch the stars come out. To comfort myself I took out my special objects, my fragments of history, but nothing seemed to work, nothing reassured. My Great-great-grandfather with the honest beard stared back at me vacantly. Whoever he was looking at, it wasn't me. The carved box had lost its lustre. It was just an ordinary box with a crudely chiselled elephant on the lid; and it wasn't really ancient, as it pretended to be - you could see the blackening stuff rubbed into the cracks. Even the thimble had lost its shine.

Holding the thimble in my hand, I began to cry. I don't know why I should have, right then, but I didn't want Adrian to see me. The tears splashed down onto my hand and into the thimble. By the time I'd finished I knew I had to go to the hospital because of Rachel, and I'd collected a thimble of tears. Even if Adrian was cursed to hell, and I didn't believe that yet, there was Rachel to consider. In my dream she had been protecting me but it was more likely that I could protect her. I had to go to the hospital even though I had no guarantee of immunity.

A moment later I heard Adrian calling.

I tucked the thimble into my pocket for no other reason than that it slipped onto my little finger as easily as it must have fitted onto my great-great-grandmother's.

◘

The last of the sun angled through the window, turning everything in the kitchen yellow. Scrubbed but uncooked potatoes sat illuminated on the cutting board looking like some fancy ripe fruit. Mum was not around and the kitchen felt empty, as if she'd just abandoned her task and had gone off forever.

When I went into Mum and Dad's bedroom, Mum was lying on the bed and Adrian was standing beside her, leaning over her.

She smiled at me. 'I'm a little bit tired,' she said. She was never just tired but always 'a little bit' tired.

Adrian straightened up. I thought he was distressed but I couldn't tell. Mum had drawn the curtains and Adrian turned his face away from me.

'Maybe you shouldn't go out tonight,' she said.

'We won't be late,' Adrian said.

Dad wasn't home yet. He was working at the farm where he was helping out doing some concreting for a friend. A cash job, he called it. Mum was feeling the weight of being responsible for us teenagers, one not quite right in the head.

'You look after your sister.' Mum's smile turned to Adrian.

'Of course I will,' Adrian said.

Mum gave me a quick anxious look. She knew I was still a baby; I couldn't hide that from her. A big blubbery baby. A weeping whale. I'd already blubbered once tonight; I didn't want to do it again.

'You're a big girl now,' she said, giving me a hug. Mum's body was frail but her love wasn't. You could feel her love from any doorway; it's just that her body wasn't strong enough to hold it.

Adrian gave me an urgent look and I felt the tide of events pulling at me. I had my choice then. I could've stayed behind, sat down beside Mum and held her hand forever.

◻

I threw a look over to Rabbitt's window when we left the house. Her blind was down. I thought I saw a crack appear, but I couldn't be sure. One way or the other, Rabbitt would be on the move tonight. The quieter Hikitarua got, the more its nocturnal life seethed. Darkness had not yet fallen, but it didn't have to. The air held that thick, after-day haze made up of dust and exhaustion that was as good as twilight.

I expected we'd go straight to the hospital, especially if Josie was there, but I was wrong. Adrian, face fixed, headed for the main road and the milk bar.

I had the privilege of trundling along behind. He had a fixed, almost ecstatic look on his face; he had such high hopes for the night. I felt suddenly sorry for him, as if I were much older than he was, and my hair really was white with age. I wanted to warn him about Josie but it would have been hopeless to even try.

As soon as we got inside the Milky Way, I saw Rachel. She was sitting at a table with some others, laughing. She had drunk something that made her lips bright red. I thought maybe, unknown to me, Adrian had agreed to meet her here, but, seeing his face, I knew that wasn't so.

Then I saw who she was sitting with.

Kahu's cheek was cut and the side of his eye bruised from Adrian and Brad's beating. He was sucking something out of a cup through a straw while Rachel watched him.

Adrian started to pretend I wasn't with him and I had to do the same. He swaggered up to the table in his Gorebag Ironclaw mode. 'Too much hangin' about and da ladz'll come t' grief,' I'd heard Gorebag say.

'You're not going t' get away with this.' Kahu spoke quietly but his voice carried everywhere. Even Rush Jimmy, behind the bar, cocked an ear in our direction.

'Get away with what?' Adrian asked airily, sculling a Coke. He didn't sound that interested in the answer. He'd grown so cool nothing could touch him, his hair so slick the light slid off it.

'I'm just telling you,' Kahu said with quiet dignity. 'You won't get away with it.' He went back to his drink.

Rachel slid across the seat to get out. Before getting up, she took Kahu's hand and gave it a friendly squeeze. 'I'll see y' tomorrow,' she said.

Kahu looked up from his drink straight into her face. His voice was shaking with emotion. 'Where're y' goin now?'

'That'd be our business,' Adrian said with heavy significance.

'I'll see y' tomorrow,' Rachel repeated.

Adrian crunched the Coke can in his fist. He was having a ball.

'We don't want any trouble in here, boys,' Rush Jimmy said. It was hard to take him seriously with that squeaky voice of his. You should have heard him sing 'You Ain't Nothing but a Hound Dog' at the Hikitarua talent quest.

Jimmy had a face spotty from drinking too much sugared milk. He boasted an Elvis Presley hair cut, dark and oily, complete with a neat duck's arse at the back. The Milky Way wouldn't have been the same without Jimmy, whose white shirts hung limp on his arms. Still, he'd put together a great milk bar with a jukebox in the corner and ducks flying up the back wall, behind the counter.

'No trouble,' he squeaked. He was Hikitarua's only foreigner; he had come from somewhere like Kosovo where people were killing one another all the time.

'Of course not,' Adrian purred. He turned his palms outward to show how good his intentions were.

Kahu turned away to hide how hurt and angry he was.

Rachel walked firmly for the door and I followed her. Adrian came out behind us, whistling between his teeth.

I took hold of Rachel's arm. It felt bare and fragile. 'Go. Don't,' I said, putting my fear before my word order again. Suddenly I thought of my mother lying on the bed, Adrian bending over her. There was something in the picture I didn't understand.

'To the hospital?' She took my arm. 'Josie's there, isn't she? It's the only reason I'm going. I couldn't tell Kahu that. If Josie needs my help, I've got to go to her, haven't I? You'd do the same, wouldn't you?'

I nodded, too dumb for tears. I couldn't bear her nearness, her love. And I saw the chain of fate that led back to Josie. I had to go to the hospital for Rachel's sake and she had to go for Josie's sake. I wouldn't have been surprised if Kahu was now going to follow us for Rachel's sake. The ties of friendship were too strong for us all.

'Then we go there,' she whispered, 'and everything will be all right.'

'Out. Her get,' I said. I was the bumpkin; I was a burnt stick in the corner of a fire.

Rachel nodded. Her curls fell like dark waves over my jacket. I wanted to stroke her head as if she were my child. Take her to my bosom, it says in books. She needed a second to decode my back-to-front words.

'Don't be afraid of your brother,' she said, still allowing me to hold her arm. 'He hasn't learned how to think yet. It takes longer for boys.' She made it sound so simple. I laughed as if we shared a great secret. I looked silly when I laughed, because of my fat lips, and made a funny noise in my nose, but Rachel didn't care about that.

'Trapdoor.' In my mind it opened like a square wooden mouth, and I looked inside, into the black depths. My body started to shake. My skeleton seemed so loosely slung together it was a miracle it could stay upright; my flesh had no firm claim upon my bones. Even my thoughts billowed out, homeless, from my words. Spoken out loud like that, the word itself was a trapdoor opening up, swallowing everything.

Then it was in my nostrils as if it had never left. The Stench. I took out my handkerchief and blew my nose as hard as I could. I blew so hard I got specks of blood on the handkerchief.

I didn't think Rachel understood me. How could she? Again she looked puzzled. Go away from me, I thought. If you value your life keep clear of me. I am already contaminated. You are too beautiful; I thought I could protect you but that was just a pretence.

Adrian had caught up to us. When he saw Rachel stroking my arm he looked suddenly very lonely, as if he had no one in the world to turn to. He flicked back his hair and it landed like a knotted whip on his neck; the great hero faced his aloneness.

'I'll take you home,' Rachel whispered to me. 'If it's too scary.'

I shook my head. She didn't know what scary meant. She had no idea. She thought it was just something that would frighten a big baby missing her mother. Something to giggle at in the dark.

She didn't understand how I loved her.

◦

There was Carpenter, sitting alone in the long grass near the window keeping a watch for us, expecting us to come down the main drive. The moon flashed in his glasses and he jerked around in fright at our arrival through the back fence behind him. He clutched at a backpack that bulged with something.

'Did y' have to come that way?' he said as Adrian pulled himself through a hole in the fence.

'Where's Rachel?' Adrian hadn't liked it when Rachel had left us a short time before, saying she'd rejoin us soon. He hated losing control of any situation. His little act in the milk bar was entirely his style.

'I thought she was with you.'

'She's come her own way,' Adrian said, shrugging carelessly.

'We can't hang around here,' Carpenter seemed jittery, clutching and unclutching his bag.

'What do y' have in the bag?'

'Lots of things.' Carpenter was suddenly eager. 'Do y' want t' see?'

'Naw. Let's wait till we get inside.'

Adrian's eyes were roving everywhere. The back of the hospital was sheltered, facing the plains rather than the town, but nowhere in Hikitarua was safe from prying eyes. Here people knew your business before you did.

'I'll show you if you want.'

'It doesn't matter.' Adrian looked irritably towards the window. I half expected it to fly open and Josie's face to appear.

At that moment Rachel slipped through the fence to join us. She was wearing a dark jacket, a white blouse and blue jeans, and her face looked very pale. 'I can't believe that Josie is in there,' she said. 'The paint's peeling.' It was a silly thing to say but it summed up a lot.

What would you expect?' Carpenter said. 'It's a condemned building.' He had the logic of bulldozers on his side. He didn't mean it but it sounded as though he were uttering a curse.

'Fucked if I care,' said Adrian, pulling his collar up under his hair, making him look very cool.

It was the turning point, when twilight gave way to night. The shadows became very possessive of their darkness, and the last of the high, light blue went from the sky. The fading nor-west arch over the Alps turned into stars. Like the night before, it was slow and mild, with a heat that never let up.

Suddenly none of us wanted to go inside.

'I can't stay very long,' Rachel said. 'My Mum and Dad are expecting me home.'

'Then don't come at all,' Adrian said, as if that put an end to it, which it pretty much did, for Rachel didn't say anything. She hadn't taken her eyes off the hospital. She knew what I knew: there was nothing inside but a long falling.

'We're probably breaking and entering or something,' Carpenter said, his old fears returning. 'If the police found out we might be charged. Some criminal offence.'

'I don't give a rat's arse,' was Adrian's majestic reply.

'The police'll be out looking for Josie soon, if she doesn't go home.'

It was already happening, but I wasn't about to try to tell them.

'That's right,' Rachel said, shivering a little. 'Let's go. I want to see Josie. She can come back to my place tonight.'

'They can't charge me and Josie,' Carpenter persisted, still following his own line of thought. 'We're minors. Under sixteen. They can't charge minors.'

'Yes they can,' said Adrian. 'They have a special law that means they can put you in prison. Special prisons. Anyway, I'm sixteen.'

'So am I,' said Rachel, her dark eyes fixed on his face.

Adrian didn't like that. He didn't want anyone up at his level.

'So I am,' I said, and everybody laughed. I didn't mean to say that, because I know I'm only fourteen, but what I meant was that I am up at his level.

'Don't diss Baby,' Rachel said, smiling at me. 'She understands more than she lets on, don't you, Baby?'

'That's what Mum says,' Adrian gave me a brief, worried look.

Suddenly everything went quiet. It was as if the town had shut down in a split second. There was nothing left to laugh or smile at.

'Why isn't Josie at the window to meet us?' Rachel said nervously. 'It's closed too. She must have shut it from the inside.'

'Me an' da ladz are gonna do some bashin',' Gorebag Ironclaw growled, and set off for the window. I knew Adrian was scared, even more scared than the first night, but he wasn't going to let Rachel see that; old Ironclaw had his uses. Casually, with one hand, he took the board off and stepped back.

Obligingly, the window swung open.

If I had thought that entering the hospital the second time would feel the same as the first - just a wriggle through a window into some musty old storeroom - I was wrong. Adrian had already gone through with Carpenter hard on his heels. Rachel stood back, waiting for me to go before her. She didn't want to go.

I didn't want to go. The window looked smaller and meaner than before. Adrian and Carpenter had disappeared through it and I would never see them again; if I went through, the same would happen to me. Rachel would be left alone with Hikitarua and the night sky.

She approached me and said in a deep whisper, 'Are y' sure Josie's in there? You're not just saying it because Adrian told y' to?'

The look on my face must have convinced her.

'Then hurry! Something must've happened t' her or she'd have been at the window by now. She'd have heard us.'

The window felt smaller than the night before too; the frame tugged at my hips. I came down awkwardly, head first on a prayer. It was like diving into a murky pool. My legs came tumbling after in their own clumsy fashion. I'd sunk to the bottom of a new world where the shadows were fuzzy and most of the light make-believe.

Rachel's face appeared above me, blocking out the light from the window. I watched her being born through the old wooden frame, trying not to rip her jeans. I looked around for Adrian but the light wasn't the same; distances lost their values, depth lost its distance. This was a world wrapped right around my face, a finger down my throat. It was the Stench, of course, suppressed in the dead air, not announcing itself outright, preferring to hide behind the shit, death and disinfectant stink that belonged to the wood and memory alone.

Adrian was there. 'Get up, Baby,' he said in the voice he used when I was being an impossible nuisance to him, an embarrassment in front of his friends. A little act for Rachel's sake, was my bet.

'Where's Josie?' Rachel said, her voice cutting through the dark air, sharp and brittle. She sounded as if she were having trouble breathing.

We were like deep-sea divers. We breathed air inherited from another world. We were holding our breath; our time was limited here, we had to hurry. Every breath we took we used up another precious portion of our life energy. We were on overtime in this place, overdrive. I could see Rachel's trajectory: she was here on a rescue mission, to get Josie out. Her love shone bright on her face. Not for me - that was an impossible dream. She was never other than gracious and caring when it came to me, I had no complaints, but it was nothing like the love that shone on her face now as she turned into the dark looking for her friend.

We are all born equal, but not all are equal in everyone's eyes.

'I don't know,' Adrian said. He was breathing through his life mask too. Once more, he was under a thousand feet of pressure. The heavy sweat was already lining his forehead like dew on a clothesline. Fear was again eating out his heart.

'Perhaps she's just asleep,' Carpenter said. His voice sounded the most normal of all of us, as if he were reading from a book in class.

Adrian shut the window behind us. I knew he was doing it so there would be less indication from the outside that we were in here, but at the same time it cut off our retreat. The wind coming through the window had brought with it the wider world of school and home, the raw smell of the mountains and the scent of pine trees. Now the musty, stale air of the empty wards enclosed us. I wanted to throw it back open, climb out and never come back.

I saw Rachel's nose twitching as the Stench hit her; it lay in a thick coating on the tongue and throat and made even the dry, musty air feel sticky.

'I don't like it in here,' Rachel said. 'I want to see Josie.'

The storeroom wasn't as small as I had remembered it either. The musty, stagnant room and grown larger, the walls pushed back to accommodate some new, unknown space.

Rachel was impatient. 'Which way do we go?'

Adrian gestured towards the door into the kitchen which, now our eyes had adjusted, glimmered faintly in the opposite wall. I remembered last night, and the way the shadow from the door and soft light from the window lay together to look like a body. Tonight it wasn't there; all the shadows were different and lay at different angles as if someone had rearranged them all since we were last here.

Rachel had her eyes fixed on Adrian. She was trusting him on this and she wasn't sure if she should be; she wasn't even sure that this wasn't some joke and that Josie was far away in a much safer place. Adrian was already setting off for the door. Rachel hung back.

'This place will give me bad dreams, I know it.'

'They're just boring old empty rooms,' Carpenter said. Like Adrian, he was pretending that this was just some ordinary old derelict building.

'There's bad dreams all over here,' Rachel backed towards the window.

'Don't be silly,' Adrian said without thinking. It was an automatic reflex, the sort of thing you say all the time to a dumb sister or a crazy girl like Josie. But Rachel was the wrong person to say it to.

'Yes, Adrian, having bad dreams is silly. You'd feel pretty silly if you had them too.'

'Dead people dreams,' I said.

Adrian tried to laugh.

'Very funny,' Rachel said, trying to recover her poise.

I noticed the same effect that had struck me the first time, how our voices sounded strange, as if the words were all new to us, as if we were hearing them being read back to us in our own voices. Everything we said was heightened, intensified; this was a stage and we were the players. For example, Adrian didn't attempt to hide the cruelty in his voice. 'I thought you wanted to find Josie.'

It stuck in the right place, for guilt and shame filled Rachel's face.

'Let's go.' Carpenter was impatient to be done with this talk and get on. He was excited and trying not to show it. You'd have thought that something wonderful and clever was about to happen.

◻

I was last into the kitchen, stepping over the doorway with some superstitious instinct. The others were just standing about without moving, like a bunch of wax dummies, looking at Josie who was lying in one corner in a heap of blankets. She was dressed in her school uniform and in front of her were some empty Coke bottles and chocolate wrappers. I'm sure they thought she was dead: her body was so still, her face so bloodless. I knew she wasn't because her face was hovering a few feet above her head watching us. Out of her dream she was watching us.

Suddenly she snapped awake. 'Rachel!' she howled, jerking to her feet almost the same moment she woke and flinging herself upon her friend. They swirled around in an ecstasy of greeting.

'What are you doing here?' Rachel said as soon as the hullabaloo quietened. 'This is a horrible place. And there's some... smell.' She wrinkled her nose. 'Let's get out of here.'

'I can't leave yet,' Josie said, as if Rachel were demanding the impossible. 'And it's not so bad as you think. You get used to that smell after a while. You don't even notice it. Fuck! What do I care about a bit of a smell. Dad can't find me here. Maro can't find me here.'

'They're worried about you, Josie.'

'Let them stew their guts out! I don't care! I've got a plan.'

Rachel cast a bleak look around the room. 'What kind of a plan?'

'You guys're going t' get me some clothes and a bit of money and stuff and after a few days I'm getting out of here for good. Fuck Hikitarua! I've had this dump. I've had it for good and all. I'm goin t' the city. Wellington. I've got a cousin who lives there. She's nineteen. I'll go and stay with her. This town is dead, man, dead dead dead!'

'They'll find you. The police'll find you.'

'No they won't because no one gives the place a second look y' see. Their eyes just pass over it like it wasn't here. When they search for you they go t' the riverbed and places like that. You guys can bring me water and stuff. And a TV. It'd be nice to have a TV. And it's just for a couple of days or so, until everybody thinks I'm dead, then I'll come back and tell them all t' get fucked, then I'll leave Hikitarua for ever an' ever and they can keep their town and stick it up their jacksies.' Josie was so feverish with words I envied her. I think Rachel tried to slap her face. That's what it looked like, but Josie wouldn't stop babbling. 'I'd just like them all t' have me dead and buried and come back and walk down the street like a zombie scaring the living shit out of the lot of them. Boy, I'd like to see the look on Maro's face.'

'They won't say you're dead for months,' Carpenter said. 'That's what happens. They just keep your file open until they find a body or dozens of years have gone past.'

But Josie didn't care about that. She was staring rapturously into Rachel's face. 'Christ, it's good to see you, Ra. Its been lonely here.' A moment later she dissolved in tears and had thrown herself on Rachel's breast. Rachel put her arm around her shoulders and stroked her hair. I was just glad that she wasn't talking about the trapdoor, and dead people and babies. Maybe she's forgotten about it, I thought with sudden hope. If she's forgotten about it then everybody can forget about it. Maybe no one will even mention the trapdoor.

'I've read about places like this,' Rachel said, hugging Josie as hard as she could. 'There's always spirits hanging around.'

'Why would they hang around?' Josie demanded.

'Because this is where they died.'

'We can do anything we like here,' Adrian said. He was looking around and breathing deep, as if he were on top of a hill. The Stench didn't bother him. Everywhere he looked, he saw what he wanted to see. The hospital was his stage and the cameras were rolling. Within the freedom of these empty rooms, Adrian could become something he couldn't be anywhere else, and it made his heart beat hard and fast.

'Everybody's looking for you,' Rachel said, as if that fact alone should bring Josie to reason.

'Huh? Let them.' Josie pulled back and tossed away her wrist in a dismissive gesture. 'They won't come here. The Stench puts them off. It's like having some resident dead rats. That little kid Rabbitt came by today, sniffing around. One whiff and she was away. I'd like to see Conk & Whiskers in here!' She laughed hysterically at the idea, and Adrian began to laugh along with her. He was falling into his old pattern of playing up to her and falling under her influence. Josie laughed by drawing her breath in backwards, fast, sounding as if she were strangling.

'Everybody was supposed to bring something,' Carpenter said suddenly. 'Let's see what you've brought.' He wanted to get on with the game, as he saw it; he wanted to show everybody what he was carrying in his bag and had been waiting for the right dramatic moment, which had never come. He was too impatient now to wait for the right build-up. He'd bring it out whether anyone wanted to see it or not. He started to unstrap his bag.

But Rachel was not to be put off. She took hold of Josie's old linen jacket and began to shake it, pulling Josie to and fro. 'You're coming out of here with me. I don't care what Maro's done. You can't possibly spend the night here. This place has come out of hell...'

Josie had gone rigid. Her hair was plastered in sweaty rat's-tails down her neck and throat. Her eyes were opaque, as if they were made of milky marble. They stood out from her face like a frog's eyes. 'He fucked me,' she said.

Everything stopped. Even Carpenter's fingers stopped fiddling with the top of his bag.

'Who?' Rachel said, being the mouth who had to give voice to the inevitable.

'Maro.'

The word hung in the air and died.

Rachel took a step backwards, as if she could put something between herself and the world. Like pale doves, her hands flew up to her face. Their wings covered her mouth and cheekbones. Her eyes were too dark to see in that diffuse light; they were shadows that bled out of her eye sockets. I think she must have known but never been able to put it into words to herself, for herself. Her family wasn't like Josie's; they were polite people, they knew the difference between soup spoons and pudding spoons. There were things you know but have no words for; of all people, I should know that.

Adrian didn't know it, and he couldn't handle it. I could see his body filling and emptying with blood as if it were a great pump. He looked like someone who had been punched in the stomach and was refusing to double over.

Finally unable to contain himself, Carpenter unzipped his bag and with one motion took out a crowbar, a real steel crowbar with a claw's foot at one end and a flat edge at the other. As he took it out the light in the room shifted; a dull silver gleam took up along its shaft. I wondered if he'd even heard what Josie had said, or if he'd heard but it hadn't registered somehow, like a bunch of nonsense syllables you don't take in.

'Where'd you get it?' Adrian said, leaving the girls to stare into each other's faces. The boys formed an alliance for a moment. Adrian eyed the crowbar covetously, but he had heard Josie and I could see the knowledge working on him deep down.

'I stole it from my Dad's workshop.' Nobody bothered to pause long enough to understand what this meant to Carpenter, so fearful of the law. The sweat was up on his face too. He hugged the crowbar to his chest.

'Y' can't stay here,' Rachel said, but her voice had broken. She was pleading now and that was the end of her, her capitulation. She didn't know what to say to Josie about Maro and neither did anybody else.

'What do you suggest I do? Go home?'

'Tell your Dad!'

'He just told me I had it coming, and he'd do the same t' me if I didn't shut up about it. And Mum's scared of Maro. He beat her up once and she won't say boo t' him now.'

'You can come and stay at my place.'

'That's the first place Maro'll look. Anyway, your Dad would ring mine.'

That was true: Rachel couldn't say anything in the face of that. Carpenter began idly picking away at the locked cupboards with the crowbar.

'They'll be empty anyway,' Adrian said.

'Then why lock them?'

'How the fuck should I know?'

It was Rachel who was crying now, and Josie was trying to comfort her. Then both girls were crying and holding each other up.

'Harder,' said Adrian. 'Hit it harder.'

Carpenter put his tongue between his teeth and chipped harder at the cupboard.

Josie was gripping Rachel's arm, babbling her head off. 'I know you'll help me, won't you Ra? I'll need clothes and money. And my shoes. Someone's got t' go t' my place and get those things. I've only got these stupid old school things and these horrid old sneakers. You've got t' help me, I'll kill meself if y' don't. It's no use asking Adrian, it's got t' be a girl. Adrian'd never get past Maro. But you could do it. Maro wouldn't dare do anything to you.'

Rachel's face looked very grave, like an adult. There was firmness and dignity. 'I'll do whatever I can for you, Josie. No more than that.'

'Just remember, if y' tell the police or anyone where I am, they'll send me home, won't they, that's what they'll do, that's what they always do. Maro's a lying bastard, he can tell lies in his sleep. That's all right for him, cos everyone believes him, no one blinks an eye. But me, I tell the truth and no one believes me. Like I've got barbed wire on my tongue, everyone starts bleeding as soon as I speak. So they'll send me home and Maro'll get me, and maybe Dad too because Maro's egging him on, saying things that make Mum cry all the time.'

'I'll remember it,' Rachel said with the same carved gravity. She sounded like a stone idol talking. I knew then that she'd gone very far away and that was dangerous; she needed to be here and on the look out, noticing things. She had gone to a place where nothing moved, nothing more than the chance collision of silences that makes a sound like singing.

Carpenter shifted position to get a better leverage. There was a square of hazy moonlight like a welcoming mat. Carpenter knelt in it and began applying the crowbar with zeal.

'But there won't be anything inside,' Adrian said with frustration. 'You're wasting time.'

'Then why did they lock them?' Carpenter asked with the same peculiar insistence. His mind clicked every time he reached that point in his thinking and the same words came out of his mouth.

Suddenly Rachel snapped out of her dream and began scrabbling around in her bag for something. A moment later she came up with two candles and a cigarette lighter. As the candles were lit, Josie began to cry. We all watched the lighting of the candles, even Carpenter who paused in his senseless chipping. Two yellow pools opened up like the irises of friendly eyes. Tall, leaning shadows clustered around us.

'I hoped we wouldn't need them,' Rachel said in defeat. 'I kept thinking of you here in the dark.'

'I knew you wouldn't betray me,' said Josie, trying to bring her streaming eyes under control. The yellow flame made everything look a bit more familiar, the glow turning the kitchen into something of a home base. 'You'll stay here with me, won't you, for as long as you can?'

'I can't. I told my Mum and Dad...'

'Don't say that! Just don't say that! I hate it when you get like that. You're sixteen now, aren't you? You're older than I am! You can stay for a couple of hours if you want, can't you? For a friend. For a best friend, won't you. Don't tell me you can't!'

Wisely, Rachel kept her counsel. I prayed she'd stand up for herself when the time came.

Josie turned to Adrian. 'What did you bring for me?' She sounded like a queen demanding tribute and I guessed that now she was an official fugitive her rule would be law. She had a hold on us all now; in a sense we were all her hostages. Rachel's gift of the candles had been gratefully, even tearfully accepted, but her generosity towards Rachel would not necessarily extend towards Adrian, who was already a slave. 'Water,' Josie said, striding up and down the room in time to the twisting shadows. 'It's amazing how much water a person uses.'

Adrian opened his bag and brought out some plastic bottles of water. Josie immediately opened one and glugged half its contents.

'I brought the crowbar!' Carpenter said, waving it under Josie's nose. 'But that's not all.'

'A great help that is,' Rachel said, of course not knowing yet about the trapdoor.

There was an awkward moment when, suddenly, it seemed that nobody knew why Carpenter had brought that crowbar. To cover up the awkwardness of the lie everybody was telling Rachel, Carpenter dived into his bag. There was more to come in the form of some small, pyramid-shaped objects he plucked from his bag and spilled onto the floor.

'Incense,' he said, pulling out more. 'Perfume and stuff.' He'd taken all sorts of goodies from his mother's dressing table: perfumes, skin creams, cleansers, lotions - stuff we didn't need but which he said might come in handy. Handy when we were lifting the trapdoor, that is, but he didn't say that. With his crowbar and his potions he was on his way to becoming a famous scientist for discovering a new kind of dead thing, maybe, and they would write about him in books. His little adventures into crime had invigorated him, flushed his cheeks and concentrated his mind on the all-important task of getting the trapdoor open as quickly as possible, so his dream could all happen straight away, and he would be famous tomorrow. He had assembled his weapons.

I wondered what his mother would say in the morning with all her tubes and squirty things gone, her cones of smelly incense, all in the name of science and fame.

'You're the best thief in the world,' Josie squealed, enraptured. Carpenter blushed.

Josie seized the perfumes and began dabbing them on Rachel and herself, tucking them in behind her ears as if she were off to some super posh party. Carpenter's mother had some fancy tastes. Looked to me as if the party was going to be so super posh she would be the only one there. Besides, the perfume didn't kill the Stench, it couldn't even mask it. Josie made silly faces at her hand as if it were a mirror, and stroked her hair. Then she turned to Rachel, a bottle of perfume in hand.

'Leave me alone,' Rachel said coldly, pushing away Josie's hand as it came towards her face. She wanted to uncouple herself from Josie, disentangle some huge knot that was tying them together.

Josie grabbed a cone and stuck it up her nostril. She made her eyes go funny to make a joke of Carpenter's things. She wanted to make Rachel laugh.

'They give off strong smells,' Rachel said. 'They have them in Buddhist temples t' keep away evil spirits.'

'That's amazing,' Josie said. 'I never knew Buddhists believed in evil spirits.'

'Well, they do,' Rachel said. 'My mother knows about them.'

Adrian looked pleased and sour at the same time; here was an idea he should have thought of first. He picked up a cone. 'Let's try them,' he said, taking the matches. He was acting smart, as if he had something up his sleeve. Everything he did was just a rehearsal for the grand act, shortly to take place, in which his dominance would be forever established.

The match flared. Adrian's face came into view, eyes darkly intent on his task. His hand shook as he lit the cone, and I had flash of what it would look like if his fingers caught fire.

Rachel inspected all the cones. 'This one's sandalwood and this one's jasmine. And these two are patchouli.' I held my breath, waiting for her to catch on that something else was happening. It was hopeless for me to try to warn her, and like the others I was prepared to let her figure it out. That way she'd believe it. She'd know for sure.

A moment later the stagnant air was being filled by lazily moving smoke wraiths. There was a riot of smells alright, and I felt downright sick from them, but that was all. The Stench was still there, of course: the incense could do nothing about that.

Carpenter got bored again and began chipping away again at the cupboard door, a restless, trapped sound. Splinters stuck out around the lock.

'That crowbar won't help.' It was the voice Josie used when she didn't know whether she was lying or telling the truth, and was in that strange territory where the truth was no more than the improvised understandings of the moment, so close to lies it doesn't matter. She was talking about the trapdoor, and all of us but Rachel knew that.

Rachel was turning towards her, puzzled, when Josie swivelled on her heel and turned to Adrian. 'I want t' know if Adrian's brought me anything else. Like some chocolate biscuits. Or some hot fish 'n' chips. When you came in I was dreaming about hot fish 'n' chips. You were behind the counter, making them for me, and I was waiting readin a magazine about this film star with the great big tits.'

You can tell when Adrian's out of his depth. He gets this dark, brooding look as if he is in control of everything, and as if his own immense cool is the centre around which everything else orbits.

'I got nothing else.' Like any slave, he began to whine. 'Water's heavy, y' know. The one thing heavier than water is books.'

'I'm hungry,' Josie said, as if this were something she was just discovering. 'You guys wouldn't let me starve in here, would you?'

I'd thought of that. It was my turn. I had something else hidden away which I knew belonged with the candles but was too shy to bring out. In the meantime, I knew what to bring out of my bag to win favour with the queen. Bread and cheese, which I had stolen from our fridge.

Josie snatched them and devoured them in front of our eyes. Everybody else's hunger stirred as they watched her eat.

She turned her back on me, however, the provider of the gift, with hardly an acknowledgement. This was not because she was cruel but because she could not meet my eye, could not admit even for a second any indebtedness to me. You had to forgive Josie things like that all the time, just as you did with Adrian.

Rachel watched her devour my offering with growing concern. 'You'll starve in here,' she said, returning to her old attack. She was trying to find the right argument and never would.

'Only if you let me.' With something resembling triumph, Josie squeezed the last hunk of bread together until it crumbled between her fingers, and ate the bits that fell. She was at our mercy, therefore we were at hers.

'Is that all you've got, Baby?' she said, the last crumbs of bread falling from her chin into her open palm. She was hungry enough to know that I was hiding something.

It wasn't anything big; its humbleness was easily swallowed by greater fates. I was ashamed to bring it out.

'She's acting strange,' Josie said nervously. 'I don't like it when she acts strange.' She turned to Adrian for support.

Everybody was suddenly looking at me. It was the one thing I hated. I had to shift the attention back onto Carpenter, somehow. There were risks in doing this but I would run them anyway.

'His pocket,' I said, pointing.

It was enough. It's funny how someone looks when they blush in candlelight; they look as if they are about to die.

From his pocket Carpenter drew forth a pure white surgical mask, like Dad used sometimes in the garage if he was spray painting. It lay like an accusation on his palm.

'What's it for?' Rachel said sharply. 'How's that going t' help Josie?'

She was close to it now, so close. She was asking Carpenter to lie and that was going to be an interesting exercise.

'It'll protect us from contamination.' He said 'us' at the last minute, because he'd brought it for himself, of course, when he used the crowbar to lift the trapdoor.

'What contamination?'

'All the junk around here.' Carpenter's crowbar resumed its clawing at the cupboard door lock, the mask back in his pocket, waiting its time, keeping its untouched white for that unspecified moment when the trapdoor came loose and he needed it the most. It was laughable to think that he believed the flimsy, sterilised cotton would or could protect him for even a microsecond from what his precious crowbar might prise loose from beneath the trapdoor. He was still under the dark enchantment of believing his own rigid, two-fingered logic.

This put him in a sweat, and gave the crowbar an excuse for further practice on the cupboard doors.

'I know what it's for.' Josie said suddenly. 'It's for playing doctors and nurses. Why don't you put it on, Carpenter?'

Rachel grinned. She was forgetting what she had been puzzled about.

'Would you like to play doctors and nursies with Baby, Carpenter?' Josie asked in her sweetest voice.

Adrian gave a snort of contempt and the two girls giggled furiously into each other's faces. Josie put her fingers to Rachel's lips as if Rachel had been about to say something too naughty, or too wonderful, for words. I didn't know if Rachel was just playing along, or had lost herself in her passion for Josie. Either way I had to hide my hurt.

Adrian, however, had picked up on the scent, the trail I thought I'd neatly left behind with Carpenter's mask. 'I still want to know what Baby's got in her pocket,' he said, completing the circle of hatred, at least for the moment.

I knew there was a certain point at which I'd have to give up on him, and I didn't know when that would be, but the time would come, sooner rather than later.

Carpenter brought the crowbar down hard and with a sharp snap the lock fell loose. The door of the cupboard fell open just as the window had opened, intentioned and of its own accord. But it was an invitation to nothingness. The cupboard was bare.

Just as Adrian had said, there was nothing inside. I was probably the only one to notice his 'I told you so' look.

◦

It's the only photograph of a dead person that I know, not counting honest beard. He's Luke, our lost brother who died a few weeks after being born; not even the hospital when it was working could save him. If he'd lived he would have been older than me. Adrian once said that I'd been born because Mum and Dad were trying to get Luke back again, but that's not true. Mum and Dad wanted me, they both said.

Sometimes he likes to come at night to share my dreams, because he died before his dreams could be made, and I don't mind.

In the photograph little Luke is lying on his back waving his legs in the air and gurgling. He has a squinty, happy face, and a flat, newly born forehead. I often stare at him, wondering what it was like for a little baby, with no memories to lose, to be dead. It's different from old people. Old people, with plenty of memories, you expect to die, and they expect it too. A baby doesn't know what to expect. It dies and not much changes.

I didn't feel like bringing out the photograph of the dead Luke, but I did it, knowing that Adrian wouldn't leave me alone until he knew what I was hiding.

I propped the photograph up between the two candles Rachel had brought. Little Luke's face was barely a blur in the moonlight.

Everybody stared.

'You shouldn't have brought that,' Adrian said, sounding almost shocked.

No one laughed and I was happy about that. Carpenter lost interest first and went back to prising open the next cupboard.

'Is that your dead brother?' Josie said, disbelieving.

'It's true,' Adrian said, staring at the photograph. Then he gave me a different look. As though he were afraid of me. As though I'd done this deliberately to get at him.

'What happened to him?' Rachel asked.

'Cot death, Mum said.' Adrian muttered the words quickly so he didn't have to think about what they meant.

'That's very sad,' Josie said, taking my hand and giving it a squeeze, but she didn't look the least bit sad.

'Y' shouldn't have done it,' Adrian said again, and I didn't know why or what he was thinking. Josie didn't know either.

'He's under the floorboards then, isn't he?' She grinned at me, hoping to freak me, waiting to see the pain.

'That's a horrible thing to say,' Rachel said, drawing away from Josie. Adrian tried to laugh it off, but it wasn't easy to recognise the sounds coming out of his throat as laughter.

They didn't understand, none of them, even Rachel. I wanted to have Luke with me to protect me; his photograph provided a link, not to the past, like Great-great-grandfather's honest beard, but with the future: unborn, unspoken, beyond the limits of Hikitarua and Highway 5, beyond the shadows and the pastels. There was some unspoken agreement between Luke and me that he would take me through the fire when the time came and I could already see the flames silently eating the flesh away from the world. The little body of Luke had been cremated, Mum told me, and his ashes scattered to heaven. Even as I placed his image between the candle flames I saw the ashes scattering to the moon, but they were not cold and dry, like ashes in an urn, but hot and cindery, like fragments of hot bone glowing above a crematorium chimney. Pieces of fireworks on a cool spring night, their brief glory spent, looping in sparks towards the earth.

There was no way, even if I had the gift of tongues, that I could tell them of this. Christ gives us our blessing by leaving us to our own salvation.

'I don't like it,' Josie said. 'It gives me the spooks.'

She was about to sweep it away with her hand when Adrian intervened. Not only was he bothered about becoming an increasingly minor character, upstaged even by his idiot sister, he didn't want to see hot wax splashed on the photograph of Luke. It was the only one our family had; there was no negative. There was no other record that such a child ever existed.

He put up his hand and blocked Josie's. If you thought Josie would oppose him and make an issue of it you would be wrong; she was far more cunning than that. She didn't give a shit about the photograph for she had the trapdoor, and the moment that was sprung, which I dared not think about, the game would change all over again and the threats would present themselves from quite different directions.

'Don't blame her,' Adrian said to Josie, firmly blocking her arm. 'She brought y' the bread, remember? It's just her little thingy.' He could have made it sound sarcastic but he didn't. He was sticking up for me, against

Josie; I could hardly believe it but it was happening. It was for Luke he was doing it, as much as for me, but in this case what he did for Luke he was doing for me.

Meanwhile, since everything was happening at once in this hyped-up time, Carpenter smashed through his second cupboard door, and scrabbled around amidst the rat shit. There was nothing there of course.

'What is that pong?' Rachel said suddenly. There were goosebumps coming up along her arm. Her hairs were standing upright as if fingers were passing close by. Finally, it was catching up with her.

'It's just the smell of the hospital,' Adrian said.

But they couldn't fool Rachel for ever. She screwed up her face. 'Smells like something rotten.'

At that moment little Luke's face ceased to be a blur, but resolved itself into a sharply outlined miniature, and floated out of the frame to hover in the candlelight the way a rainbow hovers in the air. Sharp little eyes spiked at mine. I looked around to see if anybody else could see it, but nobody had noticed a thing.

Carpenter paused in his work on the cupboard door. 'It's too dry for rotting.' He waved his crowbar in the air to prove his point. The point of the crowbar passed through Luke's hovering face, which vanished back into the photograph. The Stench, I thought. It can change things. Reach out into the real world and twist images around. Luke's photograph. The drawing of Carpenter I did yesterday.

'Under the floor,' Rachel said, getting frightened again. 'It's coming up from underneath.'

Carpenter looked thoughtful. 'You might be right,' he said, then went back to the last cupboard door.

They are playing her, all of them, I thought, like the cat and the mouse, drawing her deeper, confounding her with the appearance of normality before striking once more, closer to the jugular. All the time, softening her up. Even Carpenter with his senseless battering at empty cupboard doors was playing the same game, hiding inside the trapdoors of his own mind while raising the crowbar high. It was the love of the crowbar that drove him into the next blow. He didn't care what the cupboards revealed. The noise he made got everybody watching him, watching the crowbar, holding their breath, waiting for next, reckless blow.

'I can't smell anything,' Josie said. 'Except all that incense.'

Carpenter stood back to smash his way through the last cupboard. 'Stand back,' he said as he went into his swing. It took him a few blows before the door split.

There was something inside.

'Hit it again,' Josie said and Carpenter did. The candle flames quivered and the photograph of Luke fell forward on its face.

'Again,' Josie shouted.

'You don't have to say it every time,' Carpenter said. The noise was like a muffled explosion. The cupboard door had come away. I replaced the photo while Carpenter pulled the battered door out.

Soon we were all standing around the bucket-sized rubbish tin. It contained needles, old hypodermic needles, some with plungers attached, others fronting little cellophane sacks. These last ones, I knew, were used once and thrown away. Little frothing creatures.

Carpenter's eyes glittered as if they feasted on some great treasure he'd won from a dragon. Adrian too was interested. He knelt down beside the tin and picked up a couple of needles, holding them up for inspection in the candlelight.

'I bet some of them had drugs in them,' Carpenter said. 'Medicines and things. Inoculations,' trotting that last word out very proudly, 'like we had at school.'

'And blood,' Adrian said. 'Some would've had blood in them.'

'Oooh, that's horrible,' Josie said.

'Burn them,' I said, and everybody laughed because I always said the stupidest things. I hadn't meant to say that anyway. Josie ran her hands through my hair as if I were her pet animal, cute but silly. I noticed how hot and skinny her hands were. How they clung to the surface of my skin with their clammy touch.

'I hope I don't dream about these horrible needles,' Rachel said. 'It's like thinking about something all the time - you can't stop yourself. I just know I'm going to have bad dreams. If I do it will be your fault, Josie.'

'I'm not scared to spend the night here,' Josie said, trying to keep the quiver out of her mouth.

'I dreamed about an electron microscope,' Carpenter said. 'And I was in it, and I was just a big mass of crawly things.'

Adrian said, 'That's not a bad dream.'

'It's a stupid dream,' Josie said in a voice suggesting that all dreams were stupid. It was Rachel's comment that had bothered her.

They all stopped talking at the same moment, the way it happens sometimes, and I felt the shift, a tilt in the way everybody was standing. Carpenter had run out of cupboards to bash, and the silence of the hospital settled in deeply around us. The candle flames jerked, then leaned over as if they were bowing to the shadows, which, like a chorus of ghosts, bowed with them. It felt to me as if the trapdoor was right in front of us, about to open. I could feel Josie squirming about inside the silence, restless and unresolved, while the others breathed in and out, waiting for something to happen.

I began to hiccup, and Adrian punched me in the arm to shut me up. He'd felt the shift himself and it had frightened the hell out of him. One moment he'd been looking at Rachel, thinking how pretty she was in the candlelight with her black hair soft on her shoulders, the next he was turned around the other way facing the dark of the corridor.

'Danger!' I shouted, as if we were about to cross a busy road.

Josie gave a hateful, jagged laugh, maybe because she'd seen the way Adrian was looking at Rachel, but I don't think so. I think she was laughing because she knew that the trapdoor would win in the end.

'What does she mean?' Rachel turned to Adrian, who didn't look at me.

'Nothing,' he said. 'She's just playing her own game. Haunted hospitals.' He made a dismissive gesture.

'Danger!' I said, pointing to the corridor.

'Then she should shut up,' Josie looked at me bleakly. 'I don't like her. She has a funny look in her eyes.'

Rachel grabbed her arm. 'Josie!'

'I don't care, I think she's nuts.'

'That's right,' Adrian said. 'She's nuts, all right. I should know. She woke up in the middle of the night shouting about something.'

'Let's quit fucking around,' Josie said, nervously fingering her calves and pinching her thighs. She didn't say what we should be doing or why they all felt impelled to leave the kitchen. They drifted out into the corridor as if they weren't even moving at all, as if they were all still floating around the candles and Luke's photo and the rubbish tin. I watched them without joining them, heard their voices, full of dusty echoes, saw their shadowy figures merging and separating in the gloom.

'That smell is worse out here,' I heard Rachel say.

'It's not so bad upstairs,' Josie said.

'I thought you couldn't smell it,' Rachel said.

They don't want to tell her about the trapdoor because they don't want her to question them, I thought. It's not real forgetfulness. They're going to pretend to find it all over again. Then lift it. They'll go through this great big act.

'I don't want to go any further,' Rachel said. 'I want to go back.'

'Come back,' I said to her from behind them. Josie giggled a bit but nobody was in a laughing mood.

'I hate the way she creeps around,' Josie said to Adrian, giving me a nasty look.

'There's nothing here, you can see for yourself,' Adrian said.

'It must be under the floor,' Carpenter said in the most stupid voice you'd ever heard. Carpenter is one of those bunglers who just can't tell a lie to save their souls.

'What must?' asked Rachel.

'Whatever it is making that stink,' Josie said impatiently, as if that was what they had been talking about all along.

Rachel covered her nose with her jacket. Josie was grinning furiously. Carpenter was breathing so hard he was fogging up his glasses. 'It's stronger than last night,' he said.

'Why would it do that?' Rachel asked.

'I don't know.'

But I knew. We had disturbed its lair last night; tonight it was waiting for us.

Adrian was already kneeling on the floor, in the middle of the corridor, his back to the arch. The coloured glass crossed his face as he bent over. He wasn't about to let Josie take away the action this time.

'It's right here,' he said. 'Under here.'

Carpenter scuttled to his side, grinning like an idiot.

'What are you scared of?' Josie said to Rachel, who was hanging back. 'I never thought you'd be all wimpy like this. There's nothing here but some stink or other. It's probably just some dead cats under the floorboards.'

'It's worse than dead cats,' Rachel said. 'Far worse.'

I waited for Josie to start talking about dead people and babies, but she didn't.

'I'm going home,' Rachel said. 'I said I wouldn't be late.'

'It's not late!' said Josie, as if the idea was quite outrageous. 'I bet The Simpsons isn't even finished on TV yet. I bet y' anything y' like. You're just exaggerating everything because y' think it's going to give y' bad dreams and stuff. You'd expect an old place like this to have funny smells. Your just tryin t' make me scared so I won't stay here.'

'There's something funny though. You guys're acting strange. You've got t' get out of here, Josie.'

'What?' said Josie, sounding a bit frightened, a bit desperate at the thought that Rachel might pull out.

'Baby understands,' Rachel said, 'even if she can't talk properly.'

'Baby doesn't understand nothing,' Josie said. 'She's just a retard.'

I was too hurt to even look at her, to witness her shame. Yet she had a good soul, did Josie; she had just forgotten how to smile properly.

'Shut up,' said Rachel, suddenly furious. 'You can't say that.'

'Shut up yourself,' Josie said. 'I can say what I like. Go home if you want to, and miss the adventure.' She looked towards Adrian and Carpenter, who were conferring in whispers up by the trapdoor. She was getting impatient.

Josie and Rachel glared at each other, then Josie started crying. She didn't want to break up with her best friend of all time.

The two had a tearful reconciliation.

'It's all happening too fast,' Rachel said 'What are the boys talking about?'

'Trapdoor,' I said as loudly as I could. Adrian and Carpenter looked up. I thought Josie was going to attack me. I shouldn't have said it; it confirmed Josie as my enemy.

Rachel started shaking Josie. 'What is she talking about? What's going on here, Josie?'

'Just a silly old trapdoor. We found it last night.'

'And you didn't tell me? Why?'

Josie was all innocence; she didn't have Carpenter's problems when it came to lying. 'Why should I have? What's so special about it anyway?'

Rachel looked as if she couldn't believe her ears, turned on her heel and walked up to join the boys, Josie and I following behind. The boys had not wasted any time. The lino was already peeled back and the naked floor, with its dimly outlined trapdoor, was once more visible.

'There's no handle,' Adrian said.

'Quick thinking,' said Josie who was starting to get that cunning look she got when she thought she was plotting.

Carpenter didn't seem to be aware of the fuss. He was pondering the trapdoor deeply and had finally come up with a judgement. 'Probably some way to get at the electrics.' He sounded like his Dad, and put his hand on his chin the same way his Dad did. His eyes swam around behind his steamed-up glasses.

'Is that what it is?' Rachel was standing a few feet from the trapdoor staring hard at it.

'There has to be some way of getting underneath the building,' Carpenter said in the most reasonable tones imaginable. 'We'll need a torch to see anything properly. I should've brought one.'

'The stink is incredible.' Rachel was starting to look faint on her feet. 'It makes me want to puke.'

'Puke away,' Josie said.

'We've got t' open it,' Adrian declared. 'Go and get the crowbar, Carpenter.' Carpenter hastened to obey, heading off down the corridor to the faint yellow glow of candlelight.

'No,' I said.

Adrian sneered, 'You're getting to be a real nuisance, Baby,' he said.

'She's been a pest all along,' Josie said, slipping her hand into his. Adrian nearly died from pleasure. Josie had never done that before as far as I knew. The boy puffed himself up big enough to burst. He wasn't sixteen going on nineteen, he was immortal.

'You just butt out of it, Baby,' Adrian said. 'You're just a moron. How come I get a moron for a sister?'

Nobody knew.

'You've hurt her feelings,' Rachel said.

Adrian stamped on the trapdoor like a bull pawing at the ground. 'Tough titty. Who gives a rat's arse about her feelings?'

Josie thought that was very funny. She had to let go Adrian's hand to cover her mouth.

Rachel was biting her lower lip so hard that ugly red marks were left. And she was holding back as if about to make a run for the door. Her face, pale at the best of times, was now bloodless behind the curly shadows of her hair. 'Please, Josie,' she said, 'come away from here.'

'Let's get to work,' Carpenter said, arriving with the crowbar, pushing past her. His eyes, huge behind his glasses, were alight with excitement.

'Give me that thing,' Adrian said, reaching out his hand.

Carpenter stepped back. 'It's my father's.'

'Go and get the candle,' Josie said to Rachel.

Rachel didn't move.

'Just go and get it,' Josie snapped. 'And forget about all that bullshit.'

I didn't see why Rachel should, or what Josie was trying to prove, but to my amazement she went. Just turned on her heel and went, and without even a single glance my way.

With Rachel gone it felt as if I had lost them all. I looked back yearningly towards the kitchen and the yellowing, flickery light. Luke's photograph would be sitting between the candles. Beyond them the storeroom, the window and the world outside.

Was Rachel waiting for me to join her? Make our escape and betray Josie to the world?

The pale oval of colour on the dusty floor. The window, hovering in the alcove wall. The thin orange light from the outside seeping through the dusty front windows. The eerie sense of standing somehow at the center, the fulcrum, of the dark energy that followed us around wherever we went in the hospital. Last night it had sucked the meaning out of our words and mocked us with our own echoes; tonight it had more in store.

Rachel moved slowly bringing the candle with her, trying not to spill any light.

◦

Josie stood rigidly like a high priestess while Rachel brought the candle and placed it beside the trapdoor. Then, pushing Rachel aside with a triumphant cry, she fell onto the trapdoor and gazed at it with great yearning, as if looking into the face of a lover or someone who had just died. Her fingers raked over its surface, half caressing, half scratching.

Rachel took off her jacket, leaving her pale arms bare, wrapping it around her head and across her nose like a bandit. Then she knelt beside Josie and gently touched her shoulder. Josie flinched as if she had been struck.

Josie said, 'Maybe we shouldn't open it after all. It would spoil everything somehow. Whatever it is, it's bound to be a disappointment.'

Rachel was crying softly. When I saw the tears my fingers felt for the thimble I'd stuck in my pocket at home and forgotten about. 'You must be crazy, Josie. The stink is horrible. What're y' doing lying there for? Get up...

please.'

But Josie's fingers were already scratching the dust-filled crack that was the edge of the trapdoor.

'You'll never lift it that way,' Carpenter said. He was gripping the crowbar with both fists, so that Adrian, who was hovering nearby, couldn't grab it.

Rachel drew back and unwrapped the jacket. Her face was completely impassive, like a mask. Her arms were like those of a pale marble statue. She's changing, I thought; inside she's changing and she's put on a mask to hide it. I still couldn't understand why she had meekly obeyed Josie before, and was abandoning her now. Sometimes you think you understand people, sometimes you don't have a chance.

'It'll be dark down there,' Adrian said. There was an unexpected quiver in his voice. The sweat was coming back into his voice; he was like a diver once more, running out of oxygen.

'We'll need a torch,' Carpenter said again, in anguish now at not having one. He fumbled in his pocket and pulled out his surgical mask, which he doused in perfume. Once it was in place, with the strap behind his head, he was a pair of glasses and a white mask, like a real doctor.

Everybody stared at him.

Towering over the trapdoor with crowbar in hand, surgical face mask in place, glasses bulging on his nose, he assumed, in his own mind, leadership of our group. If anyone could crack this thing and bring the Stench to heel it would be Carpenter, the only rational one in a cage of chattering monkeys. There was not even time to pause and clean his glasses. He knelt and began to seriously apply the crowbar to the edge of the trapdoor, nostrils twitching beneath the protective gauze, taking no notice of Josie. He looked like some crazy doctor, levering open a patient's ribs. The crowbar had now grown into his arm, sinews of steel bonding with bone and tendons to make a new arm - a powerful, probing, lifting arm. A steel claw with a pair of toes.

Josie, who had been picking at the dust around the edge, gave a demented shriek and began scrabbling at the trapdoor, pushing aside the crowbar to get at the crack.

I felt something pass through the building like the shudder a gust of wind will bring to empty rooms. A hairline split appeared in the caked dust where Josie's fingers ripped. The trapdoor did not lift even a fraction out of its gunky bed, but it moved, shook as the building shook, opening a tiny fault line in its bed.

Because she was closest to that tiny crack, it hit Josie first. It was as if someone had struck her with a hammer; her head banged the floor as she passed out.

Then we all got it. It was like the smell of all the sickness and the rotting and death in the world in one place; everything horrible and infected dumped right there. You didn't just smell it; it ate into the back of your nose like acid and it licked your skin until you felt slimy all over.

Carpenter yelled and gagged. His mask hung down from his jaw like a second mouth, and it was screaming. The crowbar clattered to the floor. The candle flame bent so low it licked the floor. Adrian retched. He crawled away from the trapdoor towards the distant kitchen, heaving and groaning, a hand over his mouth and screams squeezing through his fingers. Carpenter staggered past him, clawing the air.

Rachel rocked on her heels as if she were being pushed. You could see the dark veins climbing the silver of her neck. She didn't falter for a moment, however, but bent over to drag Josie clear.

I was seeing everything through a sharp, cruel lens. I was there but I was not there. I could walk away; I owed nothing to Josie. Let her die. Let her die of some horrible toxic contamination. I wasn't moving. I was just standing there waiting for her to die. She was nothing but a wounded insect lying on the floor in the filth and dust. The sooner she dies the better, I thought. Hateful people like her have no right to live. Why should they live? Are they going to bring any joy or love into the world? No. Just misery and jealousy and horribleness.

Then Rachel looked up at me. Her eyes were huge. She didn't have to say anything. I'm strong enough to easily lift Josie without Rachel's help.

All I could think of was that outside there would be stars. Fires. Distant fires. Clean, cold and hard.

▪

Josie came-to in the dehydrated air, spitting, trying to get some moisture into her mouth. 'We've got stars,' she said.

The wan light of the open air was hard and true on our faces after the dim, waxy interior of the hospital.

'Thought I was goin t' die,' Rachel said, heaving the air in and out. 'And I saw something, and now I know I'll have bad dreams. If I have bad dreams it's your fault, Josie.'

'I didn't see anything,' said Josie. 'We just imagined it, you know, the way Baby imagines things.'

She never missed an opportunity, did Josie.

'It's in our clothes,' Rachel said in revulsion, pulling her blouse away from her skin.

'It's contaminated us,' Carpenter said. 'Like radiation.' He seemed more excited by this idea than anything else.

'That's silly,' Adrian countered. He wanted to get away but couldn't leave the conversation in this state, and was casting about for a heroic way out.

'No it isn't.' Carpenter was resolute. He would argue the point all night. 'It might be breeding inside us right now.'

'That's yuck.' Rachel hugged her shivering body as if her frail, ivory arms could save her.

'What did you see?' Adrian asked her.

'I didn't see anything,' Rachel snarled. 'There was nothing to see. We're talking about that dreadful stench.'

No one wanted to talk about it.

Rachel backed away from us, her hands outstretched, warding us off. 'You're all going to die! All of you! Carpenter is right.'

Carpenter nodded feverishly. He may not have heard what she said.

We stared at her.

'The Stench's nothing,' Josie said recklessly. 'I'm not going to die, I'm immune. You're just making a big drama.'

'You're all getting up my nose,' Adrian said.

'You're dying even now. It's inside you.' Rachel was slowly looking from one to the next, searching out the worm of death.

Carpenter said, 'She might be right. That's what dead things do. They get inside you and create illness. Microbes. They have microbes.'

Josie licked her dry lips. 'Well, I'm going back in,' she said. 'The Stench will help to hide me, keep people away. Especially the cops.'

'That's your choice then,' Rachel said, sounding very adult. It sounded like the sort of thing her mother would say.

Josie turned her back and returned to the window. Carpenter was already gone, heading for home.

Adrian didn't know which way to weasel.

Mitch

Standing outside the hospital, the voices of the others fading in my ears, I looked up at the sky and breathed deeply. The moon looked different tonight, somehow cooler and further away. That's the thing about the moon: it can look very close or impossibly far away, depending on its mood. And you can breathe it in with the silver air.

When I came back down from the moon, I was alone. Without a word, without a sound, everybody had split. And that coward Adrian had gone too, vanished like smoke into the deserted streets; Hikitarua spun around me, empty. Outside the hospital, the streetlight flared and popped. A tiny slice of darkness opened up beneath it with a tinkle of falling glass. A triangular corner of the hospital, sloping roof and wall, went dark. A shooting star flared above the roof.

A police car cruised the street, not in a hurry to go anywhere, and I pulled back into the shadows of the hospital. When it had passed I slipped through the back fence, took a good long look around and made a dash for the wall. I didn't quite make it. The police car had cruised the block and was now returning by the back street. It pulled up beside me just as I was about to take the track up onto the wall. The side window wound down and Mitch looked out.

I guessed it was Boss Hogg driving.

'Hey, Baby,' she called, her voice touched by an Australian drawl, 'you're out late. You on your own?' She was wearing her police cap and looked very official, but gave me her big wide smile, the one that made all the boys go silly.

I tried to imitate it, pointing to the wall. 'Adrian,' I said.

Mitch nodded. Like everybody else she saw me as the town's big little moron, but she didn't seem to hold it against me the way some did.

'Where you off to?'

'Home.'

'That's a good idea. You seen Josie around?'

The question was floated at me casually, as if it didn't mean anything, as if Josie hadn't been missing all day, but for me the moment had arrived, and I didn't hesitate. Well, hardly. The thought of Adrian did skip into my mind, but only for a moment.

I nodded.

'Do you know where she is?'

'Yes.'

'Where?'

You could see the back of the hospital through the fence, and the hole Adrian and I used. I pointed to the hospital.

At this point the other cop spoke, the driver. This was Boss Hogg, as everyone called him, a fat man with a bald head, the kind you might see acting as a sheriff in westerns. He sounded very tired. If there was one thing he hated it was missing kids.

'The hospital. We looked it over today. Nothing there.' When he talked, Boss Hogg looked like a bulldog chewing on a steak sandwich.

'Wouldn't hurt to take another peek,' Mitch said, sweetly.

Boss Hogg groaned and got out of the car. 'I can't get in without smashing down some boards,' he complained. 'But I'll take a look around.'

'And why don't you sit in the car, out of the cold for a while, Baby,' she said to me, even though it wasn't cold. It was an invitation I wasn't expected to refuse.

I don't know how long Boss Hogg was gone. Mitch did her best to make bright conversation with the idiot but eventually she fell silent and we both listened to the surge of static coming through the police radio. It sounded like communications from Mars.

When he returned he shook his head in negation. 'Just some old junk lying about.'

'We'll take you home, Baby,' Mitch said.

As the police car sucked me smoothly through the quiet streets of Hikitarua, Mitch pressed her face against the glass and stared out. I knew she was thinking about Josie, and where she might be. She didn't share Boss Hogg's assumption that 'the girl would turn up'; she'd seen too many girls who never turned up.

If I were to tap her on the shoulder now, what would I say? What had happened? Where was the evidence?

We took the long way, and as we passed the milk bar, we slowed enough to see Rush Jimmy wiping down the tables, getting ready to close up. He moved in jerks like a mechanical doll. It had to be around 10 p.m. There'd be nothing open after that but the all-night petrol station.

As Boss Hog pulled into our street, Mitch wound down her window and took a deep breath of air. I knew immediately what it was; even Boss Hogg's nose was twitching. The deep, comfortable smells of the police car had not been enough to overcome it.

'Come and see me any time you want, Baby' Mitch said as they dropped me off. She understood things without being told and knew something was up, but our worlds were too far apart for her to ask the right questions.

I could write to her, I thought as I got out of the car, before I remembered the muddled-looking jumble I would put down on the page.

The look she left me with was wide open. With it came a plan. Rachel would be my bridge; she would find the words. Mitch trusted me, more than even she trusted Boss Hogg, who was busy writing something down in his notebook.

Street light smashed opposite hospital, he'd written.

⊡

I didn't go home, though. My feet were too restless and besides, I didn't know if I could face Mum and Dad alone without Adrian. Would he have come home, dared show up without me?

I ran to the end of the street and up onto the wall just from the power of my own feet. I wasn't looking for Adrian exactly, but my eyes scanned the wall as I went over, down onto the stony riverbed beyond, where the stones were as white as eggshells in the moonlight.

Hikitarua was built on the edge of a river which wriggled from the Southern Alps down to the sea like a great stony worm heading for the ocean. At least a kilometre across, it was a maze, a world of shingle, broom and gorse, dying pools and trickles of water. The province of clumpy stones, it looked monstrous under moonlight, a sea of stones, like the moon, broken by lumps of water and abandoned bracken. Sometimes there were logs, white as bones, skewered on the rocks. At night the stones were all grey and the broom and lupin black. If you looked back up the river you looked right into the heart of the Southern Alps, whose spring thaw fed the river. Lately, there hadn't been that much snow and the spring floods had been sluggish, leaving the broom and gorse to take over the higher rifts of shingle.

I looked up at the sky, hoping for more stars, but a thin, shredded cloud system was getting in the way, putting a gauzy ring around the bulging moon and grey-washing the stars. There was a bit of a track to the first channel, a great hollow eaten out by greywacke under a spring thaw and overhung by a clump of lupin. I squatted down beneath it with the jostled stones, trying to think about what I should do. I felt like a tiny person lying in sand.

There was a crunch of stones and a shadow fell over me. I looked up expecting to see Adrian but it wasn't him, it was Serendipity Rabbitt, the nosy kid from across the street. I'd never seen a less welcome sight.

'Rabbitt,' I said, standing up. I ran a clumsy tongue around my lips, hating the need for words.

I wondered how she managed to get out of the house at this hour without anyone noticing. Probably a matter of how slimy you can be. I didn't know exactly why I hated Rabbitt so. Perhaps because I wanted to be on my own, with not another soul in sight, especially such a sick one as Rabbitt.

'Don't follow me,' I said.

A sly look came over her face. 'Don't follow me,' she said. She kicked over a stone with a bare foot; it was dry underneath.

'A fool are you,' I said,

'A fool are you,' she said, grinning.

I sighed. You could go on like this forever with Rabbitt. Happy just to have somebody to talk to, she would repeat what you said because she had nothing of her own to say.

I looked back at the moon as if I'd forgotten something. 'You. Us. Follow?'

Silence.

She didn't drool exactly, but her lower lip, without the thumb, was so wet it always looked as if she was about to.

'Being spies?'

A faint nod.

'Hospital?'

She gave me a look as if she wanted me to do something to her, like hurt her; once when I hurt her she gave me that look. As though she expected me to hurt her again. Wanted me to. Sometimes it was hard to refuse that sort of invitation. I had to remember that I was bigger and stronger than I felt.

'Very stupid,' I said.

Silence.

It occurred to me then I could very easily kill her right now. Nobody would know. I could kill her with one of these moonstruck stones. It wasn't impossible, far from it. Bring a stone down on her head hard enough and her skull would crack. All her brains would spill out. Better still, lure her to the hospital, if that's where she was so keen on going, and let her be the first down the trapdoor into the pit beneath. That would get the thumb out of her mouth quick enough.

You can't suck your thumb while you're trying to scream.

The thought of it, like a worm crawling into my brain, made me laugh, and when I laughed I saw these thoughts spewing out into my head as if from a broken test tube inside my brain. Putrid dreams of murder; Rabbitt's blood dripping into the trapdoor and the look on her face when she finally understood.

Maybe it was this she was seeking, some terrible flame she couldn't see but could feel on her flesh singeing the hair.

'Adrian.' I made the motions of wringing her neck. She had encountered Adrian before, and pulled her lower lip in acknowledgement, but all this was fun to her, even the thought of Adrian killing her. She didn't understand anything.

I picked up a stone large enough for the job and held it heavy in my hands. There was a moon inside it; if I broke it open on her skull, the moon would fly into the sky.

'Hothpital,' she said, giving me a sly look.

Sooner or later she'd tell someone at school and that would be the end of it. All the little kids would be lining up for Adrian to kill them. Or me. Baby the killer. They would smell the trapdoor and come crawling.

'I'm going t' tell,' Rabbitt said. She had that spongy look she got when she thought she had something on you.

'Yes,' I said, lifting the rock, testing its weight against gravity. Her body would lie there amid the tideless stones, undiscovered, until someone came along, maybe one of the search parties they'd soon be putting out for Josie.

'Yeth I will.' She carried on as if she were arguing with me. 'Tell on Adrian.'

'Adrian,' I said, trying to make it sound as little like a question as possible. Sure as something turns into a question, Rabbitt will refuse to say anything. Getting info out of her is a fine art. I didn't put the rock down though; the coldness of it grew into my fingers. I would let her have her say, then do it. I wanted to know what she had on Adrian.

She might have known that, for the thumb went straight back into her mouth, her big round eyes suggesting that maybe I didn't belong in the same world as she did, which was fine by me. Then she giggled. 'Old man thaid, "I'll pith in ya fuckin' faith".'

'Man what?'

The garbled question was too direct, too urgent. The thumb went into the mouth all the way up to the elbow, the eyes grew round and far away in her pudding face.

'You thtink,' she said, thumb still in her mouth, backing away. I guess having that thumb in her mouth made her breathe through her nose. 'A horrible thtink.'

I dropped the stone and it cracked open like a skull. There was no moon inside, but something like a white egg, densely packed.

'Adrian gave me thome withky,' she simpered. She stood for a moment looking down at the riverbed while I sat as still as a fox in twilight, then she was gone. A swift crunch of stones.

I sweated from relief. I wonder if she knew how close she'd come.

·

The house looked dark and closed up, like a house of strangers. I paused in the yard before crossing to the door. I thought I'd left the night behind but

I hadn't. It seemed as if I looked at the house and street beyond through the stagnant, worn linoleum corridors of the hospital. The empty wards with their naked spring beds were like wire skeletons, stretched across the yard and lawn. The faded patch of colour on the floor from the dusty lead-light window floated over the street lamps and the rhododendron bushes with their night echo of absent voices like the dull edge of a dream that hadn't surrendered to dawn.

The corridor was the street, the street was the town, the town stretched to the edge of the horizon, which joined the sky. It felt as if I had never left and could never leave that corridor, those peeling walls.

Inside, the passageway was dark and I got to the bathroom and into the shower unseen. I scrubbed and washed and scrubbed: no mother could dream of such a scrubbing, washing daughter. I used everything I could find, from bubble bath to Dad's aftershave, which had a bit of a smell to it.

When I couldn't go on any longer because my fingers were going all wrinkled, I dried myself down, shoved my clothes into the laundry basket, and found a dressing gown in the hot-water cupboard, which felt warm and woolly against my skin.

By the time I got back into the kitchen, where there were some leftovers on the stove, life was looking up and I was feeling better. I returned to my game plan, which was to talk to Mitch somehow, with Rachel's help; the baked beans and stew heating on the stove smelled spicy; the house was going about its business of sleep; and I was alone, which was the way I most liked to be because then I didn't have to try to talk to people.

To combat the taste of the Stench in my mouth, I mixed some water and vinegar and snorted it up my nose. I had the idea that behind my nose there were channels that led all the way up to my brain. It's the sort of idea that people laugh at me for, but I couldn't get it out of my mind. I saw these horrible little molecules clawing their way up into my brain through secret passageways and receptors. I snorted as hard as I could and felt the liquid go down the back of my throat. It's taken the wrong passage, I thought, working myself into a fear.

I coughed and spat.

When the beans were heated I took them to the settee in front of the TV, which was flickering with the sound down in the corner like a fire that someone had forgotten to douse, and started my little snack, my little midnight feast.

I was just settling into it, ready to blob out on the endless adverts that run before the late news - on the screen someone was gobbing something that glistened - when I heard a soft tread behind me. Normally, it wouldn't have mattered. It could only have been Dad or Mum or Adrian, but suddenly I didn't know who it was and the back of my neck prickled. It felt as if there was a stranger in the house, an intruder whose step was as light as sickness itself.

I turned around, a piece of meat still hanging on the fork, expecting to see the worst of whatever it might be, only to find my mother, dressing gown on too, looking down at me with compassion, reaching out to stroke my head.

'You're late up, dear.'

'Shower,' I said, pointing to my still drying hair, knowing I was kind of lying to her.

She sat down beside me and put her arms around me. 'You're my baby,' she said. 'You'll always be my baby, I won't let you grow up.' She squeezed me the way I once squeezed my teddy bears.

'You won't grow up and grow away from me, will you, Baby?' she said, stroking my arm. 'I couldn't bear it if you did. You'll always be my Baby, no matter what happens. We're a family. I don't understand Adrian anymore, but that doesn't matter, he's a teenager.' I was too, of course, but she'd forgotten that. I was the baby and he was the teenager, but that wasn't the important thing. What was important was how she looked. Only her mouth was moving. There was no liveliness in her eyes. I thought of dead fish, the skin of fish with all the scales rubbed off.

'Are you all right, Mum?' On screen somebody was driving a car across a shingle fan. An avalanche was roaring toward them. The driver, who looked like a famous writer, was quickly changing gear.

'Just a touch of a cold, that's all, love,' she said, snuggling her face into my neck.

Her body was hot, like a furnace.

'Baby, you're not a baby any more.'

She'd got it in a nutshell. Her face grew vague, crossed by currents of memory, as if she'd forgotten my name. She was watching TV and had forgotten the conversation.

◦

'I don't even know if Adrian is at home or not,' she said in a bemused voice.

Suddenly I saw something black coming out of her left nostril. It was a worm, a black worm that felt around in the air for a moment with blind inquisitiveness before retreating back inside her head.

I jumped up from the sofa, rushed for the toilet and chucked my precious warm-ups. The enamel basin was cold against my forehead.

That worm was Adrian. It was warning me. It was a sign that something would happen to Mum, and to me. Something so horrible it couldn't be said outright, because outright is in the sunlight and can be seen. This thing stayed in putrid shadows, feeding on the sickness it created.

'Where's Adrian?' Mum's voice was thin, like an old blanket; you could hear the world passing through it. A picture came into my mind then of Adrian, standing over my mother as she lay in bed. I'd seen this picture and taken no notice of it.

'I don't know,' I said, making a big show of flushing the toilet bowl.

'I'd like him to come home,' She was peevish now. 'He should touch base.'

Touching base was a very important idea in Mum's mind. It reassured her.

I could hardly look at her as we sat back down on the couch, in case I saw the worm again. I'd seen it now; I couldn't unsee it. Every time I looked at Mum I'd think of it, nestling inside her head at the back of her nose. We sat in frozen silence watching the late news.

They showed starving children in Africa - millions of them, they said. Refugees from some war. And there were sick kids, with cholera; they showed the bodies being carried out. Kids with nothing but foul air in their bloated stomachs.

Then Mum said it was late and I shouldn't be watching this stuff and I should go to bed.

She gave me a final cuddle and a kiss goodnight while I watched the cholera children being thrown into big graves by stony-faced soldiers.

Adrian's bed was empty, of course. I hadn't expected him to be home. I didn't want to speculate on where he was or what he was doing. I felt as if I'd fought a great battle, a battle that had not been won but merely delayed. A skirmish.

To distract myself, and give me something to do other than be bone-tired, I went over to Adrian's miniature display and studied the set-up. Orcs were attacking a Dwarf stronghold, which Adrian had made with paper mâché and painted grey and silver. The Dwarves had set up their artillery, bolt thrower and cannon on top of the inner citadel, out of range of Orc arrows. Old Gorebag Ironclaw himself was there with his henchman Gorefang Rotgut, chief Dwarf hater of the Orcs, ready to do some bashin'. Right by him was a Dwarf, holding out its arms in a strange manner, as if about to box with someone. Then I realised it had lost its bow. Only the idea of the bow was left. It was facing old Gorebag and smelled of nothing more lethal than plastic, but its dream arrow was pointed straight at old Gorebag's face.

Elaborate rules governed the power of each piece, hits and deaths chalked up on the roll of a dice. Adrian had had to read heaps of rule books to understand it all, and of course I'd read them too. I didn't see how the mutilated Dwarf fitted in; he looked like a left over from Adrian's bag of corpses, stray limbs and weapons, who fell by accident into the game, just happening to land in the right stance, so I removed him, restoring the delicate balance of the game. Gorebag had a fighting chance even though the Orcs were being decimated by the Dwarf's bolt throwers as they came within range.

Then I saw, off to one side, a pile of Adrian's old Fabled Lands adventure story books, now forsaken for the world of the miniatures. I knew those books. You're some kind of character, a hero of course, and when you encounter some situation you have a decision to make, and when you make it you have to turn to page such-and-such and take up your destiny from there. Like: In the deserted hospital you find a trapdoor that hides the source of the Stench. If you decide to open it, turn to page 42, chapter 5; if you decide not to open it, turn to page 36, chapter 4. Eventually, you end up back in the same place, facing the same decision, hearing the hollow sound of screaming and yelling in the wards. I'd read all these books in the school library and knew my way through their scenarios the way you can see a maze from above.

Everything had grown a layer of dust, both books and miniatures, because Adrian had neglected to make the last move. Old Gorebag's fate would have to wait on the roll of a forgotten dice. The books would never be opened again. The blade of Adrian's paring knife was getting dusty.

Seeing them made me go to my drawer and take out my special objects: the thimble, the honest beard, Bobby and the Bumpkin, the eye of a teddy, which I had forgotten, rolled into one corner. I expected these things to connect me, as they usually did, with some sense of my past, my personal past as the backward talking creature called the Bumpkin, who could make himself look like a burnt stick, my family past with the thimble and the honest beard, but this time that didn't happen. I spread these things out and they lay, inert on my bed, disconnected from everything I knew. Like Adrian's Fabled Lands books and his miniatures, they were covered in dust. It wasn't real dust as such, but the smudge of neglect. Honest beard's eyes stared out into nowhere land; the thimble was worn thin by useless drudgery. The Bumpkin, undiscovered by Mr. Brown, was finally deserted by his attendant spirits, Wumps and Woggie.

I closed my eyes, opened up an atlas and located New Zealand, and where Hikitarua was, although of course it was too small to be named on the map. You'd have to get a road map for that and even then you might miss it. Everything was in place, but it was so abstract, just lines drawn on paper. It's hard to believe in things like that. It was like the book, the photographs and the thimble.

I was suddenly terrified that the world itself didn't exist, that everything was like the map, the book, the photographs and the thimble. I rushed to the window and looked out, for there had to be a world to see. There was Hikitarua looking very normal, just as you'd expect: the sky above, clear and dry. There were things going on in the streets out there I didn't know about, but I would; our town had a very fragile surface. A single piece of news could pass like a crack over thin ice, changing everything. Tomorrow, for example, they would have to make Josie's disappearance official. Police would be talking to kids. Mitch would be around. Teachers would be smiling automatic smiles. The crack would widen. The trapdoor would open and Hikitarua would fall through.

The clouds came over and it pretended to rain. It only ever pretended to rain in Hikitarua. Dark and promising, with a light mist sometimes that swept over the dry earth, leaving nothing behind but the memory of rain. The Alps ached for snow.

I got into bed, opposite Adrian's empty bed, and tried to imagine endless space. That was a pleasure, because I vanished everywhere to the far corners of nowhere, and still didn't succeed, for there was no end of imagining space. It was a good way of approaching the City of Gates which has its own endless space to live in. The Queen of the City, in her stone and satin chamber, had the endless space of her dreams to dream in too. A mere corner of one of her dreams could swallow me whole, find me abandoned in a far-flung corner of the City or back outside even, in the world of stars, eagerly seeking entrance again at one of the gates.

I approached this world, not from a distance like a splendid sunset as I usually did, with winged beings coming and going as if from a tiny citadel, but from close enough to see its vastness, like one infinite building containing courtyards, rooms and halls, tiered valleys and pixelated skies. It was a great library; I knew this even though I saw no books. I knew it because I was now one of the creatures flying in and out, and I was here seeking knowledge from the Queen. Everything we sought was catalogued in her dreams. Whole libraries were contained there, the answer to every mystery created, and endless waiting rooms were given over to those who were pondering their question, for only if they got the right question would they get the right answer, which sounds simple enough to say until you try it. Some had been there thousands of years, but not me; I was seeking something in the worlds of the library, and was hurtling through its images with wonderful intent. I was part of the dream of the Queen of the City; it was her song that rang in my ears. The scent of her flesh, far off as it was, filled me with forests and skies and the most gentle rain falling sideways out of the sky...

When I woke sometime later in the night Adrian was there, in bed, whistling through his nose in sleep. The City of Gates was far away. I wanted to get up and tell Mum he was back but I couldn't, my legs were too heavy. I had to fend off his dreams, which I could feel creeping in and out of my head like starved rats as he mumbled and muttered and turned and did enough sweating for both of us. I had to wake up because I didn't want his Stench dreams to find the City of Gates. I had to protect the City and the Queen who was dreaming all the worlds into being.

Suddenly I thought about the hospital, and it filled up with the bodies of those kids in Africa who had died of cholera and starvation, all heaped-up fleshy sticks covered in flies. Faces with no expression on them, like teeth that aren't smiling.

I woke up later too, or dreamed I did. Adrian was in his bed, his face turned to the wall, a few strands of black hair plastered across one cheek. I thought his face was crawling over the top of his skull until I realised that it was the movement of clouds through the glass. He was a dark lump, like hills under the window.

I couldn't get back to sleep because I could still feel his thoughts eating into the side of my head. They were now like burrowing maggots, getting deeper and deeper in, hollowing themselves a hole into my head. When would those maggots break through and wriggle into my thoughts, full of death and the Stench?

I lay awake, wide-eyed, until the burrowing ceased.

⸱

Opening my eyes in the morning, the first thing I saw was Adrian, sitting up in his bed looking at me. He was very still, as if he hadn't moved for ages.

'Not going.' I said.

'Where? What do you mean?' But he knew already.

'The hospital.'

He looked at me - I mean properly focused. It might have been the first time in the last two days he'd really noticed me, and he noticed that I was deadly serious. 'You've got to come.' He spoke from absolute conviction, from sure knowledge.

I shook my head.

He was about to say something, stopped himself and thought deeply. I thought he was about to argue and bully, but he didn't.

'You'll come all right,' he said, the way you might say, 'It's a sunny day.'

I shook my head again.

'Are you a scaredy-cat?' He spoke ponderously, as if this were a real question, as if he himself had not been as frightened as any of us, as if I were the only one in Hikitarua liable to childish fears.

'Yes.'

'That won't stop you.'

He spoke with such finality it frightened me, because it meant he had some plan, something he was going to spring on me during the day.

He was full of himself, pleased as hell with himself in fact. He sprang off the bed and began rummaging violently around for his clothes.

'We'll all be there,' he said gaily, but his eyes gleamed as he spoke, as if there were already shards of night in them.

⸱

Over cornflakes and milk we heard the news that Gills McPickle had been found lying dead in the gateway of the old hospital grounds, his mouth open and his arms outstretched. He'd had a heart attack, it seemed, and tried to crawl there thinking the hospital was still open. The welcoming clamour of the emergency room ringing in his ears. Comforting lights. That was the theory.

Dad shook his head and Mum said a prayer. Mum was a bit better, or at least she said she was. She had breakfast with us, or pretended to, for she had no appetite at all. Dad was pleased to see her, grinned and made jokes, but I think he was too pleased to notice how quiet and frail she was.

Adrian didn't say anything about the hospital. He was too busy heaping up sugar on his cornflakes.

Dad was apparently amused by the manner of it all, but Mum said she was touched with the goosebumps. She didn't like the idea of mortality coming so close. Gills McPickle was as good as family; his wife was left a mortgage the pub would never pay for.

The police did not suspect foul play. Poor old Gills had choked on his own vomit after his heart attack; a fitting end for a man whose garden, into which he'd spewed a lifetime of vomit, could now produce flowers for his wreath.

'He's downed his last brown.' Dad was pensive. 'I'm surprised this didn't happen earlier, years ago.' He'd never again hear Gills, whose real name was Gilbert, singing 'Irene' to the night sky. An old sad song had died in Hikitarua with the passing of a drunk; some history had slipped away like a piece of riverbank into a darkly rushing stream. Not that Dad cared about farewells, but just for a moment he saw, and knew, that Hikitarua had changed. The laughter died in his face and suddenly he looked old. 'There's more old drunks than old doctors,' he said.

A swift look passed between Adrian and me when we heard about Gills. Adrian was very busy spooning cornflakes he couldn't taste into his mouth. He knew in the depths of his honest heart, a heart less and less willing to reveal itself, that I wasn't such a fool. And I knew, without even having to think about it, that he was a bigger fool than he ever thought he would turn out to be, and probably well past prayer.

I got goosebumps thinking how we were there, maybe trying to lift the trapdoor, while the old man was dying in the gateway, crawling towards the Stench, mouth open, fingers outstretched. Or maybe it was later. Maybe when I was sitting in the police car. I started to think of what Rabbitt had said about the old man saying some obscene thing. I'll pith in your faith, she'd reported. That had to be Gills. Or Adrian. I wanted to talk to Serendipity Rabbitt.

Adrian should have spoken to Dad then; it was his place to. I'd only muck it up and Dad had better things to do than listen to the likes of me. But Adrian didn't say a word. He listened to everything Dad said and turned away. He didn't give a rat's arse about Gills McPickle.

I tried to catch Mum's attention but it was no go. She was only just upright in her dressing gown. Every now and again she smelled her own hand, as if reassuring herself that she was alive. Whenever she looked at me she smiled and the smile cut me out. Words were so close in my mouth, so far away.

⸱

While walking to school that morning, I saw Mrs Inna standing in her garden with her nose buried deep in the heart of a rose. It was as if she were drinking the rose scent. Beside her, Softy sat quietly, his nose in the air, pretending to be a rose.

Adrian wasn't saying anything to me and I wasn't expecting him to. He was thinking furiously, hatching his schemes for the day, just as I was. I was going to talk to Mitch, with Rachel along too, if I could. Even Rabbitt. If Rabbitt had been following us around all the time spying on us then she'd know Josie was at the hospital. Mitch would be able to get that stupid thumb out of her mouth. The police would arrive before the others succeeded in lifting the trapdoor and all would be well; Hikitarua could go on as if nothing had happened which is what it usually did.

I'm sure Adrian didn't know what I was thinking, he was probably just covering his bases, for he turned on me as we got nearer to the school. 'Just remember, Baby, no one's t' know about this. No one's t' know where Josie is, or else she'll have t' go home and you know what that means, don't you?'

'You? Going. Back?'

'Of course,' he said, tossing his head. Going back had become a matter of pride to him. Just as if he'd never been scared, as if it were someone else who had been crawling away from the trapdoor last night, coughing and retching, not the great Gorebag Ironclaw.

Carpenter and Rachel joined us. We weren't far from the gate through which children were funnelling like sand through an hourglass. I hadn't promised anything. I didn't know if he noticed because he was too busy looking at Rachel. I didn't blame him for looking, and losing a bit of eternity in her dark hair, pale face and wide eyes, especially this morning when her skin looked so smooth, as if polished by wax.

Carpenter looked glum. I thought he'd be along bubbling with ideas for lifting the trapdoor but I was wrong.

'And that applies to all of you,' Adrian said, remembering his mission and ignoring Carpenter. 'We've been through all this. We know we can't say anything. We can't betray Josie.'

Rachel's eyes hid themselves behind her eyelashes. Then, abruptly, she flashed him a glance that hit me like a slap in the face; everything, the whole crucible of who she was, was contained in it.

'We should swear a proper oath,' Adrian said, our great hero, still playing pirates and gangs while someone gave him a look like that; a look that was asking him every question he hadn't asked himself. Go for him, Rachel, I said under my breath, go for his jugular, leave him bleeding at the school gate.

'No one's going to say anything,' Carpenter said sourly. 'We can beat the Stench.' He didn't elaborate. He doesn't want to go back, I realised, looking at him. It's the last thing in the world he wants to do.

'And how do you beat it,' Adrian sneered, 'wave the crowbar at it?'

'I've got my own plans,' Carpenter said.

We all waited but he said no more.

No one swore any oath, and Adrian never got to take it further, for at that point Maro pulled up on his bike, right in front of us. He was dressed in his rugby uniform, striped shirt and black shorts, I didn't know why, I'd never heard of anybody playing rugby at eight in the morning.

'The cops are on to you,' was the first thing he said to Adrian. Adrian's mouth felt around for his sneer but didn't quite find it. There were other things pressing on his mind, even Maro wasn't the biggest deal for him right now. 'You know damn well where she is.'

Adrian didn't deny it. He'd made a decision. It was suddenly easy to make because he didn't give a rat's arse any more.

'You fucked Josie,' he said, suddenly rising into hero status in my estimation. Why shouldn't he be a hero, at least for this moment? No one else had said it to Maro, not right outside the school gates.

Maro let his bike fall over. His foot missed the stand. He might have been nearly nineteen, but he was as clumsy as a twelve year old at that moment. If we'd thought he'd come in swinging, we couldn't have been more wrong.

'That's a lie,' he said, tears sprouting from his eyes. 'That's what she says to people, makin it all up and goin schizo. They had t' give her pills for it, y' know. But she won't take them.' He rocked back and forth in sudden grief. 'She just tells lies all the time. She's got to make things up. They sent her to a doctor in Christchurch, and she told all these stories about me, and Dad, and even old Conk & Whiskers...'

'What do you mean?' Rachel said sharply, her voice as brittle and as prickly as a piece of bone.

'That's what she said.' Maro looked desperately about as if there might be some source of salvation lying handy. 'You guys think I'm your enemy, I'm not. It's not true what she says. She says old Conk felt her up in his office cos she came onto him. She says all kinds of weird things. That's why the doctors are onto her. And you,' he poked Adrian in the chest. 'You are full of shit.'

We listened to this, and the lead up to the final insult, the attack on our great leader.

The strange thing was that chaos did not break loose ; Adrian did not haul off and start bashin, as Gorebag Ironclaw would have advised. Rachel did not start screaming. She was just looking at Maro, looking at his legs and his hips and his chest and face and out staring her own embarrassment. My guess was that she believed him, and it shook her to the core, that's why she couldn't stop staring. It rang too true. Josie was always lying; lying came naturally to her, or it was something she learned very early.

Maro noticed her stare. She made him feel ashamed of how naked he suddenly was. I liked him then because he misjudged the world somehow, like I did.

'So you say,' Adrian said, which was the best he could find. You had to love him in his great inadequacy, his complete inability to follow through.

'So I say,' Maro said, 'I never touched her, Dad never touched her. I told you what the doctors said. She keeps makin up stories. And unless you believe the stories you can't be her friend. But then she'll keep changin the stories. Y' got to tell me where she is. She's sick. She's got t' come home, maybe even t' the hospital. If you kept tellin lies all the time you'd be sick too.'

Then Adrian did something brilliant, with a touch of class to it.

He reached out and grasped a piece of Maro's sleeve, the rugby top. 'This is an Avengers top,' he said, half accusing.

'That's right.'

'They're a crap team.'

Maro didn't make any more speeches. He looked at Adrian and then at all of us. All of us were lying. We were all lying because he could have been lying and Josie's fate lay in our hands. We hadn't sworn an oath, but the unsworn oath held for the moment.

He tried to get a good look at the lot of us, like a witness at a crime. He was puzzled about me; not sure if I was a retard like people said; he couldn't make up his mind. Josie had probably said all kinds of stuff about me, and the rest of us, lies, lies.

He got his bike up, tears were coming back into his eyes. Ignoring Adrian, who was still basking in his own glory, he appealed to Rachel.

'You're her friend,' he said, accusingly. 'She might be dead. That's what I think. I think she's dead because she done something stupid, like trying t' hitch hike out of town and gettin murdered. Did she ever talk t' you about hitching out of town.'

Rachel nodded her head.

'She talked about it all the time. Now if she's not dead, and you know she's alive, you have t' tell me. If she's alive you have t' say so.'

No one spoke. Each of us had our reasons for staying quiet just then. For me, Maro was not the right person to tell. It had to be Mitch. Me and Rachel and Mitch.

The bell rang for morning assembly.

⊡

The kids knew something was up. There was an expectant buzz as the assembly hall filled and solemn-faced teachers took their seats on stage. They were always solemn whenever we had an assembly but today they were more solemn than ever.

Old Conk & Whiskers came forward, blowing his conk loudly on a red and white handkerchief and stroking down his recalcitrant whiskers. As soon as he approached the microphone a hush fell, which was unusual enough, and everybody listened very carefully when he took up a Bible and read the story of the three men who were thrown into a furnace to test their faith, and of course they came through unscathed because their faith held strong. When he'd finished reading he fastidiously placed the book to one side and announced that Josie Summers had gone missing and that our faith, too, was being tested. But, like the men in the story, we had to hold on to our faith.

He said he was sure that everybody in the school shared the horror that Josie's family must be going through at this time. Their tears were our own, he said, with rare inspiration, his whiskers quivering. Everybody at the school knew Josie and what a fine girl she was. All the kids looked embarrassed. Some of the girls snuffled. He urged any of us who knew anything to go to him or to the police, no matter how minor it might seem.

Then he introduced Josie's father, who came on stage from the side where he'd been waiting unseen. He wore a suit and tie, which I'd never seen him wear before, and his voice held a sob. She was the most beautiful daughter in the world, he said. The light of his life. He and his wife were devastated. His wife would be with him now, supporting him, if she weren't so devastated. Her brother too, Maro, had been searching from morning till night. No one who hadn't had such a tragedy happen to them could imagine what it felt like to face every hour not knowing, the huge uncertainty, and he appreciated all the expressions of support he'd had from all around the community, from everyone, which made him think that Hikitarua must be the most wonderful place in the world. He paused to wipe his eyes. From where I sat I could see Carpenter, his jaw was moving sideways as if he were chewing.

Then he invited Mitch to talk to us, and Mitch came out from the side of the stage and, very friendly and reassuring, said we mustn't walk home alone or wander around alone at night, and that anyone who knew anything should talk to her, and so on. The kids all listened wide-eyed to this, their eyes straying to the side of the stage to see what other wonders might step forth.

But there were no more wonders and we were all sent to class. As everybody scattered, I caught a glimpse of Rachel walking very rapidly towards her classroom. Adrian was standing behind her, dithering, apparently torn between running after her and walking the other way. He had a look of terrific concentration on his face. Then he saw Kahu and some guys coming and cleared off.

We went through the motions of going to class. I stayed in the Library away from everybody and wondered how I'd go about it. Finding Rachel at morning break was the first part; she'd understand me, I had no doubts, in fact she was probably already summoning up the courage, just as I was, and would be glad of an ally. And maybe she would cry with relief, I could see her doing that, grabbing hold of my hand and dragging us off to see Mitch.

Mrs Manui talked to me for a while, but it was just about my writing. She patted me on the shoulder and said she believed in me, and that I was a 'fine girl.'

I didn't waste any time when the morning bell rang, and set off in search of her. The first person I saw was Carpenter, sitting on his own looking up into the sky as if all the answers were there, and would be reflected off his glasses somehow. He always looks up like that when he wants to give the impression of being in deep thought. His lunch, untouched, sat beside him. I saw cucumber edging out of his sandwiches, the stain of butter on the wrapping paper.

'Rachel?' I asked him. He shrugged his shoulders. He wasn't interested in Rachel, or even Josie for that matter.

'I don't want to steal anything more,' he blurted out. 'I've already stolen enough.' Then he lapsed into silence and stared without interest at his sandwich.

'Don't then,' I said, wondering what he'd been stealing. I was impatient to find Rachel but Carpenter intrigued me. I knew now what was bothering him. He had a plan for lifting the trapdoor all right, but he had to steal lots of stuff to do it. 'Don't go.'

He looked at me then, or at least it seemed he did, but because of the angle of the light on his glasses I couldn't see his eyes.

'Maybe I won't,' he said. 'Adrian just wants to be stupid, he won't take it seriously. He's just being stupid with the girls all the time.'

I was pleased but didn't show it. 'Why go?'

He didn't answer. His glasses flashed light. He toyed with one of his sandwiches. A piece of cucumber fell out onto the grass. He looked back at the sky like an adult who, having fulfilled his duty to a child, turns back to what he is doing. There were two skies reflected in his face.

'Go not I,' I said, testing him.

I waited again. You have to be patient with Carpenter sometimes.

'Why?' he asked finally, not sounding too interested in the answer. There was a bead of sweat along his fatty upper lip.

'Because.' I said.

He nodded as if I had really said something.

'I have to go,' he said sadly. 'I've got no choice. I left the crowbar behind.'

He looked suddenly depressed.

Then I saw Kahu dusting along looking lost and sad and thought there was a good chance that he was looking for Rachel, like I was. I was on my feet again and away with hardly a goodbye to Carpenter. He didn't notice anyway.

I followed Kahu for a while but that didn't get either of us very far. I kept half an eye out for Rabbitt; usually it was impossible to get rid of Rabbitt, tailing us around, but now I wanted the little sniveler she was nowhere to be found.

Finally, I checked smokers corner down the bottom field.. Rachel was up against the back fence, facing Adrian; they were leaning towards one another as if they'd just been kissing and were taking a breath. Rachel's face was inflamed and her mouth was open, as if she were about to speak or drink, her plump lower lip pouting. Adrian's face was fixed in the same concentrated look I'd seen earlier.

I skipped away before they could see me. It was no use with Adrian hanging around. All the moments were slipping by with the right one never coming along; half the morning was gone and I was no closer.

The bell rang for late morning classes all too soon, and a final scout around the thinning playing field showed no signs of Rabbitt. I didn't go back to the library, but sat outside and thought about it. The best thing to do, I decided, although it was scary for me, was to go to Rachel's classroom and call her out as if on some official business, because I couldn't guarantee catching up with her at lunch time either. It was almost as if she were avoiding me, but I couldn't bear thinking that.

Suddenly I saw kids trooping to the hall and followed to see what was happening. The medical team had arrived to give us our measles booster shots. We all had to line up by name rather than by class, and I soon found myself herded along into the right group. Adrian should have been in that group but he wasn't; I didn't see him anywhere.

Then I saw Rachel. She was in another group, talking to some girls. She was laughing and her hands were moving around quickly. I didn't hesitate, I headed straight for her, running headlong into a teacher who patiently returned me to my line.

Carpenter was in the line next to me, I noticed, and he looked scared. At least I think he was scared because he kept casting doomed looks at the medical team and the hypodermics that were going into the kids' arms. We could see all that when we got close enough. He was fascinated and couldn't stop looking. Nobody was crying because everybody was trying to be brave. The nurses, who all looked very pretty in their white and red uniforms, were wearing out their smiles on nervous kids. When Carpenter turned around, I could see the damp on his forehead, the glint of closed windows on his glasses. Carpenter was sweating it out.

Conk & Whiskers walked past the rows of waiting children with his hands behind his back and his famous conk in the air.

When the time came for me to roll up my sleeve to the friendly needle, I couldn't help but think of the empty, used needles in the rubbish bin at the hospital, the droplets of coloured water at the bottom of them.

There was a wrinkling of the pretty, powdered nose of the nurse who slipped the needle under my skin.

◦

There was no return to normality, or a further chance to track down Rachel, for as soon as the medical team had departed, a second assembly was called, and the mood was very different from the first.

Grim faced teachers lined the hall. The kids sat in their seats but there was no silencing them; shocked chatter ran up and down the rows like bursts of electricity and the volume of sound was steadily increasing when Conk & Whiskers made his grand entrance, looking particularly grave and solemn.

I still didn't know what was going on but the news of it was spreading through the hall like wind through corn.

Conk & Whiskers squared his shoulders.

'We have called this assembly,' he said without any introduction or Bible reading, 'so that rumours will not spread. Yes, we have a second missing child, Serendipity Rabbitt who has not been seen since yesterday afternoon.'

He stopped at that point; I think it must have dawned on him that for the first time since the ice age something had actually happened in Hikitarua. The shocked chatter had given way to a hushed, expectant whisper. He had everybody's undivided attention for the second time that day, and he didn't quite know what to do with it. He urged us all to walk home together, to not go out at night alone and all the things Mitch'd said in the morning. The police were here, on the school grounds, so if anyone wanted to see them, now was the time.

For once I took his advice to heart. I couldn't wait for Rachel any more. I could get enough across to Mitch on my own, all I needed was my courage.

I kept a firm eye out for Adrian as I slipped into the office building. The police had set up in the staff room and I saw Mitch as soon as I came in, her back to me, talking to a crowd of excited children.

Boss Hogg saw me coming and intercepted me. 'Come along Baby,' he said, 'we're very busy.' He took off his peaked cap and fanned his head with it.

'Rabbitt,' I said. 'At the hospital.'

'Sure,' he said soothingly, 'We checked there last night Baby, remember?' He passed his hand over his bald patch, which was sweating.

'Mitch.' I turned and pointed, and I could feel my eye-glands swelling up with ready tears. 'Talk to.' A tearful wobble came into my voice.

'She's very busy right now,' he said escorting me out. I cursed my useless, helpless tears. Crying only confirmed Boss Hogg in his opinion of me. Some passing teachers gave me a sympathetic look.

It was back to the library for the big little moron.

Kids were sitting around the tables either pretending to read or openly talking. I hung about as I usually did, putting books back in the shelves. The last person I expected to see walking through the door was Mitch. All the kids looked up as she came in but she went straight into the back room and talked to the librarian. A moment later she came out and over to me, took me by the arm and said a few words in a low voice. The kids' eyes all glued onto me as I followed Mitch out. A rage of whispering started up as the door shut behind us.

We didn't say anything until we got to the staff room, now cleared of kids. Boss Hogg was there and a couple of other cops I'd never seen before. Mitch took me to a quiet corner. Boss Hogg hung around nearby but not too obviously, which was hard for him; it looked like he'd been told to back off a bit.

'Adrian is Josie's friend, isn't he?' Mitch said. Her chestnut hair was pulled tightly into a bun at the back. It made her small face look smaller and unexpectedly severe.

I nodded.

'Are they, do you think, like girlfriend and boyfriend?'

I nodded again but I wasn't sure, I didn't know if they were sure themselves.

'We're trying to find Adrian now,' she said in the same pleasant voice, 'He's not around the school, do you know where he is?'

I looked from her to Boss Hogg, who was trying badly to pretend he wasn't listening. If I told them he was at the hospital I would get nowhere; Mitch would write me off as a dead loss.

'Rachel.' I said with sudden inspiration. 'She knows. Rachel!'

Mitch nodded to Boss Hogg who walked quietly off. While he was away Mitch got me a cup of tea and some biscuits. It made me sad to think she didn't want to try and talk to me further, but she hadn't given up on me yet, and there was still hope.

Calmly, Rachel walked into the room, Boss Hogg behind her, hardly glancing at me; her eyes were on Mitch who had risen to greet her.

'You are Josie's friend, aren't you?' Mitch said sympathetically. 'Do you know if they were emotionally involved...' seeing Rachel's hesitation '... I mean do you know if they were having sex together?'

'Hardly,' Rachel said involuntarily; it came out with sort of a laugh behind it. She was wearing perfume, probably her mother's, and had put too much on.

'But you don't know?'

'Josie would have told me.'

'Did she tell you stories about her brother and her father?'

'No, not until...' She hid behind a sweep of curls.

'Until when?'

'When I last saw her.' she went stony-faced.

'When was that?'

Rachel shrugged carelessly, her beautiful dark curls tossed on her shoulder. 'At school a few days ago.'

Then it dawned on me that she was going to lie; that's why she wasn't looking at me, that's why her curls were in action.

'And what did she say?'

'She said Maro....had sex with her.'

'Did you believe her?'

The shrug again. 'She told lots of stories.'

'Do you think it's connected to her disappearance?'

Rachel looked Mitch straight in the eye. 'I don't know,' she said.

I could see what Mitch was after, what she was trying to uncover, but it wasn't the point, none of this was the point at all. I had to say it out loud, just once.

'The trapdoor.' I said.

They both turned towards me. Rachel looked at me for the first time, and the glance was hard, the look you give a stranger approaching you for a favour.

'What trapdoor, Baby?' Mitch asked ever so gently, as if I were a precious crystal that might break.

'The hospital. At,' I said, finding the word with relief and putting it in its right place. 'At the hospital.'

I must have blurted it in a shout, for Mitch recoiled a little, and the other cops in the room looked up. Boss Hogg, standing nearby, was keeping a careful eye on me. All the muscles of his cheeks were screwed up in the effort to hold me in focus.

'Baby thinks that Serendipity and Josie are at the hospital,' Mitch said, watching Rachel carefully.

Rachel turned a pitying gaze on me. She put her arm over my shoulder and her face close to mine. I could smell her breath and body and the inevitable, bitter taint of the Stench. 'I'm sorry, Baby,' she said softly, 'if only it was that easy. If Josie was so close, it would be wonderful, we could just drive around and get her now.' Still cuddling me, she faced Mitch. 'Baby's got a bit of a thing about the hospital,' she said, then hesitated, as out of delicacy, 'Her young brother died there as a baby.'

The look that switched between Mitch and Boss Hogg told me it was all over.

'We're wasting time,' Boss Hogg muttered. He shouldn't have said it. Mitch gave him a sharp look. She tried one more question on Rachel, a final throw before she put it all out of conscience.

'Would Adrian have gone to the hospital to look for Josie?'

'No way.' Rachel said, 'He knows she's not there; he'd be more likely to be looking along the river bed, some of the places they used to go together.' She left an implication in the last remark for Mitch to pick up, and she did, nodding, satisfied. Boss Hogg grunted in agreement.

With a howl of fury, I knocked Rachel's arm aside and laid into her, trying to smash her beautiful face; that same face I'd loved was now a torment to me.

Boss Hogg jumped in to hold me back. He'd been expecting something like this from me. Mitch said soothing words while Rachel was hurried out by other cops. Before going through the door she turned and looked at me, and the old Rachel was back, just for a moment, in a flash of anguish.

I was returned to the library, and was allowed to sit in the back room with the librarian and think about my defeat. All I could do was think about Rachel. Was it that her loyalty to Josie had won out, or was there something more I hadn't seen, something to do with her and Adrian?

Or was it yet simpler than that? She was covering for the trapdoor. The Stench itself.

·

At lunchtime I sat alone under a pine out of the wretched heat and watched the other kids, all of them talking about Rabbitt and Josie. Mostly about Rabbitt and Josie, for, besides the death of Gills McPickle, other strange events had taken place in Hikitarua that the disappearance of the girls had overshadowed. Mrs. Crayford, who lived a couple of streets from us, a crippled old lady who'd spent the last five years in a wheelchair sitting in her living room twisting her hair in her hands and staring out of her window, had been found crawling along the road, unable to explain where she thought she was going. Since it had all happened in the middle of the night, her daughter, who was looking after her, had heard or seen nothing. How could a crippled woman who had to be lifted from her wheelchair to her bed drag herself a hundred yards? I had only one memory of her, glimpsed at her window, white-haired and pale faced, running her fingers through her hair as if she were weaving wool.

There was an even stranger rumour that had surfaced concerning Gills McPickle. Joan Martian, whose father was the doctor who had examined the body, said that the old drunk did not die where he was lying, but a few yards further back. In other words it looked as if he had died, then crawled a few yards further. This strange detail had been completely lost in the hullabaloo over Josie and Rabbitt.

My schoolmates looked so stupid, with their faces hanging open, stuffing food and horror into their mouths in equal measure, every tiny detail that was known, every speculation, gone over again and again as if it were fresh. Everybody was pretending to know things others didn't. I could show them. Get them along to the hospital, get a whiff of the Stench seeping up around the disturbed trapdoor, that would give them something to gape over.

I saw Donna, and realised with a sinking heart that I would have to sit beside her all afternoon. It wasn't that I disliked Donna that much, she was no more or less stupid than the rest of them, it was just she was a part of it all, a much larger stupidity that lay at the heart of Hikitarua; a wilful lethargy, a monstrous self-inflicted ignorance. It scarred them, turned their faces into open wounds. Even Rachel had not escaped it.

Then it unfolded before me in simple, lurid detail. I would lure Donna to the hospital; it would be easy, all I would have to do is tell her I knew where Josie was but nobody would believe me; she was gullible and I would convince her, particularly since I'd be telling the truth. Josie and Adrian would welcome me at the hospital because I'd brought them Donna. At this point the action became blurred. I saw Adrian dragging Donna to the trapdoor. The open trapdoor. Josie was helping, screaming at him all the while. Rachel was sitting off to one side, observing all this with a tender pleasure, like someone in love or watching a flower unfold.

My eyes snapped open and Donna was standing in front of me. A group of girls nearby giggled behind their hands.

Donna said, 'Baby, you can't talk properly, I know, but it doesn't matter. I can understand if y' use y' hands and a few words.' I could feel her hunger for whatever it was I had to say. They needed something new to feed on. I could be the oracle of the hour. I could sit her beside me and tell her, just as I had done in my fantasy, and the next step would be just as easy - invite her along, make her promise not to tell anyone.

Instead I did something I shall never forgive myself for; I pretended to be the moron they all took me for, it was easier for me that way. I don't know if Donna believed my nobody home act, but the girls behind her did. They stopped giggling behind their hands and giggled openly.

Before Donna turned away she gave me a curious, hostile look, as if I'd somehow set her up to make her look like a fool in front of the others. Maybe I'd played the vacant stare too hard. Belatedly, I remembered that Donna had seen the piece of paper with my drawing of Carpenter creep across the desk top.

When she had gone I opened up my lunch box to find a small packet of chips and an apple. The apple was almost mushy and the chips hurt my gums. I chucked the apple and went over to the giggling girls who were quick enough to take my chips in return for an orange.

Only an idiot would make a swap like that.

▫

Adrian didn't turn up at school that afternoon. Boss Hogg offered to drive me home, on the instructions of Mitch no doubt, but much to his relief I turned him down; he had a lot on his mind did our local cop.

For a moment I hung around the gates in the vague hope that Rachel or Carpenter might turn up. I had things to say to Rachel. The gate crowd thinned out pretty quickly; no one hung around school if they could help it. There was no sign of Rachel. The caretaker was wandering across the playground.

I did see Carpenter though. He went past with his head averted, so he didn't have to look at me. I didn't have to look at him either.

Right then I hated all my friends. And my brother. My brother most of all. They were all cowards or fools.

It occurred to me then that I might have to kill my brother. I don't know exactly why that thought occurred to me when it did; perhaps it was the realisation that he must've known this morning that he was going to disappear. That's why he was so sure I'd go to the hospital, and he was right. He'd planned the whole thing.

Up until that moment I'd held out hope for Adrian, shallow and cynical as I knew him to be. The deeper parts to him, the nicer parts, were gone.

He was a big shot now, so besotted with himself he couldn't see what was coming. I had to give up on him. I had to comprehend that my brother was dead. Maybe not dead the way others might die, yet effectively dead as far as his sister was concerned. I had no brother, that was the reality of it. I thought I had a brother but all I had was a poser, a posturer, a monumental bullshit artist and a sad-arse sadist to boot. That wasn't a brother, that was a hobgoblin. That elder brother, who always fell victim to what he imagined to be his own evil genius, a wondrous self inflation.

I walked home on my own with tears just behind my eyes.

Hikitarua had never looked as shabby.

My mouth had never felt so dry.

・

The last thing I wanted to do was to go home to face Mum and Dad, especially if Adrian was still missing; the thought of what the look on Mum's face might be like was unbearable. I wondered if Mitch had been to talk to Mum. I took the main road, Highway 5, home, which is the long way, and watched the cars zooming past from somewhere important to somewhere else important. They were big and smooth and slid along the road like fast, silent silver slugs.

I took a look in the milk bar to see if Rachel or Adrian were there. Just Brad sucking at a straw at one of the tables, Kahu was sitting opposite him. They were deep in conversation. It looked to me as if Kahu was hardly listening, his slender, sensitive face like a reed in the wind. Brad was shooting his mouth off to no great effect. When he saw me coming, Brad came running out.

'You know where he is, don't you?' he said excitedly. He took me by the arm.

I grinned vacantly.

'You tell him, when you see him, that he's got something coming his way for what he did to Rachel.'

'Rachel?'

'So you can speak. Yes Rachel. Kahu's very upset?'

Then I saw that Kahu's face was red, like someone trying not to cry.

'He'll pay.' Brad promised.

I wondered what could have made Brad switch sides and Kahu want to cry. Beating up Kahu one day, trying to be his friend the next. Probably because he felt that Adrian had deserted him, left him behind.

I didn't like the feel of Brad's hand on my arm; his fingers were too eager.

'Don't know,' I said, and backed away.

I ran from him, conscious of Kahu's blank stare through the window, remembering Adrian with his face up close to Rachel's at smoker's corner.

I scuttled over Highway 5 to the service station where I was just in time to catch an oil truck with its hose in the ground, watch this huge beast pumping its breath, funnelling liquid fire down into the huge cool storage tanks below. The burly driver didn't belong to any town or time or place, it seemed, but to the tanker he serviced, the road animal. He was its creature, like one of those birds that live on the backs of rhinos picking the bugs out of their ears and even the dead meat from between their teeth. The driver was like that, scampering along the top of his big rig to turn some valve that allowed the tanker to relieve itself into the service station storage tanks. The tanker itself lived on the stuff it sold, pumping and spitting fire, using that same fuel to take it to every little Hikitarua you could find on the road map of New Zealand.

The great beast coughed as its motor turned.

I couldn't delay for forever, and soon found myself on our home street. When I got closer I could see a commotion going on at Rabbitt's house. There were cars coming and going, and the police cruised by. Mitch gave me a wave out the window. They pulled up in the Rabbitt's drive. I saw Mr. and Mrs. Rabbitt come running out to meet it. Mitch and Boss Hogg got out of the car. Boss Hogg was holding something in his hand.

I'd come to a stop by this time, right by our gate, and I could feel the silence of our house behind me. Mitch glanced over at me again and I moved up our drive, trying not to look too curious, but I didn't look away until I had observed that Boss Hogg was holding a schoolbag in his hand and from the look on Mrs Rabbitt's face it wasn't hard to guess who the bag belonged to.

I ran down the drive and round the back of our house with a new idea forming; I could go through the back way, across our back yard, over the fence into another back yard and down their drive to the next street. That way I'd avoid having to see Mum at all. I hated doing it, for I knew she'd worry and blame herself; and Dad, he'd get angry and stamp around and leave the house and go looking for Adrian and me to give us a good thumping, that's what he'd do.

My chances were pretty good of making my escape now, even during the day, because the house over the back only had a woman and her two-year-old child. Her husband didn't get back from the plant until after dark, and she didn't like to leave the house. She always pulled lace curtains across her windows to protect stuff inside from the sun and I could probably zip down her drive while she was busy inside somewhere.

It was a gamble, and it didn't work out. I'd just got over the fence into her garden when she came out her back door, a bunch of washing on one hip, the kid on the other. The kid was bawling, as usual. She was heading for her rotating washing line on the lawn near he back garden. She looked up and saw me standing by her withered potato stems.

'A ball,' I said, not having to pretend to be embarrassed and feeling pretty low on invention. 'Lost ball.'

'That's alright,' she said, giving out a smile that might have been pretty before her teeth started going brown. 'I never saw any ball.'

The rotating line gave out an anguished groan as she heaved it around.

'The drive,' I said, racing for her gate.

She watched me, open mouthed, as I hit the street. I was the most interesting thing that had happened to her all day.

When I got to the top of the wall I could hear the sounds of the search teams calling to one another as they scoured the river bed.

PrisOner

The first thing I saw when I came through the hole in the hedge behind the hospital was a mess of glossy black curls - she knew I was there anyway and turned to face me. Her face was as pale as ever and tonight she was wearing dark lipstick; a purple that looked black in the fading light. There was no pretending that nothing had happened; she knew what lay between us. One look at her too and I knew that, like me, she hadn't been home after school; she was getting that same haunted look that Josie and Adrian and even Carpenter had, although with him it came out as impatience. I'd surely see it if I looked in the mirror.

'I thought y' might not come,' Rachel said in a husky voice. 'Look, I have t' tell you, I'm sorry for what I did today but I had t' do it. Josie must have one more chance before the police come and haul her away. I have t' give her that chance, you just watch me. I'll give it to her straight. I've had t' lie for her.' A tremble came into her voice. 'I don't like lying.'

She didn't know what to do, she was lost just like the rest of us; it was in me to forgive her, but I didn't. Something stuck in my throat. It was like phlegm but it was something else, something I couldn't spit. I wanted to fall at her feet making wild speeches and protestations of love, as if I was the one who had wronged her, as if I was the one who had all that ground to make up.

I turned away from her, trying not to cry. Crying wasn't the answer right now.

'I'll stand by you Baby, when the moment comes,' she said from deep in her throat. I met her eye and she held me steadily in her gaze, as if there was no need of the earth beneath to support us. 'I promise.'

'Lets get moving now,' Carpenter said. There were pimples coming up under his skin, little strained lumps. I noticed his bag was bulging again, and guessed he'd been stealing more stuff from his father. I was surprised Carpenter hadn't gone straight in. He'd been intent enough; his precious crowbar was inside. And Rachel too, also carrying a heavily laden bag. Had she waited just to make me a pretty speech? It was more as if they had to wait for me because I was a part of the key they needed to unlock the back window of the hospital and climb inside. Nobody would go in until everybody was assembled, as if altogether we made up some magic number that allowed us to get in.

Now I was here there wasn't a lot more to talk about. In Adrian's absence, Carpenter led the way this time, making as big a show as Adrian of pulling off the loose board and opening the window. Wriggling through was undignified, there wasn't much he could do about that; even Rachel, who was always graceful, couldn't do much about that; her jeans would get scraped again. She kept her denim jacket on to protect her arms.

Before going through I took a last look up at the sky. I was like one of those condemned to execution who takes that last look at the world. With the nor-wester still flowing over the plains towards us the heat didn't much lessen in the evening; the same dry, abrasive air. The sharp orange that edged the nor-west arch had faded to a wispy grey. All around me Hikitarua was turning over quietly for the night.

Next thing I was through.

◻

The Stench hit us as soon as we hit the floor of the storeroom, where we paused, as we always did, to try to get used to breathing it. Rachel stood very still, her breath coming in shallow gasps, her chest rising and falling. Carpenter gagged. His eyes streamed, forming tears beneath his glasses, but he held up, stayed on his feet, pulled a large wrapped parcel out of his backpack, placed it to one side on the floor, then clutched the backpack to his breast as if it were a life jacket.

Once more I looked across towards the door where, on the first night, I had imagined I'd seen a body lying; that was two nights ago, but it might as well have been another lifetime. It was hard to believe that this was only our third visit.

A body was there once more, a curved shape of dense shadow in the same place. And the silence was all wrong; there should have been the sound of voices to go with the flickering shadows beyond the door of the storeroom. There should have been a greeting.

I grabbed Rachel's arm and pointed. She grabbed my arm just as hard. I thought she was about to scream. She opened her mouth but the body screamed first, springing into life at the same time, turning into Adrian, while the scream was Josie's, just behind him in the kitchen, turning into hysterical laughter.

'Josie!' Rachel howled, gripping onto me so hard she made marks in the skin.

Carpenter was staring dumbfounded at the place on the floor where Adrian had been lying - how come he hadn't noticed?

The hysterical laughter switched off.

'What's so funny?' Rachel asked.

'Yeah, what's so funny?' Adrian said, trying to make the question sound original.

'That wasn't funny,' Rachel said, unhinged. 'It wasn't funny at all.' She turned on Adrian. 'You had no right to do that.'

'Get stuffed.' Josie called out from the kitchen. There was something funny about her voice. 'You can get fuckin stuffed!'

In the kitchen, the first thing I saw was that several candles were burning on the bench and that, strangely, the picture of little Luke's squinty, baby face still held pride of place between two flames. There were candles on the floor too, along with a half drunk bottle of whisky and a packet of tobacco. Josie was lounging back on a couple of long pillows, a blanket which came from our place making a temporary mattress, with a lit cigarette dangling between her fingers, watching us with a mixture of amusement and aggression. Her straggly blonde hair was plastered down on her head as if wet.

'They shit their pants,' Adrian said, flopping down beside her, giggling, and she giggled in return. There was something else different about them, besides being drunk or pretending to be drunk. They looked as if they had been living there for years.

'I wasn't scared,' Carpenter said.

'Goody for you,' Josie snapped at him. She relit her cigarette and started abusing her face with it. In the candlelight her pixy face looked thinner than ever, full of hollows. The shadows were like black mascara around her eyes.

Adrian followed suit, blowing blue smoke and looking at the three of us as if he had a great deal in mind for us. 'Good,' he said,' we're all here.' His voice sounded empty, as if he were talking into a drum. I wondered why it was so important that we were all there.

Josie rolled over and supported herself momentarily by putting her elbow on Adrian's thigh. He grinned at her and they both giggled again. Then I understood what was different about them and why they were giggling; they had had sex. Once, Adrian had proudly told me that he'd been having sex since he was eleven; he was already a hero, even then. He'd been born a hero.

That was why he'd skipped school after lunch and come here with the whisky, the tobacco - wherever they had come from - and the candles. The lonely Josie would have greeted him with open arms.

I closed my eyes and saw them, naked and wriggling around on the floor just as they must have really done. When I opened my eyes Rachel was looking at me, shocked. She saw it too and it rocked her; it was something she hadn't counted on, the way things could twist out of your hands just when you thought you had a grip on them.

Suddenly, for no reason I could fathom, Josie honed in on me, scrabbling up over her mattress on all fours.

'Baaaby!' she screeched in the most insincere voice you'd ever heard; a voice not even trying to be sincere, that had given up the struggle. 'I've been such a bitch,' She said, looking bleakly at me when I didn't respond to her greeting; she knew the truth when she heard it out of her own mouth. She'd figured it out for herself some time back; she was already doomed. She'd been doomed since her first hit of the Stench. Her fair skin was blotchy with terror and alcohol; her freckles glowed like flakes of gold paint, her eyes turned amber.

She leapt up and gave me a big hug. Her body was thin, full of small, vulnerable bones. 'You're alright, Baby,' she said, as if the problems were all mine. 'You're just a big lunk with nothing in your head.'

She laughed at her own cleverness as she turned to Rachel, but at the sight of her friend a huge change came over her and she fell onto her knees, arms outstretched to Rachel as to a long lost love. 'Raaaaaaa,' she said in a cracked voice that pleaded for forgiveness. 'Oh Raaaaaa...' She looked around helplessly as if she didn't know where she was. 'Would y' like a cigarette? Some whisky? It makes y' feel good.' She giggled again and Adrian imitated it.

Rachel stepped back as if one touch from Josie and she'd burst into flame. 'I've had enough of this.'

'Enough of what?' Josie demanded, all abasement vanished. 'Enough of what? You're not the one who can't go home, are you? You're not the one who has t' stay here in the dust and the shit all the time, hiding.' A wheedling tone entered her voice, 'Come on Ra, be an angel. Pretty please.' She hiccuped and Adrian giggled for her. She jabbed him in the ribs to shut him up.

Boosted by her fury, Rachel tipped her bag upside down; out came a shower of clothes, outside clothes, good clothes, food including chocolate and biscuits. 'You just wanted to hide out for a while, remember? A day or two while we got some stuff together, right? Clothes and money and stuff we had to steal, right?'

'Yeah, right,' Josie said vaguely, as if she couldn't actually remember but didn't want to doubt Rachel's word.

'And then you would go to Wellington to stay with your cousin, remember? The one who's nineteen.' From her jeans pocket she pulled out a fifty dollar note with a ten and some change. Her voice trembled with rage. 'Here's the money. Enough to get you on the bus to Wellington.' With revulsion, she threw the money down on the makeshift bed. 'And that's the last time I'll steal and lie and betray people for you.'

'Did you really steal the money?' Carpenter asked, morbidly interested. 'Where did you find it?' He'd found his crowbar and was hanging onto it for dear life.

'In her mother's purse, of course,' Josie said carelessly, 'where she usually gets it. She's stolen money before you know. It's not some big new thing she's done just now.' She waved a dismissive hand, but her eyes were locked on the fifty dollar note.

'I had to lie to the police,' Rachel went on. 'I lied to them and betrayed

Baby.'

'Really?' Adrian sat up, tobacco in hand. 'How did you betray Baby?'

Rachel opened her mouth before she realised what she was doing. She gave me a quick, ambushed glance. Adrian was on to it immediately. He thought about it while he ostentatiously fingered his cigarette. Calmly, he lit it on one of the candles, holding the candle up to the cigarette; it was Adrian's way of acting super cool, a sickening display if ever I saw one. Then, to cap off the performance, he took a deep breath and blew heaps of blue smoke up into the air where it pushed aggressively at the stagnant air. While he was doing all these stylish things, his mind was working furiously enough to come up with the truth.

'Baby tried to blab to the police. Baby is a traitor,' His voice became hollow again. He put the cigarette in the side of his mouth so it bounced up and down as he spoke. He had to shut his eye on that side because the smoke was going straight up into it, and that made his face look all twisted up. 'Tried t' tell the police t' come here. And they did come here.' He gave a crooked grin.

'What happened?' Carpenter asked eagerly.

'They didn't find her.' He let that hang there for a moment, for us to appreciate along with his smoking style, then turned to Josie. 'They won't be back, will they Josie?'

'No.' Josie's voice sounded like a piece of wire being rubbed against something rusty.

I tried to imagine the police stomping around the hospital, their torches bouncing off the yellowing walls. I tried to imagine where Josie would hide. I didn't get any further than that.

'But what happened?' Carpenter insisted. He was clinging to his crowbar as if someone were about to wrench it from him and take it to his father.

By tortuous way of reply, Adrian slowly and carefully unscrewed the lid of the whisky bottle and a new smell entered the room to join the gang. It was heavy and sharp. He lifted it to his lips and took a sip, rolling his eyes up towards the ceiling as the liquid rolled down his throat. It was a performance every bit as sickening as the put-on with the cigarette. 'Old Boss Hogg's too fucking lazy t' do more than flash his torch around.' He gave a contemptuous laugh. 'But that doesn't stop Baby being a traitor. We can't trust her any more,' he said serenely, his eyeballs filling up with water from the sting of the tobacco and the fumes of the alcohol. If he hadn't been sitting down he might have fallen over.

Carpenter said, 'What does it matter now? We're here, let's get on with it.'

Carpenter had forgotten that Josie had taken some enormous step into nothingness; the idea of leaving home and taking to the street was beyond him. He only cared about the trapdoor, and lifting it. As far as he was concerned Josie was just raving, which was what she usually did, while he got on with the real business. He had retrieved his crowbar, which was firm in his hands, and his mind had once more returned to its single track.

'Matter?' Adrian sounded aggrieved. 'We made a pledge.'

'No we didn't,' Rachel said quickly.

I don't think Adrian heard her. He went to sneer at me and the sneer turned into a snarl. For a moment I didn't recognise my brother. Right then he wanted to kill me, just as I had wanted to kill Rabbit on the river bed the night before. I remembered the worm crawling out of Mum's nose. My lower lip quivered. I knew what a baby I looked like, a big blubbering baby, but I couldn't help that.

Adrian changed again and the creature looking out at me crouched inside his skin still only half born.

'I hate you,' he said, and I despaired. He had never pushed any difference between us this far. The quivering of my lower lip degenerated into blubbering. I depended on him; I thought of Mother, watching us go, trusting him because big and clumsy me was his sister.

I turned to where the candles lit little Luke who glowed between them like a baby saint.

'You're a fuckwit.' Adrian turned brusquely away, as if I wasn't even worth stepping on. 'A big little moron.'

The words were out. Because I was crying the others said nothing. I turned to the glow of the candle and the wavering shadows, both of which looked bulbous and drippy through my tears. Squeezed by the wetness in my eyes, the shadows pulsed and took on strange shapes. I thought I could see figures in them, starving, screaming beings, creatures of the Stench. I blinked to drive them away, and tried to hold a little prayer steady in my throat.

It's too late, I thought, as Mitch's face came into my mind, I've left it too late.

Josie made a snarling sound. 'Fuck Baby, we'll deal with her later.' She snatched up the chocolate and opened it.

'That's not for now,' Rachel said, swiftly snatching it out of Josie's hand. 'That's for the trip.'

'What are you talking about? I can't go right now. I'll go in the morning.' Josie waved an airy hand. 'There's no rush for fuck's sake, calm down Rachel, just calm down. Y' come in here all aggro, tryin t' throw your weight around. Why don't y' sit down. Relax. Stop panicking, that's what you're doing; you're in a big panic. You tip everything upside down, shout and yell, put on a big drama and there's no bus until the morning anyway.'

'Yes there is. The nine forty-five, you can get it at the petrol station.'

'The cops'll catch me.' Josie said instantly.

'Same in the morning,' Rachel hit back, not giving Josie any quarter at all. 'You'll be on it. Tonight.'

'Stop trying to organise my fucking life!' Josie screamed. She grabbed the bottle off Adrian and took a slug. Still holding the chocolate bar, Rachel stood above her, staring down at the thin body below; I thought she was going to kill Josie, grab the crowbar out of Carpenter's hands and smash it into the back of her head. That's what I saw. All of us were on the edge of something like that.

'Sit down, why the fuck won't you sit down?' Josie said, cringing away. 'You're just standing there like an idiot.'

Rachel didn't sit but knelt beside her friend, staring intently into her face. 'Maro says it's not true, what you say about him. He said you tell lies all the time.'

A bitter, cynical look made Josie's face ugly. 'Of course he would say that, wouldn't he? He's not likely to tell you guys, let the whole world know. He's got his story worked out, don't you worry. He'll tell the cops his story and Dad will back him up, that's what, don't talk t' me about Maro, he's a cunning bastard. He'll tell the same story t' you too, so you'll tell the cops. Then everybody can think I'm crazy. That's what you think, isn't it? You think I'm crazy.'

'I believed him when he said it.'

'Did you?' Josie gave a faint shriek. It was like somebody dying a long way off. 'You believe him then?' Her voice went very cold. 'Why don't you fuck him instead, you'd like that wouldn't you, wouldn't you? I've seen the way you look at him.'

Rachel got off the bed and threw the clothes and the money in Josie's face. Her own face was covered by dark blotches of red, but whether from fury or embarrassment I couldn't tell. She turned for the storeroom. Her voice, like her body was full of trembles, as if she'd been gripped by a fever. 'I'm getting the cops. Now. Mitch will come.'

'Yes,' I said, bringing my hands together.

Adrian started to move but Josie put her hand on his arm. Her fingers were like tight, wrinkled tentacles.

'You can't do that!' Carpenter said. He looked horrified at the idea.

Josie threw away her cigarette and stood up. She was nothing but anguish and bone. 'I'll kill myself,' she said in the new, flat, dead voice she was developing.

She let the statement fall into the silence.

'She was goin t' kill herself before we found the hospital,' Adrian announced. There was almost a touch of pride in his voice, as if he had been a major instrument in her salvation. 'If we hadn't found this place, she'd be dead now. She told me.'

Rachel was poised in the middle of a movement, half way through the storeroom door.

'And I'm still goin t' do it if I'm forced to go home.' Josie took Adrian's cigarette out of his hand. 'I'll still do it. I know how t' do it. There's no trouble there. I've worked out how t' hang myself in the garage.' She threw a quick look at Rachel's frozen back. 'Y' just climb up on a chair, loop a rope over one of the supports, put it around your neck, kick the chair away and you swing.' Her lower arm swung loosely in the air, hinged at the elbow.

'You wouldn't though,' Rachel said, 'you just wouldn't. You might think you would but you wouldn't. When the last moment came to it.'

'I would.' Josie said flatly. She took a deep, destructive drag at the cigarette. Rachel had paused at the door, looking into the gloom of the storeroom ahead; Josie held her there by the spell of her words. 'And you'd never know when it was coming, tomorrow or the next day.' She gave a quick, jagged laugh. 'I might even not wait that long. I could be dead before the cops get here. That would probably be the best way, actually. For you too, then y' wouldn't have t' wake up every morning wondering if I'd done it or not yet.' She flung her cigarette down where it glowed for a moment in the dry dust.

'And I'll do it with you.' Adrian said, apparently deeply impressed with Josie's stand. 'We'll both do it together. I don't care what happens t' me.' He gave everybody a reckless look; he wanted to let everybody know that no matter how high the stakes got, he was in. Rachel would have two souls on her conscience.

If he expected gratitude from Josie for his heroic declaration then he was disappointed; Josie was ignoring him, concentrating all her energy on Rachel who had not moved from the doorway. A shudder went through her as she tried to step through into the storeroom and found herself unable to move, as if her limbs were bound.

'It would be very easy, even here,' Josie said softly. 'I'd use a rope. I know how t' make them slip knots. I'd tie it t' the top and throw meself down the stairs. It would only take a moment.'

No one listening to her could have doubted her words; even Adrian was silenced by the gravity of them.

The strength went out of Rachel; her shoulders slumped, her arms collapsed limply by her sides and her head tipped forward, exposing the delicate white skin at the nape of her neck where her hair parted as it fell each side of her face.

'You wouldn't really do that, would you?' said Carpenter, fascinated.

'Sure I would. Why shouldn't I?'

'Because then you wouldn't exist.'

Josie shrugged. 'You can't prove you exist even now, can you?' She spoke with that same flat certainty that already sounded as if came from beyond the grave, already possessed that coldness and distance where existence was only a memory. Just the ashes of a cigarette ground out on the floor.

'Of course I can.' Carpenter stopped in confusion. How do you prove the obvious?

'You can't. You can't prove anythin about anythin. We're just fiery atoms and electrons and things racing about everywhere and nowhere. The Science teacher told us that, remember? The rope that's going t' hang me when Rachel dobs me in, does that exist? It's just more fiery things racing around, isn't it? The science teacher told us.'

Carpenter looked dumbfounded. The crowbar in his hands of course was real, he knew that, it was cold and dense. Josie would know about the rope too when it broke her neck.

Rachel turned slowly around to face everybody. Her face looked small and white inside her curls. Her eyes were huge, as if her pupils had swallowed her irises. Slowly she took off her denim jacket. She wore a light, white short-sleeved blouse and her bare arms gleamed in the half light like milky marble, slender and fragile.

'What have y' done with Rabbitt?' she asked in a whisper, looking from Josie to Adrian and back again. 'Just tell me that.'

Josie put her head on one side, as if she'd heard something screwy. 'What are y' talking about?' She was staring at Rachel's arms.

'Serendipity Rabbitt. She's gone missing.'

'Maybe she swallowed her thumb,' Adrian said and Josie giggled as if she'd just been containing that giggle all along.

'You haven't seen her?'

'She wouldn't show her fat face around here,' Adrian said.

That was not what I understood. I thought that Rabbitt had followed us here, maybe even come into the building on the very first night, successfully hiding from us.

'You haven't seen her,' Rachel repeated. She had been so sure Rabbitt was here she couldn't believe it. Like an old woman, she shuffled forward a few steps.

Josie stepped to met her. 'Did you have any nightmares?' There was a peace offer in her voice; the suggestion of concern.

'No.'

'That's good.' She took hold of one of Rachel's fascinating arms and stroked it.

'No, it isn't.' Rachel pulled her arm away.

'Why not?'

'I didn't sleep. That's why. Y' can't have nightmares if y' don't go t' sleep.' The same flat chill had entered Rachel's voice. The slender arms hung limp by her sides.

I tried to read what was happening inside Rachel but the block was up. I'd met that block before, when Mitch had been talking to Rachel about the hospital. I was afraid that, like Adrian, some new creature would be born in her that I would not recognise. She couldn't overcome Josie and Adrian, not after they had had sex together, they were too united in their purpose.

I saw it happening before it could happen. I saw her slump onto the end of the bed like an unwelcome visitor, grab the whisky bottle and lift it up to her mouth. I saw the bubbles coming up through the amber liquid as her throat opened. It was something I imagined, then it was happening.

Rachel puffed away on a cigarette without inhaling. Then she inhaled by accident and started coughing. Josie showed her how to do it, all sophisticated with the cigarette between her fingers and her wrist dangling conspicuously in front of her face. When you talked to her you thought you were talking to the cigarette. She drew in the smoke in little sharp gasps and didn't cough.

'You don't smoke like that,' Adrian told her. 'That's how you smoke dope,' as if he knew all about it. 'You smoke tobacco smooth and even, like this, and you don't hold it in.'

'I know,' Rachel giggled and pretended that she didn't have a brain. I had to look the other way. I was glad this part was just a dream.

'It tastes like soot,' Rachel said.

'That's what it's like at first,' Adrian said, sounding like the biggest smoker of all time, 'but after a while you get used to it.'

'Why?' asked Carpenter.

'Why what?'

'If it tastes like soot, why should you get used to it? I mean what's the point of it?'

Adrian gestured helplessly at Carpenter's dorkish comments. 'It doesn't have a point. It's fun.'

'At school they show you photographs of smokers' lungs all black and eaten away,' Carpenter said.

Rachel gave a grin of intense inner pleasure. She looked up and her eyes were glassy. I realised with a shock that she was drunk. She had a bottle between her legs. Everything was happening too fast.

'That's after years and years,' Josie said.

'We're not doing this,' Rachel said, passing the bottle to Adrian without meeting his eye and stubbing out her cigarette all at once.

That was a signal for the scene to dissolve. Even a slave has her choices. As Josie had argued, death was always an option, so was screaming. A slave could scream and scream until a song was born, Rachel had no other way out; so great was the power of her intent at that moment that she could change fate, alter the time line, avoid the whisky and the cigarettes and the craven talk, but the cost was enormous.

She shattered the whole delicate balance to the conversation by opening her mouth and starting to scream. But it wasn't really her that screamed; she just opened her mouth and the screams came floating out of their own accord like a warped prayer. She didn't have to do anything. Her eyes were all screwed up, buried in the scream, her mouth was wide open and you'd have thought the scream would be loud enough to wake the neighbourhood if not the dead, but it wasn't. It sounded far away, like a huge sigh, some ancient throat giving up the ghost.

I thought Josie was going to slap her or beat her to shut her up, for everything had seemed to be going on in hushed whispers, but I couldn't have been more wrong. Josie joined in, tearing the screams out of her body as if they were big, rough splinters. They were louder than Rachel's.

'People might come,' Carpenter said to Adrian.

Adrian grinned. His teeth were clenched together so he could keep his cigarette in his mouth; he liked the screaming. He treated it as if were an accolade; he basked in it as if he'd created it. Carpenter didn't feel that way. He put his hands over his ears. His feet shuffled around and the sweat broke out all over his face, shining in little white beads. His glasses were opaque and his jaw kept moving sideways. I'd seen him doing that when Josie's father had made his appeal to the school.

Josie was the first to carry her scream out into the corridor to let it loose in the wards. She moved slowly, like someone walking up the aisle of a church to get married. Her voice filled the old hospital the way air fills a balloon. Rachel, following behind, feet seeming to move her upper body along independently, provided an ethereal descant the way we learned in the choir, rising above the main theme with a higher voice. The building vibrated with the sound.

Carpenter put his hands over his ears. The cops were sure to come and his Dad would find out about the theft of the crowbar; his Dad was very strict about thieving.

I went to the doorway and looked into the corridor. Rachel was standing at the bottom of the stairs by the banister; she had one arm on the banister, not for its support but to support it, and the whole building it seemed. Screams were coming up out of her like bubbles; some of them not so much loud as far inside the ear, deep in the brain. Rachel was testing out her screaming, trying to find how many worlds she could scream into. Her voice ascended to heaven, at least as far as the corrugated iron roof of the hospital would allow. Josie was moving up the stairs ahead of her, letting her screams loose in the upper story. Throwing them from one corner to the other. Long hard sounds with barbed ends.

I joined in. It was a pleasure to scream instead of trying to talk and say things that would never sound right. No one expected that. Just because

I couldn't talk didn't mean I couldn't scream. I channeled my scream to Mitch, who was far off down the river bed searching the stagnant pools for Josie's body. I wanted her to come here before someone died, otherwise someone would have to die, that's what the screaming was all about; my scream was a lament, a mourning chant for deaths yet to come. In the enchantment of the scream I saw them, many deaths laid out before me as if a plague had struck, their dying arms lifted in supplication, like the branches of the tree in Hone Tuwhare's poem. Death was not the end for them, however, that was why I was screaming.

The screaming went on for hours. In the meantime, Adrian amused himself by staring into Carpenter's eyes, apparently trying to hypnotise him. Carpenter stared back, glasses flashing defiantly. There was a moment of truth between them I couldn't fathom, perhaps because they were boys and I was not meant to understand; perhaps because Adrian didn't understand himself. Mostly Adrian sided with Josie against Carpenter, but now he seemed to need a male alliance. 'They're crazy,' he said, as if to console Carpenter who maybe couldn't hear the note of triumph in his voice.

Carpenter wasn't much of a prospect alliance-wise. He was upset and shaking. 'Stop them' he shouted, banging his hands against his ears. Sweat dripped off the end of his nose. The old building shook with a sudden hard gust of the nor-west.

Our screams shut off abruptly. The three of us, at the same moment, in mid scream. There was a long silence while the echo ate into the timber.

When I opened my eyes Rachel had moved up the first flight of stairs to join Josie on the landing. Josie seized her and hugged her fiercely, burying her body into Rachel's. Rachel had a tiny, sad smile on her face. Josie was babbling, words bubbling from her mouth like blood from a wound. 'You'll let me, Rachel, won't you? You'll let me. I love you so much, just so much, fuck...' she started crying, 'We'll open the trapdoor tonight, Rachel, we'll let out the dead people, let them out so they can go up to heaven, let the Stench out because it's just a lot of pus.' she laughed hysterically, 'Then they won't come anywhere near me. Maro won't find me, will he, will he, Rachel? Kiss me. We used to kiss when we were little. You'll let me, won't you?'

And she met Rachel's black-tipped lips with a slow death kiss. It was more than a kiss; it was a pact, a promise. It was more like a slip knot than a kiss. When she pulled away Rachel's lips were still half open; she had received it like a blessing. She tasted it and swallowed it.

The sight was too much for Carpenter, who turned away, having no eyes for something like this; in that respect he was innocent. He was drawn by the trapdoor at the end of the hall and the unfinished business he had with it. He took a few steps in that direction. Then he swung right around and did something completely different. Maybe he thought it was like playing zombies, God knows what he thought as he went gallumping up the stairs with heffalump breaths and a hooting sound, pumping his arms up and down, trying as hard as he could to look like a ghost or dead person. His shirt was plastered with dark patches where his sweat had soaked through. When he got to the landing, he didn't know what to do. Puffing and blowing, he stared at the girls and did nothing

Josie gave a nervous laugh. She reached out her tongue and tasted Rachel's arm. Rachel shuddered. Carpenter took a step forward, towards Rachel. 'Keep away from her, four-eyes,' Josie screeched, lashing out at Carpenter who stepped back, rubbing the scratch on his cheek.

'The cops'll come,' Carpenter said, which really didn't have anything to do with anything except the screaming, which had already stopped. He spoke in a wounded voice like an eight year old, flapping his arms aimlessly as if he were a bird that couldn't lift off.

Then Adrian took over the action; he'd been left out of the mainstream far too long. He came up the stairs like a hot spring flood, bearing down on Rachel. He looked as if somebody had just slapped him across the mouth and his lips were still white from the sting of it. He grabbed hold of Rachel's arm and she opened her mouth to say something but he squeezed the words back. I know how he could do that; he'd done it with me. His fingers tightened around her arm, cutting off the life flow, the birth and death of every pulse. I knew what it was like when he did that. It could really hurt. He knew where to take hold. Where to squeeze. As he did that he smiled at me and his smile was as tight as his grip.

For a long moment no sound came out of Rachel's mouth.

'Let go,' she whined at last.

I don't think Adrian knew what he was doing, or why he desperately wanted to hurt her. He let her go just as easily, when the attention shifted elsewhere. He was too indifferent to care, even for cruelty.

'Open the trapdoor.' Josie's expression was deadly serious as she walked back down the stairs. She might have been announcing the burning down of the school.

The trapdoor awaited her pleasure. Already she was thinking over some of the more delightful things she could do. 'We could send Baby down first,' she said brightly, 'to have a look around.' She giggled. Adrian joined her, even Carpenter who was usually a bit slow in the humour department.

The laughter died in their throats as we hit the lower floor; the Stench was all around us, sucking the laughter out of everything. I wasn't the only one to feel it, but I felt it first because I wasn't laughing.

'We have to hurry,' Josie spoke as if she were about to vomit. She was thinking hard and biting her nails to the core. It occurred to me then that she was frightened, more frightened than the rest of us even.

Adrian vanished into the kitchen and returned with the whisky. As soon as it appeared under her nose she grabbed it and had a swig. She was building herself into it, smashing herself in the face to make it numb.

Then Rachel started talking, just unwinding the words, anything to delay the final moment; there was a deep quiver in her voice. This was her last throw, her last appeal. She spoke from a dream, a ritual.

'Right now we're being attacked by creatures we can't see or hear. We can only smell them.' Her voice seemed to have lowered two or three registers. 'You can feel them everywhere, everywhere around us.'

They were there, she said, wafting around the dead air in invisible bodies which were just densities of the Stench. Stench creatures. We could feel them in our throats and on our teeth, feel their sticky touch on the inside of our mouths. The maggoty crawl along our gums. She spelt it out in detail.

' Ha ha! You're just tryin to make me scared so I'll leave here,' Josie said, and from the tone of her voice it sounded as if the strategy might be working.

'It's not just a few old bones down there, a few grinning skeletons t' give us a nice little scare. Or just a few nasty rotting things. Whatever is down there is the mother of all these creatures,' Rachel's fingers flickered down her arms in revulsion, 'and already, before it is even let loose, it is squeezing us between its fingers, hollowing us out, fingering us...'

'Ha ha ha!' Josie said, 'I know what you're up to.' Her nails raked down her own arm leaving a red trail.

'..feeding on us. That's why I couldn't sleep. Every time I fell asleep I could feel it coming for me. It wasn't my dreams I was afraid of, it was the

Stench. It was coming to feed off my dreams.' She took a deep, shuddering breath and threw a heavy glance towards the trapdoor.

'You're just making it up!' Josie jeered, 'just makin it up! It's just a silly old stench down there. I made up stuff for fun too about dead people under the trapdoor. I was just playing spooks.' She tried to make her voice sound casual but it cracked open, like a fissure opening in rock.

'Not that old thing again.' Carpenter let out an explosion of breath. He tried to laugh but his eyes were swimming around naked in the aquarium of his glasses.

'I'm not playing spooks,' Rachel said, grabbing Josie's arm and staring deeply into her eyes. Josie gave an embarrassed laugh.

Adrian had a conspicuous swig at the whisky. He took too much, couldn't hold it down, and squirted it back out, covering everybody with a spray of alcohol. That made everybody laugh, and Josie laughed so much she went half mental, doubling right over and twisting her face up.

At the same time everybody was edging down the corridor towards the trapdoor; inch by inch it was reeling us in.

Josie came up for air, pulled the bottle out of Adrian's hand and took another drink. The more she drank the more she thought everything was all right.

'You'll piss in their faces, won't you, Adrian darling?' she said, simpering in front of him. 'That's what y' said you'd do.'

'Get the crowbar,' Adrian said to Carpenter out of the corner of his mouth.

'He'd better not get too close,' Rachel said, turning her seriousness into a stupid giggle in an apparent complete reversal of mood; her giggle was forced and deliberate, a travesty of Josie's laugh, enough to start Josie going. Both girls went hysterical, wrapping their arms around each other's shoulders and screaming in each other's ears. At the same time Rachel kept subtly pulling at her friend, trying to reverse the drift towards the trapdoor. Finally they collapsed in a disorganised heap on the floor, rolling and flailing their arms, punching and grabbing at each other. They were not rolling on the floor laughing but fighting. At some point giggling gave way to scratching. Rachel came out on top, holding Josie down.

'It's killing us even now,' she screamed, shaking Josie like a rag doll.

Her voice echoed in the air as if trapped in a canyon of sound, and the shore on which everyone was flung in the wake of it was further and bleaker than any of us had seen before. A rotting ocean stirred against a putrid coast. Dead trees spiked the sky. Crops lay flat on the stinking earth and there was the slap of flesh against sickness, over and over. An eye with a toxic glaze. A great desert staring down at Hikitarua out of the sky. The Stench, it seemed, had memories of these things; images that quickened in the thickening air.

Suddenly Carpenter's voice floated in faintly from beyond the corridor. His voice filtered out of the tallest shadows. 'Be really quiet,' he called. 'The cops are here.'

We traced Carpenter up to the second floor, into one of the wards with a view over the front street, Adrian taking the steps two at a time, gracefully, like a young buck on his way up the mountainside to lock horns for the first time.

Soundlessly, Carpenter gestured to the window.

The police car was sitting opposite the hospital, sitting there under the still popped street lamp, not doing anything. I looked in vain for Mitch's coppery hair.

'Where are they?' Adrian said quickly.

'In the car, I think.'

'What are they doing?'

'Eating fish and chips?'

'Are they watching the hospital?'

'How would I know?' Carpenter's lower lip quivered.

'I'll be in deep shit if they catch me here,' said Rachel. She looked at the window as if she were peering into another world.

I came and stood beside her, ready to do battle for her as she'd done for me. 'Rachel,' I whispered. She turned and looked at me and the old Rachel was there, calm, ageless as rock, looking out from a time before the world.

The first thing she did was to step forward and lift her arm to smash a window and alert the police, but she was too slow. Josie was right in front of her, rigid, brittle.

'I'll kill myself if they come in and try to take me,' Josie said, reminding Rachel of her old power over her. 'And you'll be responsible. I'll use a piece of glass that y' break t' cut me throat.'

It was a battle Rachel had already lost.

'We left the candles on downstairs,' Carpenter said in panic. He had the same look on his face as when he was facing the inoculation jab.

'The cops are pretty stupid,' Adrian said, looking at them gloatingly. It was a Gorebag Ironclaw moment.

'Maybe you should just wander over there and sort them out, Adrian,' Rachel said. 'Piss in their faces. Tell them what a big-shot you are.'

'Fuck off.'

'Tell them that then. Tell them to fuck off.'

'I will,' Adrian said, and leaned forward towards the window as if he were going to spit.

Suddenly, without fuss, the police car slid off into the night.

Adrian gave his most sublime smile.

◦

I didn't follow the others down directly. They were going down to open the trapdoor, I had no doubt of that; nothing would stop them from destroying themselves unless I tried again and what hope did I have?

I stood alone in the corridor of the upper storey in the creaking silence, and tried to reach the City of Gates where I might find some answers, but it was nowhere to be found. A huge greasy darkness lay all around me, letting in no other worlds, no other universes, for there was no language to reach them; all the words in the world, and their histories, had become hemmed into one tiny putrid space. This is how the Stench works, I told myself; like a blindfold placed around the world, around the words that make the worlds; how can a big little moron fight a thing like that?

And how was it, I wondered, that Josie and Adrian were so eager to serve it, to make it their own and plunge their faces into it like pigs into the trough. But was Josie so eager? Wasn't that terror I had seen in her face tonight, when she'd been listening to Rachel, and hadn't I heard that terror like a knife's edge in her giggling. Then I remembered the worm coming out of Mum's nose, and shivered in the warm night. There are no words for it, I thought, that's how it operates, by blocking out the field so it cannot be seen. But there was a price to pay for its success - it could not conceal its odour, its Stench. The more concealed it was from the eyes, the more it got up the nose.

At that moment I heard a sound. It might have been a rat, it might have been the shadow of a branch scraping across the floor of one of the wards; whatever it was it pulled me out of my thinking. I'd been busy falling into time, into the holes between thoughts, between worlds.

I followed the sound, more with my hands than my ears, for all I could hear was the deafness of the hospital. The voices from downstairs had fallen away. I had closed my eyes because, for the moment, they too were useless, and their light only distracted me. I followed the shapes my hands were making out of the darkness; muffled shapes, shapes buried thickly somewhere.

I felt my way through a door and some metal beds, stopped when the shape grew too large to hold, and opened my eyes.

There was a large furry creature whose belly had been ripped open and guts spread around. In the moonlight all the blood looked black, bits of coagulated fur stood up, sharp and shiny, from the edges of the wounds. Finally I located an opossum head, and remembered the thump I'd heard on the roof the night before.

Behind this mess, almost in the middle of it, was Serendipity Rabbitt, tied up in a knot of moonlight from the window, a gag across her face. When she saw me she made a buzzing noise, like a hive of tired bees, and her head jerked up and down. A rope secured her hands.

'I can't put my thumb in my mouth,' was what I thought I heard her say.

MaSk

The trapdoor lay blurred in the wan moonlight, the lino peeled back like a top sheet on a well made bed. It didn't look like anything special, just a dusty piece of flooring; from a distance you couldn't see the line where it fitted snug against the rest of the floor, or the orb of light which marked the spot with a soft brand from the coloured pane above.

It was just another part of the floor.

But it was rapidly being transformed. Incense had been placed at each of the four corners, and Josie was busy placing two candles along each side, giving the trapdoor the appearance of a place of worship. Above it, wreathes of incense hung in the air like ghostly clothes swinging on an invisible line. The bottle of whisky, half empty, and the cigarette packet sat upright to one side like presiding judges.

Adrian was standing tall, apparently director of operations, throwing out useless orders. They were all, except Carpenter, abusing their faces. Tiny lights glowed like fireflies in front of their mouths. Even Rachel had joined in. She liked to smoke, I could see by the way she sucked it in. Cigarettes were lit and stubbed out, the whisky was handed around and everybody talked in false voices, as if they were all at some sort of cool party waiting for the music to start.

They were psyching themselves up to it, each in their own way, trying to convince the rest that they were not scared and drinking as much whisky as their throats would allow. Smoking as fast as coolness permitted. All the time the trapdoor lay at their feet waiting to be opened.

As I approached, I decided to say nothing about the bound girl upstairs; it was more dangerous for her down here anyway, than where she was. Her captivity was of course what Adrian and Josie had been covering up all the while they were beating down on Rachel, trying to break her so they could use her. They must have captured Rabbitt, the foolish, while on one of her normal sneaking missions, bound her up and had sex in the kitchen below while Rabbitt wriggled and squirmed above in the struggle to get her thumb in her mouth. At that moment I wished I'd been born anywhere else in the Cosmic Map. Anywhere but Hikitarua.

They already had their sacrifice stashed in the wings; why had I been so stupid as to not see how fast events would move?

They were moving fast now. Carpenter had his bag by him and was hauling something out. He must have gone back into the storeroom and got it. I imagined he'd just returned for he was working feverishly to find what he was looking for.

Suddenly a bright eye sprang out from among them and went bouncing off across the dingy cream walls which suddenly sprang into relief; a crazy creature made of brightness jumped around the room. Under that ruthless eye with its leaping shadows, the place looked tatty and abandoned; all cracks and cobwebs.

'Turn it off!' Adrian commanded.

Before he could be obeyed, its piercing, unseeing gaze landed on my face and ate into my eyes as I walked towards them, burning its circular image deep into my brain.

'Turn the fucking thing off,' Adrian repeated.

Carpenter laughed. As he pulled the light away, I screwed up my eyes and saw dancing red demons. Now Carpenter was the one who was stealing the show, pulling out a torch and flashing it around, jerking the shadows out of the corners and raising dust with his sudden light. There was a fixed grin on his face and his glasses made his eyes look bigger than they were, especially when he shone the torch underneath his chin to throw the shadows upward, making shiny, arched cathedrals out of his eyes.

'We'll get a decent look this time,' he said, waving his torch like some holy object. 'We'll get some actual scientific proof.'

'You look really demented,' Josie said with desperate contempt.

Carpenter shone the light on her, showing us a scared girl looking younger than her age with the white pimply face and straggly blond hair curling into rats tails. Her mouth was like a double ribbon with a twist at each end. 'Fuck off.' she said, as if she were lip-syncing. We're all doing it, I thought, everybody's lip-syncing. Carpenter jerked the torch away, maybe because he could see Josie's face, tearless, hot and dry and all bone, or maybe because, like Adrian, he didn't want to see it.

'Fuck off,' I said, seeing if I could get it right.

Everybody laughed; it relieved their feelings to laugh at me and it made them leave me alone, at least for the moment, but Adrian didn't laugh for long.

'Turn the fuckin thing off or I'll wrap it around your face.'

I was the only one that laughed because Adrian always makes me laugh when he says things like that, which he thinks are so tough. I laughed because it was such a relief to hear Gorefang Ironclaw in echo and not have to think too much about the bound, frantic girl upstairs. He was almost just his old silly self. For him, however, the bright light defiled the darkness of the place, its deeper, spookier mysteries, the hidden places like under the trapdoor from which Adrian fancied he was drawing his power.

As if in obedience to this thought, the single eye fell to the floor, to the trapdoor, which lay in the fuzzy, haloed circle; the circle squared. We could see dust along its edges and the faint disturbances we had made the night before. It seemed like a short distance for the torch to probe down into the interior once the trapdoor was open and to bring its secrets into the light of reason. A torch with the beam still strong, the battery hardly touched.

Carpenter let it hover there long enough to make that point, to bring everybody back to business, then the eye snapped off like a dry branch breaking and we were back in the dark again. He took his glasses off in a vain attempt to wipe them down as if he could bring back the light that way.

'I've got a secret weapon, if we need it,' he said. 'But I'm not telling y' what it is.'

As I joined the group, Adrian wasted no time in turning on me, as if I was responsible for everything, as if he were resuming an offensive delayed only by more pressing matters. 'You hate us all, don't you Baby?' His lips fell back into their familiar, contemptuous shape. 'I see y' lookin at us with those little pink piggy eyes of yours, decidin what's this and what's that. You think, don't y' baby, y' keep thinkin and y' hate and you think at the same time. You hate everybody because of what y' are. Because y' can't think straight, y' can't even put one word after another and make sense. You don't know what's goin' on here at all. You're makin it all up t' suit yourself. You scare me sometimes.'

Josie hissed in agreement. 'I told y' not t' bring her,' she said. 'Having her around is like having a rope around your neck.'

'She'd never kill herself,' Rachel said with stark conviction. I saw the after-light of the torch in her eyes and wondered what she was thinking.

'There's worse things than that,' Josie assured her. 'She could kill all of us. Y' never know what she's thinking. She's always making plans about goin t' the police. Y'r own sister. I reckon she could go down into the trapdoor first. Head first.' She sounded in deadly earnest.

'No, me first,' Carpenter said, absurdly waving his torch and his crowbar, his two great claims to fame. 'I've got my secret weapon.'

'We're ready,' Josie said.

At the last minute, no one wanted to make the first move. Even Carpenter the dauntless was pale and sweating. Everyone was intent on the trapdoor and the fascination of what might lie beneath. If you stared at it long enough without blinking too much, you could see the trapdoor move. Not across the floor, but move the way the surface of simmering water moves, seething within itself. Waves of motion passed through it. It crawled within itself and yet remained motionless. It was, I decided, a sign that the trapdoor was a pretence; something made to look like an ordinary thing, hidden and inconspicuous. It did not belong to the world the way ordinary trapdoors do, but mimicked reality to hide what lay beneath.

Nobody was making the first move.

Rachel's eyes were fixed hypnotically on the trapdoor, her pupils had grown round and dark enough to swallow the whole town, and her chest heaved like someone after a hard run.

'Rachel,' I said softly. She looked up at me blankly, apparently not recognising me. The Stench feels us as shapes inside its body, I thought. And once it has discerned us completely, the shape of every thought, it then destroys us. 'Rachel!' I hoped that the tone of my voice in this one word, her name, would say everything I needed to say and the urgency of it all.

Then she recognised me and tried to smile. 'Baby.' she said. Her curls hung around her temples like bruises. Behind her Adrian snatched the whisky out of Josie's hand and gave it a buccaneer tilt. I tried to stare Rachel out, to make her come into my eyes.

'Give me a hug, Baby,' she said. 'You're very beautiful.'

She must be drunk, I thought, stepping back.

'You're right Baby,' she said, 'I know you're right.'

Carpenter knelt down. The moment had come, but before Josie could do anything and before Adrian could snatch the crowbar out of Carpenter's hand to take over the action, Rachel stepped onto the trapdoor, first foot forward as if over an abyss. She banged her foot against it and looked mockingly at Josie.

'Yes!' Josie hissed, her eyes rolling up into the middle of her head. 'Yes! Now!'

Rachel swung around and brought her left heel down hard.

'No,' she said, 'You won't lift it.'

Josie shrieked and clutched her heart as if she had been stabbed.

'You have t' get off it, if we're goin t' lift it,' Carpenter said, labouring his way through the logic. He turned to Adrian for leadership.

'Just step away from it,' Adrian said to Rachel, indicating the short distance with his hands. Rachel saw him and knew him for what he was. She didn't sneer, like Josie would've, rather her face softened, as if she could have loved him.

'I'm not moving,' she said softly, as if she were saying goodnight to a sweetheart. How easy it was to love her then, and how easy to step up beside her on the trapdoor and add my weight to hers. They didn't call me the big lug and the big little moron for nothing. I had legs like young tree trunks and a stomach like an over boiled potato. If push came to shove, I could shove as hard as anyone would like to push.

Rachel took my arm. We didn't care about the Stench. You got used to it after a while anyway.

The battle of the trapdoor had begun.

⸱

Josie made a last minute appeal to Rachel. 'Don't desert me now, Ra,' she said. 'I need you.' She broke down and started crying. 'I love you Ra and I need you now at this time more than ever, more than ever Ra.'

Ra was unmoved. Her dark eyes in her pale face were huge, like lumps of coal in the face of a snowman. 'Go fuck Maro,' she said leaning forward to deliver the blow with as much cruelty as she could muster.

Josie gripped herself between the legs and sank to the floor, moaning.

Carpenter turned again to Adrian for guidance; he was lost, was Carpenter, he kept turning the torch on and off but nothing changed. His head waggled. His glasses flashed.

'But we've got t' lift the trapdoor,' he said dully, his voice full of metal and heavy, radioactive things. His hands were growing ponderous with the torch and the crowbar.

Adrian steeled himself to spring. I knew the signs and so did Josie. 'Get her, Adrian,' she hissed, back in her evil, snake woman mode, drawing herself up off the floor.

Adrian sucked air in over his top teeth. 'Get out of the way, Baby,' he said. He made the word, my name, sound pregnant with corruption. He raised one eyebrow and it turned into a magpie's wing.

Rachel was talking urgently to Josie, 'I don't want t' come back here when I die,' her voice trembling as hard as her lower lip, 'I don't want to be recycled through this place because it's all cobwebby and nothing moves. If we don't destroy it, we'll come back here when we're dead, we'll become part of the Stench.' She stared down at the coloured spot which lay at her feet from the glass above and kicked at it softly, as if she could move it. Her foot came to life with muted colour.

'How do you know what happens when you're dead?' Josie demanded, 'You have no idea.'

'Yes I do, I heard at school about the old man who died. He was coming here, wasn't he? And he died but he kept coming, he crawled across the road after he was dead, Adrian knows because Adrian was there. Where do you think he got the whisky and the tobacco? He stole them off the dead body of the old man.'

My fingers found hers and laced with them. We were like stone, immovable, nothing could shift us off this trapdoor. If I had a sister, I would want her to be someone like Rachel. A brave person. Can there be an insignificant prayer? That's a prayer from a small, insignificant person like me, for a prayer went through me, from my feet to the crown of my head, just a tiny shiver, for Rachel, that she might hold onto her understanding and not lose it again, and help us all get away from here. I say it passed through me because I didn't make it up like words, rather it came out of the body involuntarily, like a sigh of love.

Josie lit another cigarette from the dead man's tobacco. 'That's just nonsense,' she said sulkily. 'You think I'm stupid, you should hear yourself. Listen to her, Adrian. Anyway, you wouldn't come here after you died.'

'What do you mean?'

'That old man, he wanted to come, he was coming here when he died, he could smell it. Christ! I'm sick of all this talking!' She swung to Adrian, 'Why're y' waiting?' she hissed, turning herself inside out with frustrated desire. 'Get her off there,' she laughed at Adrian's incompetence, 'just shove her out of the way.' Her laugher was like a shirt of needles.

'Yeah,' said Adrian in his tough voice. He thought that if he talked tough he would feel tough. Neither Rachel nor I moved an inch from on top of that trapdoor.

Carpenter switched on the torch and the beam leapt out like a laser through the gloom. It burned into the surface of the trapdoor as if it would set it alight. Then he turned it around and shone it back into his own face, as if he could see something in the quivering light.

Josie kept smoking. She needed something besides words to do with her mouth. She needed an acrid flame in her lungs, the ignition of fire. I could see the way it burned up her body. 'Get out of the way, Baby,' she said out of the corner of her mouth, as if they were words she could never be accused of later, 'go fuck yourself with your fat finger.'

'We're wasting time,' Adrian said, grabbing hold of me, but there was something wrong with Mr Hero. His mask was slipping; his face was strained and sweat stood out on his forehead. I only had to take one look at him to know that he was shit scared, and he only had to take one look at me to know that I knew he wasn't what he pretended to be.

He dropped my arm and backed off; his knees jarred, his neck was made of rubber; I could hardly believe what I was seeing. Nor could Josie. Adrian was too confused to move either forward or back. He was straining against something, some invisible leash, some web laced into his skin, growing there. He'd just done something he couldn't comprehend and he didn't like it. Fear had got the better of him.

'We'll come back another night,' he mumbled, his head weaving back and forward, like a stubborn ox. He offered the world his shoulders; fate could beat down upon them all it liked, the shoulders hunched over the vulnerable neck.

Josie spat on the floor in disgust.

Carpenter went down on his knees before the trapdoor and began picking at the edge with his crowbar. He didn't believe he could lift it with us on it, it was just that he couldn't stop himself, he had to pick and pick away at the scab.

'You're tit useless,' Josie said, starting to work herself into a foam. 'Can't even push a couple of girls out of the way.'

'I could.' Adrian was gritting his teeth; he always fell for Josie's little traps.

'Then what's stopping you?'

'Get fucked,' was all he could manage. He kicked some perfume bottles across the floor. Some pieces skidded between our feet. Nothing changed.

'You're a worm,' Josie said. 'I'll do it meself. Get out of the way Rachel or I'll hurt you.'

Rachel stood her ground. 'You've already hurt me, Josie.'

No one knew what she was talking about except Josie, maybe, and she didn't stop to ask any questions. She grabbed Rachel's slender arm, lifted it to her face and bit deep into the muscle. Rachel screamed. Like before, her scream was not completely connected to her body; she opened her mouth first and the scream followed a few seconds afterwards. When Josie's face came away from Rachel's arm there was blood on her teeth.

Then Adrian revved up. It started in his arms, which jerked downwards, propelling him into the air, then moved to his legs which came in under him like an engine running hot; that's what he was, a hot rod with the engine stripped down and flames painted on the wings.

A sharp blow landed on my ear. It went from one side of my head to the other like lightning. Blood filled my nose. Then came the thunder, which was his body hurling into mine at a thousand miles an hour. I was about the same size as him, probably heavier, but I didn't pack down the way he did, I was clumsier, looser in the limbs; he was an arrow of muscle and I went over, heels dragging at the trapdoor.

Adrian and Josie screamed at the same time. Carpenter stood back, his crowbar held warlike in front of his face.

Adrian was standing over me, his arm raised, his mouth working although I couldn't hear any words coming out. Whatever the words were, they were pulling his lips out of shape. A rotting smell clawed its way out of his mouth.

'Hit her again,' Josie said to Adrian. Still holding Rachel's arm, she swung around like a rock and roll dancer, and Rachel went down before Adrian's fist landed on the other side of my head.

We'd just lost the battle of the trapdoor.

・

When I opened by eyes, there were Josie and Rachel sitting propped up against the wall, Josie with her arms around Rachel's shoulder and her head close to hers, apparently whispering something into her ear. I didn't know how much time had passed or even where I was exactly except that I was seeing everything sideways, and could feel the cold, greasy lino against my cheek. Every so often Josie's head would pull back, so as to get a better view of Rachel's divine face, then she would fervently kiss her eyelids, which were shuttered by long, dark lashes. 'It'll be alright, darling,' she said. Rachel opened her eyes and her irises were submerged in a bitter sea.

She said, 'You've hurt my arm.' Her half chewed arm lay like a maimed white snake over her lap.

'Your arm will be fine, darling.' Josie was smiling wistfully, stroking Rachel's arm, taking care not to touch the wounded bits. Tears were forming in Josie's eyes. 'I love you, you know that, Ra?' As she kissed Rachel's injured arm, right where her teeth had gone in, and sucked gently at the wound, her eyes filled with a penitent bliss. She was all over Rachel like a rash, hugging her and stroking her. 'I didn't mean to, Ra. It's alright, isn't it.'

'You did it deliberately,' Rachel said.

'Of course I didn't. It was an accident.'

Rachel wanted to get up, take action for herself, but Josie's arm lay casually across her shoulders, holding her down.

I went to move and found the weight of Adrian's heel on my neck. Then I understood. I was supposed to be dead. That was the deal Adrian offered after my treachery at the battle of the trapdoor. My only role, to lie dead at his feet. I looked better dead. It felt better for him for me to be dead, for he could be tender, even compassionate towards the plump and maggoty. He could find a tear gathering in the wasteland behind his eyeballs somewhere; crying might be heroic, in the right context, like over the body of a sister you have just murdered. He could wonder what he was going to tell Dad and Mum; he was learning how to live with a dead sister; the hunch of a shoulder over a grave. A new Adrian in the making.

Or perhaps I imagined all that.

'There's nothing to stop you now,' Josie said to Adrian so sincerely you'd have thought it was the final truth. There was a horrible tone in her voice, as if she was talking about the worst possible thing imaginable. 'Are you goin t' let her get up?'

'But she's dead,' Adrian said and Josie laughed. Adrian kicked me in the arse. 'See how dead she is.' I played dead and counted from ten backwards to zero.

Josie was still laughing when her forehead slammed against Rachel's, 'I thought you were my friend, ' she said, head butting her again, 'Y' pretty soon learn about friends.' Down came the head again, you could hear the smack of skulls.

The light went out of Rachel's eyes.

▫

When the light went out of Rachel's eyes she took me with her, and when I opened my eyes this time I was lying at a completely different angle. Adrian's heel was no longer on my neck.

My new angle of vision showed Carpenter with his steamed up glasses and piggy face, hanging over his precious can of needles, his mouth open, apparently about to vomit. But nothing happened; he just looked like that when he was thinking.

I tried to remember when he'd brought the useless can here to the trapdoor. I had no way of knowing how long I had missed, except to register that the trapdoor was still not open. That much at least.

Josie lay alone nearby, huddled in herself, as still as a rag doll, the flickering candle light making rubbery shapes out of her face. She was watching Adrian and Rachel who were huddled together against the wall, whispering. He looked tormented by what she was saying.

It's too late now, I thought. Too late for last minute deals.

Adrian kissed Rachel. It wasn't a passionate kiss on the mouth, the way the kids do at school down by the trees with their tongues all big and lumpy in their mouths, but a humble, devoted kiss on the cheek, as if he were forever indebted for something, some priceless gift he could never pay back. At the same time it was a very public kiss, probably for Josie's consumption.

'I've still got my secret weapon!' Carpenter pronounced, and lifted up one finger as if everyone was hanging on his every word and he should say no more in present company. A little dribble came from the side of his mouth, which was nothing special. I've seen him look like that when he's doing his arithmetic. He was very pleased with himself and wiped away the dribble with the back of his hand. 'You'll never guess what it is.'

Nobody took him up on it.

He spat some of the Stench into the can where it festered among the needles, picked up his precious crowbar, hefting it uncertainly. There was no one standing on top of the trapdoor to stop him this time. Without even bothering with the pretence of his white mask, he knelt again by the trapdoor. Something like enthusiasm shone on his face. The Stench would be discovered, conquered, its mystery exploded. His father, and others like him, would stand around with serious faces, making plans. There would be bulldozers, bombs even, to root it out and destroy it if need be. Or better still, harness it, use it to improve the lot of suffering mankind.

There wasn't any music, it was a stopped, flickery moment while he worked and thought. Everyone was between frames. The Stench seeped out from around the exposed edges of the trapdoor with fuming intent. These were nothing but tendrils; in colour, they were violet, in sound they were like brass. Wispy candle flames of darkness, in themselves they were nothing to what lay behind, licking against the underside of the trapdoor.

Then Carpenter, suffocating from the Stench and everything else, began to weaken. It wasn't cowardice, like Adrian, it was just that his body couldn't go through with it. The crowbar turned to jelly in his hands. His brain rattled in its petri dish. I had the sudden wild hope that none of them would be able to lift it, that the Stench would overcome them all before any of them could free it. Or that none of them would prove worthy enough for it.

'I need some help,' he said, fumbling into one pocket and sneezing. 'I thought of everything. Everything!' He took a moment to marvel at his own genius. He had a wedge. A few inches wide. Just enough.

'I need help,' he called again.

Josie crawled forward, grasping for the wedge.

'I need something around my face,' she croaked.

'Someone's shirt,' Carpenter rasped, 'Quickly.'

Josie looked at Adrian who was on his feet. He looked thin and blue around the mouth. 'Baby's.' He was gulping air and trying to swallow.

'Yeah.' Josie swung back to the trapdoor, still on her hands and knees. 'Hurry.' She sounded like someone who only had a few moments to live.

Adrian was suddenly leaning over me to make me stop playing dead. He didn't want me dead any more. 'Take it off,' he said, gesturing to my top. I was confused. I didn't know if I had really seen him at the wall with Rachel or not. It was like the scene at the back fence of the school, like something I might have made up.

'I'll hit you again,' He was regaining his courage and that was a bad sign. I decided to stay with dignity and hand him my shirt, and sat up to do it. I had only a bra on underneath, and as soon as the shirt came off, I could feel the Stench prickle across my skin like tiny, slimy fingers, and shivered as if to shake it off.

'Watch her, Adrian. Y' can't trust her.' She was a snake again; she couldn't get onto her feet but she could wriggle, wriggle towards the trapdoor, my shirt around her face like a bandit.

I went to Rachel who was sitting against the wall and knelt by her side. With her good arm she grabbed hold of me and whispered hotly in my ear. 'You have t' escape. Get help. Do y' understand, Baby?'

There was something building up inside me like grief, but it wasn't that; it was darker than grief. I didn't know how much pain she was in, but she was slipping away from herself, losing her grip, forgetting who she was and where she had come from. A darkness was stealing over her, blotting out the peaks and valleys, the smiles and the tears. The words came out of her mouth like a straggle of refugees, 'Help me.'

The teeth of the crowbar bit crudely into the wood along the trapdoor line, seeking leverage. It wasn't as easy as it looked, for the join was crusted with age, cementing the trapdoor to the floor, and the damage Josie had done to it last night with her fingernails could no longer be seen.

'All I have to do is lift one end, and Josie puts the wedge in,' Carpenter repeated to himself over and over, such a simple procedure. But it wasn't working. He couldn't even see the trapdoor any more, there was so much trickling fog over his glasses.

Adrian hung back, looking useless, but not for long. His previous cowardice had made him reckless. He strode forward, snatched the crowbar out of Carpenter's hand, pushed Carpenter aside and brought the instrument down with a whack, chipping the floor. He didn't even succeed in hitting the trapdoor. He made the floor bounce and dust spurt into the air. Josie drew back and Adrian went on, slashing at the floor with wild strokes, heedless of the fact that he had no nose cover. It looked like he was going to go on until he'd smashed the trapdoor to pieces, although he didn't seem to be doing that much damage.

Carpenter scuttled away. It was just a sideways movement out of the corner of my eye, as quick as a rat moves, and he was gone.

'Get out of my fuckin way,' Adrian said, which sounded brave, except there was no one in his fucking way.

Suddenly his crowbar rattled down on top of the unmoving trapdoor and he staggered backwards, tearing at his nose.

It's like a big clumsy beast, I thought, ripping its own creatures to pieces before they can do its will.

Rachel tried to scream but not much sound came out. I thought she was reacting to Josie, who was making a spidery approach across the floor towards her, but then I saw that a creature had entered the room and was looking about with uncertainty, as if it could not see clearly. It had a short, pig like snout and two huge oval eyes that shone with a glassy light. When it moved its head, its rubbery jowls moved loosely.

Its bobbing snout moved in our direction, it said something in a muffled booming voice and walked towards the trapdoor with hesitant steps, its breath sounding thickly, like an asthmatic. 'Open the trapdoor,' it said.

'What the fuck?' Adrian reached for the crowbar.

Then a hand pulled at the head, which came off to reveal a second head. Carpenter's.

'It's called a gas mask,' Carpenter said with great importance. 'You breathe through this here,' tapping the snout, 'all the air y' breathe gets filtered. It's from some old war or other when they used poisoned bombs. The soldiers used to wear them in the trenches. They had to wear them in the trenches otherwise they'd get gassed.' He loved to say that word, 'trenches', but I don't think he knew what it meant. I did because I had looked at the pictures in the school library and found they were big long ditches which filled up with water when it rained, and men died in them the way men die, with their heads at funny angles to their bodies.

'Maybe we've discovered some new kind of super fungus.' He got a bulging, frog-like look on his face, his neck blew in and out; he didn't look like he needed a gas mask any more. He looked very pleased with himself. He now had his crowbar, the torch and his pig snout. He waved them around the air, doing a little dance of authority. 'We'll soon have this thing nailed down,' he crowed.

'We don't all have gas masks,' Josie said in a snarky voice. 'What about us? Does it really shut it out?'

Carpenter put it over his head and looked like a creature from outer space. Insect eyes turned towards us. Time had rotted and mildewed several patches in the concertina snout, the buckle didn't fit tight at the back of his head.

'I've only got one mask,' the mask said.

He flicked on the torch. An empty piece of window glowed with dust and cobwebs; its illuminated space was proof of everything to Carpenter.

'Turn it off,' Adrian said.

'That thing won't help.' Rachel was still on the floor. She pointed with her one good arm at the mask.

'Why not?' the mask said.

'Because you'll be dead.' Her face shone, as if it were polished with wax. 'We're all dying now. It's only a matter of time. It's killing us.'

Maybe we'll die before we can get it opened, I thought, and the thought came like a hope.

Josie shook her head so that her blonde rats' tails slapped together. 'Give me that party hat,' she said in a flat voice. 'If anyone has it I should, after all I was the one who found the trapdoor.'

The snout waggled backwards and forwards. 'No way,' it boomed. 'This belongs to my father.' Having that stuffy thing on his head seemed to give Carpenter strength.

'I'll take it,' Adrian said, 'and settle all this once and for all.' He made a grab for the mask.

'It's my mask, get your hands off it.' His voice sounded thick and distant. He headed back towards the kitchen brandishing his crowbar and torch. 'I've had enough of you crazy bastards,' he yelled.

Adrian grabbed him and spun him around. 'Take y' mask off so I can smash your face in.'

'You can't stop me,' The snout said.

It wasn't much of a struggle. Adrian was bigger and meaner than

Carpenter will ever be, and proved it with a swift hard punch into Carpenter's stomach. Carpenter went down like a sandbag falling into a swollen river. 'I don't want to have to rip your balls out,' Adrian said in a horrible kind of lifeless voice I'd never heard before. It was all over, he was bending down to get the mask when Josie hit him. She came in, scratching for his eyeballs. Adrian was scared because he could see that she was going to rip his eyes out of his head, and he began to fight desperate and dirty. He couldn't understand why Josie had attacked him so viciously, although I had a few ideas. I stood clear, hoping that once more they would fail, and that this time they would destroy themselves utterly. Rachel hung back too, still unable to rise. Once though, when Josie's foot came near, she snarled at it like a vicious dog.

'Go!' Rachel shouted to me, just before her teeth connected with Josie's flesh.

But I was locked inside of chaos. Chaos ruled. The Stench was thick on the air, hot on everyone's breath. Everybody was yelling and barking and screeching like a bunch of animals being tortured, and the empty wards echoed to the sound. It wasn't like the battle of the trapdoor, swift and sharp; everyone but me got kicked and gouged and scratched and bruised. Blood spattered onto faces. Hands clawed for the nearest flesh. No one knew, or seemed to care, what they were fighting for, but eventually the mask surfaced and Josie was holding it like a mace, threatening to smash anyone who came her way.

Everybody was puffing and aching and hating, wheezing the Stench in and out of their lungs full speed. I didn't know Josie, her eyes were like bits of stone that'd had something obscene scratched on them and her hair was glued to her face and shoulders in thick clumps. She was standing on top of the trapdoor, mask in hand, blood coming out of her nose. She wiped the back of her hand across it and stared at the blood, stupefied. She took out a broken cigarette from her pocket and lit it up with shaky fingers, pulling the smoke in hard and blowing it up towards the circle of coloured glass in the upper window, where it billowed towards the hanging cobwebs.

Carpenter was crying because he thought his precious mask had been broken. I'd never seen him cry before and he cried like a baby does, lying on the floor holding himself between the legs, groaning in between times as if he were pulling the groan up from beneath the floor.

The incense burned on, filling the air with hanging layers of sooty clouds. Then I saw, or thought I saw, a line of golden flame blink along the edges of the trapdoor. It only lasted a moment, a flicker of time, but the lick of it, like a tiny St Elmo's fire, set the dust and crud of the floor crackling like sparklers. Josie was suddenly surrounded by the impression of flames.

'Dad'll beat me if I bust his gas mask,' Carpenter said in a fractured voice. 'It belonged to his grandfather or somebody.'

'It won't matter,' said Adrian, smacking the crowbar into the palm of his hand, watching Josie trying to put on the mask and smoke at the same time.

Adrian approached her. 'We'll share the mask.' He had the same rubbery smile the snout had. I wanted to laugh. I could just see them taking turns.

The cigarette rolled away and smoked up large all on its own.

'Me first,' the snout said.

'We'll never lift it if we keep fighting,' Carpenter said. Adrian and the mask stared at each other but said nothing.

'We've got to do it with the proper scientific spirit.'

'That's right.' Adrian and the mask said at the same time.

Then Josie took the mask off and threw it at the bemused Carpenter. 'I don't want the silly old mask anyway,' she said carelessly. 'It's too stuffy.'

The battle of the mask was over.

⬚

This time the lifting of the trapdoor was to be done with true scientific precision, and there'd be no cock ups or failures of nerve. Carpenter had it all worked out. It would have to be a team effort. Adrian was to take the crowbar and prise up one end while Josie was to be ready with the wedge for when the crowbar had done its work. Once it was open they would move to each end and lift it, while Carpenter himself would come forth brandishing his torch and wearing his mask to crack the final mystery.

He would shine the torch down the hole and everybody would see what there was to be seen.

Adrian agreed to all this, I guess because he hadn't thought it through himself, and possession of the crowbar and the lead role in getting the trapdoor up was enough to maintain him as chief hero of his story. Besides, the chief hero seemed to have other things on his mind. He kept looking at Rachel, puzzled, like someone trying to remember something maddeningly close to recall, something of the hugest importance.

Rachel and I were to stand back, or sit back, and watch. Carpenter said that we would be 'independent observers'. It meant we didn't have to do anything unless there was an emergency, and we had to report back to him afterwards and tell him what we'd seen. Witnesses, he said, we were witnesses, and what witnesses did was witness things, and give a true report of what took place. He kept looking at me all the time when he said it, doubting, I would say, my ability to give a true report on anything.

Carpenter took his time, too, getting himself and his mask together, testing the snout and the straps and everything to make sure nothing had been busted in the battle, issuing instructions the whole time. Adrian had to get the crowbar into one of the chips he made before; he could wear the white, surgical mask soaked in perfume. Josie was to remember to get the wedge in the right way round. If it fell into the hole, he might never get it back and his Dad would get suspicious.

He had a lot of wounded pride to show off to everybody, especially to Adrian. He was very prickly towards Adrian.

'Don't lose the crowbar down the hole,' he said pointedly.

'Go piss your pants.' was Adrian's bold reply. He seemed to have shaken off whatever was bothering him and was back in the race. I waited for the titter of approval from Josie but I was mistaken; Josie was staring at him with such pitilessness it should have burned two black holes in his skull. She hadn't forgotten the fight either, or Adrian's cowardice, or his sudden, clumsy siding with Rachel.

As for Rachel, she made one last hopeless attempt to stop them by crawling across the floor in looped movements, like a caterpillar, making a huge effort to do it, as if she were traversing miles of lino, before slumping onto the trapdoor.

Carpenter was ready to go. He didn't want any more sideshows. He said something in his mask and gestured to Rachel.

It took both Adrian and Josie, true soul mates, to move Rachel off the trapdoor, which she clung to with a maniacal strength. Her body seemed to weigh ten times its normal weight. In the end they rolled her, Adrian ripping her fingers free. She took her defeat in silence and sat up. I could see she'd passed some threshold, her eyes were so calm; she looked as if she were a million years old.

Now there was nothing to stop them, the three of them, from seeing it through. Adrian, who'd rejected the surgical mask for a perfume-soaked scarf he wrapped around his face, making him look like some Arab terrorist, knelt, crowbar to the ready. Josie was right by him, with the wedge pointing in the right direction, my shirt wrapped around her face. The snout lurked behind, torch in hand.

They couldn't do it. The trapdoor wouldn't budge. It wasn't Adrian's fault. It was Carpenter who worked it out. It needed some sort of even pressure all round. He produced more wedges as if he could command them into existence. His breath was coming so hard through his snout, it sounded like the honks of geese.

Then came the hard part. He had to get Rachel and me to cooperate. We could no longer be impartial observers, we had to join the experiment.

They dragged Rachel over from the wall and made her hold the wedge where it needed to go. Rachel did it on remote control, as if she were being guided by someone on the moon. I recognised that side of her now. A side she could flick into as quickly as you can flick into an inane giggle. I dreaded to hear it; I knew this part of her could be worse than anything the others could come up with, and I didn't know why. She took the wedge and rubbed it down her cheek as if it were a piece of silk.

The four of them tried it and still it didn't work. I knew by that stage that it wouldn't. All four swung their heads my way. It was my moment and they all hated me for that. At the last minute everything depended on me, the dark horse, the unknown quantity, the despised, the ignored, abhorred, and now they all turned to me, their eyes bleeding out of their faces wanting something from me.

I laughed, because it is one of the easiest sounds the human body can make; the diaphragm prepares for it, the lungs make it happen. The funniest thing of all was how easily it could be done. One moment I was standing there laughing, the next I was kneeling over the trapdoor. I didn't need a wedge, crowbar, mask or anything. I didn't need to do anything. The fever was in my fingertips.

I only had to bend over and touch it. It was laughably simple, the caked dust of years was merely a sham.

It came up to meet me as I bent my hands over it, lifting up out of the floor at the touch of my fingers. It rose into the air kicked from below, and fell sideways, clattering onto the floor.

The gaping square darkness in the floor was revealed.

Baby

No one said anything. For a moment it seemed there was nothing, and this whole business had been some hot imagining. Something we'd made up out of boredom and nor-west fever. A bunch of kids with nothing better to do than scare the hell out of themselves.

After all, we all knew there'd be nothing there. No slimy monster to crawl out of the pit, at least none that the eye could see. No flesh trickling dead, at least not apparently. Things like that didn't happen in Hikitarua. Nothing ever happened in Hikitarua.

All that happened was that everything went quiet, very quiet. Even the hospital ceased to creak and move and change its shape around us. The trapdoor, a few pieces of tongue-in-groove nailed together by a couple of cross pieces, lay skewered sideways over the pit, utterly still.

It felt as if Hikitarua itself had stopped moving.

We were frozen where we stood, in that vacuity. None of us could see down the hole because of the trapdoor still obscuring it, and the mass of shadows beneath. There is nothing underneath, I told myself. Just the space between the floorboards and the ground. Framed by joists and bearers, there will be nothing but bare, hard earth beneath. All the rest was hysteria.

Then Josie giggled. A nervous rattle in her throat. Nobody knew what to do.

Carpenter, all brave and scientific, steadied the trembling torch, his breath wheezing through his tattered snout. He managed to probe the torchlight for a moment or two down into the black guts underneath the floor. I saw the light get eaten up; all the light in the room was sucked up and showed nothing in return. The beam got buried in the blackness. There was no form beneath but a quickening darkness.

That was about as far as he got in his grand plan before it hit them. Before it hit all of us. Rachel and I saw the other three get it before it reached us and slid its fingers up our nostrils and through the pores of our skin.

Forget the fancy perfumes and billowing incense, the smell just clawed them aside like they weren't there. Something that was in there was getting out, invading us. Eating us. I saw it. It had a body, and, being a smell like the Africa that swallows children in greedy flies, it had no mercy. It didn't spare you because you were a nice person or anything. It was like skeleton hands remembering how to be fingers, but badly, having to crush and maim in order to learn how to hold. Something that knew you were there but couldn't see you, had no hands but could feel you. While you could not comprehend it, it comprehended you all right. Knew you by your warmth and your terrified breathing. You could feel it all over your body like a wet mouth sucking. It was something that could talk, but only in the voice of dead spiders and musty spider webs growing over rotting bones. A voice to call in the dead. It didn't have a mouth but an empty space behind its jaw where its hunger was. It went through your nose up into your head where it flowered against the inside of your skull. Then hit you in the guts to make you vomit.

A living odour. A rushing, putrefying, presence. A smell that could wrap itself around a human life and snuff it out the way wind could douse a candle flame.

Adrian and Josie were the first to go down because they were the closest to the edge; they keeled over backwards together like a pair of collapsed puppets. Carpenter, perhaps because of his great mask, lasted a moment or two longer, then reeled back, the torchlight spinning across the ceiling, waving his arms in front of his snout like he was warding off a pack of butterflies, tripped backwards and came down on his arse. Rachel, standing right beside me, her eyes huge, making no attempt to cover her nose, was the next to go. She opened her mouth and a tube of grey porridgy stuff came out. Her face was giving birth to something monstrous.

I turned to run but it was too late, far too late.

Abruptly, the Stench as I had known it shut off, vanished. There was no Stench. Then there was something as sweet as the morning dew on Mrs Inna's roses; it cleared out all my nasal passages as if by magic, like those decongestants they advertise on TV. There was no longer the Stench, nor even the senseless, gritty undertone of the incense.

It was as if I had died.

I saw everything with immense clarity, and I was clean.

All the passages of my body were clean.

I could breathe even in the heart of the Stench, fill my lungs with the sweetest of ambrosia, the most lush rose. I was filled with the odour of sanctity, the sweetness of grace.

I didn't understand what was happening to me, slow to see that the Stench had the opposite effect on me, or that perhaps I was immune, and the rinse of morning dew through my body was my defence system kicking in.

It didn't matter, what mattered was that some kind of miracle had taken place. I was there because I was spared. In this clarity I could see the others and the walls and the distant door into the kitchen all lit up by searchlights behind my eyes, see through the open doors to the empty wards, their wire beds gleaming with wire bones, see the pane of coloured glass floating on the grey wall with burning luminosity.

Carpenter got back onto his feet. His absurdity was reassuring. Perhaps it was the mask that gave him the courage or the madness. Whatever, he lumbered to his feet, stood swaying, his great insect eyes fragmenting, then sat down heavily on the edge, kicked the trapdoor aside, and lowered his legs into the opening in the true analytical spirit. Here was a pioneer! His head raised for one last snoutful of life, Carpenter's moment had come, and he pushed himself off the edge of the floor like a deep sea diver heading for the bottom of the ocean.

Then the unbelievable happened. The world reversed. Instead of falling through the shadow into the black hole beneath, Carpenter rose, like a football that had been kicked good and hard in the guts, in slow motion, his cloth and wire pig-face twisting grotesquely in mid air. The careering torch clattered down into the hole and was gone.

He came down, limbs flailing, right on top of the discarded trapdoor and lay still, his body twitching in a thousand places.

I approached the pit, no longer afraid; like the saints in the story old Conk & Whiskers read out, I could walk through the flames and not get burned. I walked through the murk to the edge of the opening and looked down. There was no torch, no stairway, nothing. Just a steady sheet of blackness that seemed to ripple to the touch of the coloured light from above.

I knelt down by the edge and stared at the dark, shimmering surface. Tiny points of light came and went like distant stars. I put my hand down to just above the surface. Nothing. No chill. No vibration at all.

I touched the surface. Still nothing.

I dipped a finger beneath and it came back whole.

I dipped a hand beneath and felt around in the nothingness. The hand came back unchanged.

I looked up and they were all watching me, even Carpenter. Adrian and Josie were side by side like twins, their mouths open expectantly - they were waiting for me to do something.

Rachel was behind them, still standing. Her face was like a dancer's mask with holes cut out for her eyes to stare through.

Watch me then! I bent lower and lower until my face was within a finger's breadth from the shimmery surface. I felt I was looking into the essence of depth, depth with no end. A vast expanse of emptiness.

I looked up at the others. Oh they were watching alright. I gave them a Baby smile and pushed my head through.

◘

At first I thought there was nothing but blackness but that was because I had my eyes shut.

When I opened them I was looking down on a world. It was as if the trapdoor opened in the sky of this world, and there was my little face peeking through.

It was a great red, dusty, murky planet, the home of the Stench, so powerful now that even its disguise as the smell of roses could hardly hold, and behind the ambrosia I could smell the true Stench.

I had to laugh at my big miracle of before. It hadn't been a miracle at all, just the Stench trying to camouflage itself in sweet memories.

As I watched, I seemed to zoom closer, as if their sky was contracting. The landscape came into focus, a red desert lying under a dying sun, bloated with red and yellow dust.

Directly beneath me, there was a castle. Something about it reminded me of the City of Gates, but this castle had no gates, not even a drawbridge or a window. It had carried that passion for isolation one step further, the last step, into complete inner darkness.

Then I was inside the castle, which was big enough to have its own landscape, its own hills of iron, a stone sky. Its own rusty light.

At the centre of the castle there was an enormous bed; an iron, hospital-style bed piled up with festering sheets and pillows, upon which lay the hideous figure of a semi-decomposed woman. She sat up on the bed as if it were a throne and I knew that she was a Queen. The Queen of the sickbed, the Queen of all who died of sickness and old age.

Slowly her head turned upwards, turned back until it lay at right angles to her spine and she looked up at me. One side of her face living, one side rotting, perpetually rotting away. The living half was as fresh as spring, skin like the blush of a newly opened rose, the lips full and moist. The eye was alive with light, the hair dark and glossy like Rachel's, full of interior colours. The rotting side was of putrid flesh dropping from the bones. Dry, ragged hair. Everything was caving in. Everything ravaged. Only the eyeball remained, connected to the skull by tiny filaments of red.

She was not alone. Behind her, kneeling, there were rows of her sad followers, souls of the old, sick or mad who suffered ceaseless pain and hunger in their cheerless drear homes. Beside her were silent attendants, kneeling at the bed, their heads bowed in supplication.

As soon as she saw me her face began to grow larger. I was contracting into her face. I knew then that the Stench was coming from her body, the rotting half, and its beautiful counterpart, the smell of paradise, came from the living half.

Her eyeballs sprang towards mine.

I jerked my head back and I was once more among the tall shadows of the hospital.

They were all watching expectantly.

'You wants She.' I said, getting it completely wrong.

I knew why the Queen of Sickness and Death was here in Hikitarua. The town was ready to die, die from heat and dehydration - the exhaustion of hope. Opening the trapdoor was like pulling the plug in a bath; all that pressure had already built up - everything living would be sucked down through the trapdoor opening by the Stench. The Stench would pull them in. The Queen would reap a new harvest of acolytes.

A town would vanish off the map. The big tankers would no longer stop here. The lights would wink out in the Milky Way. Highway 5 would fall silent. Death would creep over everything and the Stench would reign supreme everywhere.

It's out now, I thought. Loose in the world, and we've done it, we've let it out. The Queen of Sickness already had one hand in our world. Maybe more and more of it will go, more and more of the world slipping into her realm.

When I looked up from thinking, Adrian wasn't there. Carpenter still lay where he'd been thrown, his head turned in my direction. He was trying to sit up and not succeeding. He was struggling to say something too, but was having difficulty with his mouth.

Josie was watching, never taking her eyes off me, but at the same time her hand strayed to one side, seeking the crowbar, finding it and clamping over it like a vice. She couldn't get to her feet, but began to advance on me, her legs dragging on the floor. I thought she was going to attack but at a certain point she stopped, dead still, as if the crowbar had turned her to iron.

She was guarding me.

Behind her Adrian came down the stairs, pushing Rabbitt along in front of him. He had untied her feet and taken the gag out of her mouth but her arms remained bound to her side.

She stumbled on the lower step and Adrian plodded on, unheeding, pushing her across the floor. I wanted to laugh because he looked the way he had on that first night, when we had played at being zombies.

I made a gesture to move and Josie did the same. I stopped and Josie stopped. Rachel moaned. It sounded like a song she was trying to sing. She stepped forward to try to say something to him but was silenced by his unseeing gaze. He looked right through her, his eyes themselves dead. His eyes were like the open trapdoor; they opened onto blackness - that same shimmery surface.

Adrian prodded Rabbitt towards the trapdoor. When she shrank away, he prodded her harder.

'What'h down there?'

Her voice broke into a scream and she made a run for it. With her arms tied, she ran like an awkward chicken, bandy legs flying. Adrian caught her with ease and dragged her back.

It occurred to me then that perhaps not everybody would see the same thing if they looked down through the trapdoor as I had. After all, something had kicked Carpenter back into this world - why hadn't he just floated through the sky to the Queen of Sickness's castle?

When he got to the edge of the opening Adrian stopped, picked Rabbitt up and held her above his shoulders, like the weightlifters you see on TV. Then she was away, hurled with all his force down into the darkness of the pit. There was a brief glitter, like the sparkle of sunlight on swiftly moving water and she was gone.

Josie let out a great sigh.

Adrian stood with his arms upraised as if he were still holding something. Atlas holding up the world.

I pushed Josie aside and went to the trapdoor to have a look. I lay down this time, on the floor, and just took a quick look beneath the surface; it had to be quick because I didn't trust what was happening around me.

I saw nothing I recognised from before. Everything was furious swirling colour. Then I saw Rabbitt, still wriggling while the colours ate into her. They were colours that fed. They ate away her flesh, leaving her a pulsing mass of raw muscle and organs. They were Stench creatures. I'd felt them once, on my skin, but here, in their element, they had become so dense they could be seen. The colours were their auras - garish, jangling.

Then, just before I pulled my head back, the rope fell from her arms and she walked towards me, her mouth opening and shutting. Instead of words, stinking yellow pus was pouring out of her mouth.

Then I felt hands grip my ankles. A knee went into my back.

I was unable to move, unable to pull my head back out of the pit.

I watched Death walk towards me in the flayed body of my little neighbour. She was joined by others. She was joined by others, more Stench creatures whose form changed as I tried to look at them, for they were half body half odour.

A hand arrived at the back of my neck and pushed my head in deeper.

Within a few seconds I would die. Rabbitt, the Rabbitt creature, was very close. I could see her ribs, now rotting away to reveal the still beating heart;

but it was not blood that flowed in the arteries and veins, rather vapour, dense and sluggish - the watery form of the Stench.

Just as this creature reached out to touch me, the pressure on my body suddenly lightened. I struggled, strained to break free and the pressure returned.

A bloodied finger touched my face.

I gave an enormous heave and at the same time the pressure went off.

I was back in the hospital in the middle of a screaming melee. Josie and Adrian were bending over me, scrabbling at me, trying to tip me into the pit.

Rachel was on the floor, gripping Adrian's leg. Her lips and chin ran with blood, Adrian's blood. She had taken one chunk out of his shanks and was taking another. Clamping on like a bulldog and tearing back with all the strength in her spine.

Adrian was beating on her back, using his arm like a club.

I wrenched free of Josie and pulled away. Just above my left eyebrow, where I'd been touched, burned with a pale fire, as if some chill coin had been sewn into my skin.

I had to get out of there. I had to get out of the hospital.

Meanwhile Josie and Adrian seemed to have forgotten me. Josie, her face haggard, the shadows spooling under her eyes, took hold of Adrian's sleeve like a beggar woman beseeching alms. She pointed at Rachel and her mouth moved. I don't know if any sound came out, or if it couldn't reach me through the Stench, but Adrian reacted. He stopped beating on Rachel's back, ripped his leg free with a howl of pain, and began to push her towards the pit. When she struggled, he hit her a couple of times and she fainted.

He kicked her and she didn't stir.

Moving as if his bones were welded to wires, Adrian took her underneath the arms, tenderly, about to kiss her perhaps, then swung her towards the pit.

Her ankles had already hit the edge of the opening when I came at him charging like a bull. I am the BIG little moron remember, I can't fight very well but I'm a force to be reckoned with when I'm moving at speed.

Adrian wasn't expecting it, and I took him at the shoulder and sent him staggering over backwards, hands clutching the air as if he were falling over a cliff. He almost went into the pit, but at the last moment sprang, like a cat, and landed on his feet.

Josie came at me with the crowbar. She had it raised in her thin arms with all the steel of her hatred in them. At the last minute she stopped as if she'd hit something. She was staring at my face, above my left eyebrow. The crowbar fell to the floor with a clatter.

Rachel rolled over, pulled her feet from the abyss and crawled away. Carpenter moaned. He was still feebly trying to get up, pulling at his mask with hands too weak to move it.

Josie looked frightened again, and, looking frightened, looked more human. This was a Josie I knew, the Josie I had always known. The bold tomboy, only a terrified tomboy this time.

'Don't go near her, Adrian,' she said warningly.

Adrian looked at me, saw what Josie saw, and the heat went out of him too. The big time murderer, the big evil hero of the piece, went into a state of shock. 'Fucking hell...' he said. He turned to Josie.

'We have to kill her now,' Josie said bleakly.

I grabbed one of the candles and ran for the toilet where the dirty mirror still hung. I rubbed it furiously with my fist to get off the dirt and gunk, and held the candle up.

Where the Stench creature had touched me there was a hole about the size of my small fingernail. It was a hole, not a wound. Not a healthy slash of pink flesh and oozing blood. Not the livid skin of a burn.

The hole was like a tiny piece of the dead, rotting half of the Queen of Sickness's face. Inside it the thick bone of the skull looked old and dry. Shreds of decaying meat hung from the top. Even as I watched one piece fell away and rolled out of the hole down my face.

I shuddered and brushed it away.

Deeper inside the hole there was movement, a twisting, wriggling movement. It was not light enough for me to see what it was that was happening deep in that hole, but enough for me to know one thing.

The hole was getting bigger.

They were waiting for me outside the toilet door. Adrian had the crowbar. Carpenter was on his knees and had joined them, the mask dangling in one hand like an animal trophy. His face was like an overcooked steam pudding, and his glasses had a crack across one of the eye-pieces.

He stared at the hole in my forehead. It was the first time he'd seen it.

'It will infect us,' he said wildly. 'It will get inside our bodies.' He scratched at his body as if he'd been stung all over. 'It's already doing it. We need an inoculation against it, like with the measles.' I could see his mind scrabbling for safety amid the clean, pressed, white blouses and the cheerful smiles of the nurses at school, and not quite making it. His thoughts were like screams.

I expected Adrian and Josie to attack but they didn't. They just stared at me.

'We have t' have an inoculation.' Carpenter said desperately. 'They'd have them at hospitals, that's where they keep them.' He spat onto his fingers to clean them, then walked on his knees to the bucket of old needles. He picked up one of the hypodermics that had a little clear liquid at one end and turned towards us, the candle light on his glasses making his frog eyes jump up and down. 'This is probably what they used these for,' he said.

'What are we goin t' do?' Josie asked Adrian. It was great to see the way she was putting it on him now.

She hadn't noticed yet that Adrian was too scared to attack me. Even with the crowbar, disposing of me wasn't as easy as throwing a bound child into the pit.

'We've got to be protected,' Carpenter said, as if that logic alone carried the day. He put the needle into one of the bottles Adrian had brought and drew a little water into the barrel. Then he jiggled it around to mix the water with the liquid. He inspected it the way the nurses had done at the school.

'I bet you won't,' Adrian said over his shoulder, not taking his eyes off me, 'I bet you won't really do it.'

'How much will you bet?' Carpenter sounded like a three year old. His eyes were crazy and staring like those of a small baby or very old person.

'You'll chicken out at the last minute,' Adrian said.

'You're not going to just let her get away are you?' Josie said.

Adrian walked away from her and me. He just turned his back and walked away. He went over to Carpenter. 'You are a chicken,' he said.

'That's what youuuu think.' Carpenter was three years old. He didn't know what he was doing. He took the needle and held out his other arm. The needle was shaking as it approached the skin.

'You've got to find a vein,' Adrian jeered. 'What kind of doctor do you think you're going to be if you don't know about finding veins?'

'I do know,' Carpenter said. 'So shut up!'

The needle wobbled, then connected with the skin. Carpenter's face was bloated with concentration, his glasses steamed up with heat and sweat.

'You know when you've found a vein,' Adrian said, 'because a little bit of blood squirts into the barrel.'

With grim determination, Carpenter pushed the needle deeper into his arm, then, screwing up his face and closing his eyes, pushed the plunger home. He screamed and stood up, the needle still hanging from his arm. He brushed at it frantically with his other hand as if it were a clinging cockroach until it came out and clattered on the floor. There was blood trickling down his arm and splashing onto the floor.

Then Carpenter went into a huge tantrum. He screamed and threshed on the floor.

I had a new power over Josie. She was afraid of me. I used it to push past her. She had no more substance than a scarecrow in a windy field.

I picked up my blouse from where Josie had let it drop, ripped off one sleeve and wrapped it around my head, covering the hole. Then I got hold of Rachel and pulled her to her feet. She felt light, as if her body had already left her. Her head lolled on my shoulders, sending a spray of black curls across my chest. I hugged her tight.

'You're letting her get away.' Josie said to Adrian. 'You're letting her walk out of here.' Her face was stripped down to her eyes and cheekbones.

Adrian threw her the crowbar. 'Here. You kill her.'

Josie screamed and dropped the crowbar as if it had become red hot.

Carpenter's frenzy had finally got him to his feet. The three of us, he and Rachel and me, staggered for the kitchen, the storeroom, and the distant window that glowed with the promise of outside.

◘

Outside the clouds were tearing rags at the moon. Warm, gritty air brushed our faces. It seemed like a miracle that Hikitarua was still here around us, looking the same as always. But not quite sounding the same as always; instead of that familiar flat quiet, there was an uneasy, restless under-throb of sound, cars, distant voices, doors slamming.

'I've left everything in there,' said Carpenter, broken, 'mask, crowbar, torch, God, the torch!' He clutched at his face.

The open air revived Rachel. She drew in great gulps of it, dry and grit notwithstanding.

She took me in her arms and held me with infinite tenderness. 'I won't desert you Baby, I'll be there at the end.' She stroked my ugly face as if it were a flowering rose, but she didn't touch my makeshift bandage. 'You're very beautiful,' she whispered, because she hardly had any voice left by now. 'You never knew that. Now you know. Don't forget what I said.' Her lips touched mine like a blessing.

Then, drawing my ear close to her lips she spoke a few words, whispered them into my ear as if the great hostile universe might be listening. It was such a secret thing she said I could never repeat them, but I knew that she was right and what I had to do.

The words were like a curse I couldn't escape.

She left like a long, sweet, exhalation. 'I can find my own way home.' Her voice sounded distant as she faded towards the road.

'Me too,' Carpenter said in haste, not wanting to be left alone with me.

I took hold of his arm. 'Tomorrow.' I said, choosing my words through a minefield of words, 'You help me. Must help me. Help.'

He got the idea. He nodded like a wounded dog. I doubted he'd hold up until tomorrow.

'An experiment,' I said. 'Scientific experiment.'

He nodded, a gleam coming back into his eye.

It was all I needed.

I turned to the wall although I knew there would be searchers. I wasn't worried by them. They didn't have any idea what they were dealing with and I did.

And that gave me the only advantage I was ever going to have.

▫

I needed something only the mountains could give me, and I moved across the river bank like a moonwalker, heading for the nearest trickle of icy water. I wanted the taste of mountain snow in my mouth; that taste which prickled like gorse and stung like thyme.

Cloudless, the sky made a huge arch from mountains to ocean, the stars a great scattering. I walked beneath them with awkwardness, negotiating every stone like a child who has just learned to walk. I couldn't look up at the stars and keep my feet.

When I found the water, a swift unobtrusive stream, I leaned close to the black velvet surface and took a deep breath through my nose, hoping to catch the mineral smell and the dark yellow smell of broom. It was there because I knew how to find it.

The hole in my forehead felt like a cold, silvery burn. As if a piece of moonlight had become stuck to the bone. I unwrapped the blouse sleeve and bent down to the water. Several tiny pieces of decaying flesh fell out of my head into the water and wriggled into the depths like tiny fish. I remembered a piece of paper crawling across my desk with the same caterpillar motions.

I splashed my face and head until my sight filled up with cold tears. The water had the tang of moss and melted snow, the crystalline feel of glaciers, those flowers of ice that come up between mountain folds. Then I put my head beneath the water until it touched the cold stones beneath.

It felt as though the icy stream was hollowing out my head.

I was half in fever, I realised. The mountain stream was drawing my heat, but not enough. I wanted to throw myself like a hot moon into flowers of ice. I wanted to forget everything that had happened at the hospital, forget the chill circle boring into my head, but I could not; the stench was still there, like something old and rotten you burp back hours afterwards. It was out in the world, too, seeping out of the stones. It had entered the landscape of smells and had taken up permanent residence there. An aftertaste. A taint.

Everything I touched stank.

When I got back onto the wall, I hardly knew north from south except for an old cunning. Hikitarua stretched off into the distance forever, straggled along Highway 5 as stars were straggled across the sky.

I took the first street I found to the main road in time to see a big-rig pulling out, taking a little bit of Hikitarua with it, festooned with lights on its trailers. It drifted out of town with snorts of diesel.

Then I heard Gills McPickle singing his song, just across in the next street. My head ran all over the place. I knew it couldn't be. It was a sad, deathly song approaching on deathly feet. I could even hear the break in his voice where he had to clear his throat.

> Sometimes I live in the country
> some times I live in the town
> sometimes I'm gonna get lucky
> and jump in the river and drown.

And why would it be lucky, I wondered, to be drowned? Then I understood the message this herald was bringing to Hikitarua, most of the inhabitants of which wouldn't understand even if it was spelled out in plain English and not sung by a drunken ghost in the dead of night.

It was the very thing that Rachel had spoken of, hot and intense in my ear.

I laughed as if I had drunk with such a ghost; I had never known the sky to be so lucid, the outcome so clear. I wanted to shout it into the fading roar of the rig, pulling away upwind, but my voice was lost in the hugeness of everything else.

A greater dynamic was at work or all was madness. Adrian hadn't seen that. He thought he had it all under control. He thought he was directing it all; a movie director, ordering everything around to suit his purposes. Setting up Josie in the hospital. Reducing Rachel to a pulp. Lording it over Carpenter. Mincing and miming. Killing people.

Only at the end, when he saw the hole in my head, did he start to understand.

Illusion dies very hard.

There was a helicopter coming from upstream, riveting the distant sky. They had infra-reds and could see heat spots at night. I would stand out like a red chestnut on the their screens.

I made a run for home under fitful street lamps. With this hunt on, there was an effective curfew. They might be looking for Josie, but if they thought she was already dead they might be looking for someone else; who knows, I might be their roving killer. It wasn't far to run. Nothing was very far from anywhere in Hikitarua.

◉

I felt like Rip Van Wrinkle returning after a hundred years of absence to my old home. It looked the same, sat the same way under the same street lamp, presented the same face to the world but all the paint had peeled, and all the front yards had grown strange with extra distances; trees that had taken over new areas of the sky.

I sneaked in the back way. There was an empty, cold feeling about the place as if it had been abruptly abandoned. I paused at the door, listening. I seemed to have new ears for comprehending shades of silence.

The kitchen was chill and empty, with no warm-blooded, left-over smells of cooked food. Despite the restless, gusty nor-west there was a tomb-like silence to the house. There were ants all over the bench; a great spidery mash of them feasting on something spilled. There were black lines running back into the woodwork. I didn't care about them enough to kill them. I had eyes only for Dad sprawled out in a kitchen chair, his head back, his mouth open enough to catch a few flies, his breath see-sawing in his throat. His Adam's apple stuck out like a piece of bone. When he's asleep, Dad doesn't look like Dad, rather like someone else, older; a stranger.

There was a half empty can of beer on the table in front of him and a plate of dead leftovers, fried sausages and half cooked chips.

I loitered at the door to Mum's room, in an agony of indecision. Surely I could creep in quietly enough not to wake her up if she were asleep. Of course I could, I just needed to see her, to look at her face and reassure myself. A few moments later I entered the gloom of her room, for all the blinds had been pulled down.

Crept over to Mum's bed and peered at her. She was asleep, not with a vacant, snorer's mask like Dad, rather a restless sweaty look, not asleep but deeply involved in some other life that required her eyes to be closed; another world stitched on the back of her eyelids. Not a reassuring face, more disturbing a person with its own disturbance; maybe she was awake in some other place that wasn't nice. A place that required all her attention and energy.

Even asleep Mum couldn't stop working.

But she was not just my Mum, this restless, fevered woman; she was a person named Rosemarie, a special name which Nana always said was beautiful because it could either be Rose, which is a flower, or Marie, who is a sacred person. So Rosemarie is a sacred rose. When I asked Nana what a sacred person was she wrote it down for me and it looked like scared person but she said that it meant a person who was loved by God. That couldn't be quite right because in that case we would all be sacred and sacred then wouldn't be that special. Or so scared.

Anyway, Mum's face didn't look sacred at all by Nana's reckoning of the word, because there was nothing loved by God about that look which was just the look of a person suffering, and what's so sacred about that? I wished she'd open her eyes because this world, with my face looking down at her, must be a better world than the one she was in. And if that was the case why shouldn't I wake her up? Surely my face would be a welcome sight. She would return to her body as soon as she saw me, smile at me and put her arms flowingly around me and my Mum would be back again.

I could get into bed with her and she would cuddle me, murmuring things.

I touched her arm which was clammy, like your skin after you have run a race then sat in the shade for a while, still sweating.

She didn't wake up. That was ok, it was actually better that she didn't wake up because she would have to tell me she was sick, and that would make me scared. Scared was more common than sacred.

I'm a carrier, I thought, as I had once before, then stopped at the memory of Adrian, leaning over the bed. All of us, even Carpenter, feeding off the living as if we were already dead. The black hole sitting in my head.

I looked back at Mum. There was a hugeness around her eyes, but not much to the rest of her.

I turned around and tiptoed out.

It was shower time.

▫

In the hard, cruel light of the bathroom, the hole above my eye stood out in all its hideousness. What was hideous about it was that there was no blood or healthy gore. When I looked deep into it, I saw a miniature world of death and putrefaction; slowly, bit by bit, flesh and bone were turning to rot. It looked ancient inside there, bits of bone already yellow and flaking with age.

I wondered if it would go over just half my face, like the Goddess of Sickness, or all of it.

Deep inside, the movement that I saw was the writhing of the Stench maggots I'd seen devour Rabbitt.

I had only the few hours left to achieve my mission here in Hikitarua.

Then I could dwell in her drear cities forever; they could hardly be worse than Hikitarua.

◘

The room I shared with Adrian had never looked so deserted. I thought I could see the dust on his sheets, the frame to which the wire was strung; easy to imagine that the ordinary, domestic silence of my room was the larger, creakier, cobwebby silence of the empty wards and the moon-rusted corridors of the hospital.

I sat on my bed and thought about my mission. There lay a secret I had to hold fast. No one would stop me. It was the last thing I could do on earth. For Rachel. For Hikitarua.

I would need all the resources of my cunning but I knew I could do it. If Donna had believed my moron act others would do the same. Nobody would suspect Baby.

Except Mitch.

It was Mitch I was worried about now. Mitch might be the one person who could stop me.

I went to the frozen miniature display. There were the inks Adrian had used, two bottles of the crimson he'd painted onto the bodies of the corpses he'd created in the course of his battles. Other colours were lined up behind, silver for the swords, bronze for the dwarfs' beards and the Orcs' helms, a colour for every piece of armour, for every weapon.

They were helpless without their master to move them; they didn't mean anything. Only the colours still gleamed with life inside their bottles. I picked up his paring knife and felt the point against my skin.

I wanted to sleep but the burning coin in my forehead kept me wired to the night. I closed my eyes and was falling into the face of the Queen of Sickness. Her face, with one half rotting and one half living, had become a planet, still with forehead, eyes, nose and chin, but the living half was forested, with crystal rivers and lush plains. The dead half was blasted by desert, decaying vegetation and toxic waterways. Inside the skull of the dead half toiled slaves, some meaningless trivial work I could not make out.

I had to open my eyes to remember the real nightmare. I got up and sat by the side window. The moon was like a big blind orb turned to the horizon. There were necklaces of mist along the hedges of the side streets and on the paired steel gates that held hands of latched metal here and there on the newer houses.

It was Hikitarua at the dead hour, and it wasn't a gripping sight. The houses, mostly with drawn blinds, lay wrapped in their silence. The only living thing I saw was a dog, trotting cool and quiet as you like down the middle of the main street looking neither left nor right nor round about, intent on its own purpose.

It took me a moment to recognise Softy, off on important business on behalf of Mrs Inna and her roses. He had his head in the air, sniffing.

Softy knew.

It wouldn't take him long to find it.

◦

I woke regretting the sleep I'd had. The dull, pearly light of dawn was already bright.

I rushed to the bathroom and checked the hole. It was as big as the nail on my thumb and deeper into the bone. I could see the slaves of decomposition at work, hard at work, taking apart my skull, but there was no blood. There was never any blood. The juice was sucked out of everything as soon as it appeared. The skin around the hole looked old and dead, almost black with age.

It looked so dark in the white, albino cast of my face.

I found a large plaster in the first aid kit and stuck it carefully over the hole. Nothing showed. The skin around it looked clean and healthy. Only I knew what festering lay beneath.

I'd just arrived back in my room, and had started dressing when there was a gentle tap on the door .

 Mitch was there with Dad standing behind looking awkward. She had gone for the softly-softly approach, her gentle red hair spread across her shoulders at the back, her cap off, almost informal but for the uniform. Yet there were the dark rings of sleeplessness under her eyes. She glanced up at the patch on my forehead

'Where were you last night, Baby?' she asked. She didn't stuff around with niceties.

'Adrian.' I said. 'Searching.' I nodded my head, the bright-eyed dumb-arse trying to wake up.

'Where?'

I gestured helplessly. I was helpless anyway so it wasn't such an act. 'Everywhere.'

'Nobody saw you.'

I smiled. It was a hard idea I had to try to say to her. Lying, it was especially hard to convey it. In the end I got it over to her that I had looked in places where no one else had thought to look.

She just shook her head.

She took a good long shifty around the room, at Adrian's bed, at mine. She put her hand in to feel the warmth of my sheets and had a good eyeful of Gorebag and his crew.

She also got a good eyeful of the plaster on my forehead. 'Did you have an accident?'

'Just a pimple,' I said with what I hoped was the right, morose tone of voice.

It was a dangerous moment. She was about to ask again, but held back.

We went downstairs where Dad, acting very sober and responsible, was cooking me porridge while Mitch continued to ask me questions. Actually, she didn't ask me that many questions, she was just trying to get a handle on me, trying to figure out what made me tick.

'Did Adrian and Josie have a secret place, where they used to go?'

I shook my head and indicated that they wouldn't tell me if they did.

She sat and watched me while I ate my porridge. Dad watched me too, standing quietly by the stove,. They were like people waiting for something. As it turned out they were waiting until I had finished my porridge.

'Rachel killed herself this morning,' Mitch said quietly as I put down my spoon. 'She hanged herself from a beam in the garage.' She waited until that had sunk in, then kept going. 'She climbed up on a stool, threw a rope over the supports, put it around her neck and kicked the stool away.'

Mitch's face went all lumpy as the tears came out of my eyes. I didn't try to hold them. I'd always loved Rachel best.

Mitch was very patient. For a police officer who now had one dead as well as three missing children, she was very patient indeed.

'Rachel left a note, Baby. Do you want to hear what it said?' Her voice was so deathly quiet you could hear a pin drop behind it. 'The dead can't smell themselves. For them, nothing smells so sweet. Do you know what it means?'

I shook my head. I thought of the death growing in my forehead. There was nothing sweet smelling about that.

'A line from a song, maybe?'

I shook my head again.

'Why would Rachel want to kill herself?'

'Upset. Upset Adrian and Josie gone.'

'Did she talk to you?'

'Rachel cry.'

Mitch looked at me as if she wanted to climb inside my brain.

'Please, Baby, listen. When Rachel got home last night she went straight into the garage without speaking to anyone. She must have been somewhere. Do you know where?'

I looked her straight in the face and took an enormous risk. The last place I wanted Mitch to go to now was the hospital; if she cottoned on to the hospital, my mission went down the drain and the Stench would triumph. That's what it boiled down to; she would never allow me to complete my mission, not in a million years.

'Hospital,' I said.

For a moment I thought she wasn't going to take the same bait twice. 'You told us about the hospital, we checked it out.'

I didn't tell her that Boss Hogg had been too lazy, tired or scared to do his job properly.

'What's this about the hospital?' Dad wanted to know. He was surrounding himself in the smell of coffee.

'Luke,' I said, creating as big a smoke screen as I could. Poor Rachel had laid the foundations for this. Mitch sighed. I was playing the same card, I just had to hope she didn't notice.

Dad got it before Mitch had to explain it to him. 'Oh sweet Jesus,' he said. I felt sorry for Dad. Now he was making all sorts of wrong connections and feeling responsible for things he didn't need to bear. That's what happens when you start lying to people; their reality gets all distorted.

Mitch was ready to go, but she had a social duty to perform first. 'Your Mum's still sick, Baby, and your Dad has to work at the Plant today. Do you want to stay home with your Mum or go to school?'

'School,' I said and held my breath.

Mitch and Dad looked at each other.

'It's probably best,' Mitch said. 'Her friends are there.'

And nobody said a word about the Stench. It was still something too impolite to mention.

Then Dad came over and gave me a hug. It was a shamelessly warm hug that told me everything would be all right.

If I would just hold on a bit longer, everything would be all right.

I held onto him for a moment, forever.

⸫

Being delivered to school in a police car, an event which would normally have drawn enormous interest, passed with hardly a ripple. The school was agog with Rachel's death. All the stories were different; Rachel had been found hanging naked from the washing line, Rachel had gone to bed and stabbed herself. Rachel and Josie were members of a secret suicide cult and it wouldn't be long until they found Josie's body too. I was glad that Mitch had told me what really happened.

A fever lay over the school. There were ripples of hysteria, outbreaks of sobbing and shouting. Clusters of girls broke up and reformed as teachers and police tried to keep everyone moving.

There were police everywhere and rumours were rife that the school would be closed at lunchtime. I could taste the Stench in the air but no one said anything; I was sensitised to it now, I could even hear the odd echo it produced in people's voices, as if their thoughts didn't quite match their speech. I only heard it mentioned a couple of times, and someone said it was something they were doing at the Plant. Everybody was too busy going nuts to notice it, just like we had been on that first night at the hospital.

Nobody commented on the plaster over my left eye.

Mostly kids walked around blinking in the sunlight as if they didn't understand where they were or what they were looking at. Class bells rang meaninglessly.

And wherever I looked, whether at the black asphalt of the courts, the green grass of the playing fields or the rows of brown desks in the classrooms, I saw the moon-grey, dingy corridors of the hospital, the dusty windows and the greasy walls. I saw the trapdoor lifting up from the floor, heard a rush of feet through the abandoned wards and the echo of Josie giggling backwards.

Hikitarua had become one big hospital, the hospital itself had become the trapdoor, about to spring the Stench on the whole town.

There was no school assembly with cheering readings from the Bible; Conk & Whiskers stayed holed up in his office and talked on the telephone or met with a constant stream of dignitaries.

When the first TV crew arrived, I realised how little time I had, the town had. While Mrs Manui tried to herd us specials into the library for sanctuary, there was no real pretence that there'd be school as usual. She walked along the shelves looking for a story and she just kept walking, her fingers running along the books. They kept running but found no book. I knew what had happened. Her library angel had deserted her and there was nothing she could find to read us. None of the stories were whispering to her.

I ducked out unnoticed and went to find Carpenter. Carpenter had to help me. He was the last chance I had, and I had to find words for him, I had to convince him of something and it looked like it was going to be the hardest thing I ever did. I'd sort of brushed over this bit in my mind when the idea had come to me. I'd simply foreseen Carpenter helping me, I had no idea how it was to come about.

As I crossed the ground to his block I saw a pack of dogs in wing formation, purposeful, intent, like Softy had been the night before. There were maybe eight of them and they were utterly silent, looking neither right nor left. It was like seeing a slice of night spliced into the middle of the day.

I found Carpenter lying on the ground. Someone had pushed him over and instead of getting up he just lay still, his cucumber sandwich in his hand, looking at the sky as if the dead were up there parading around for him to watch. It appeared he'd been trying to eat his lunch when it happened although lunch hour was still hours off. The greasy sweats were bad on him, and the heat was poaching his eyes, turning them white and milky. His face was breaking out in ugly red spots.

I thought he hadn't seen me but he had, or at least he spoke as if he had.

'I'm going t' tell,' he said in a mechanical voice. It sounded as if he were going to hell. 'We've got t' tell now. Now that Rachel's dead.' There was leaden certainty in his voice. He scratched at one of his spots.

I looked up and saw Kahu, his lean face still turned in our direction. I knew from the miserable look on his face how much he'd loved Rachel. He was hooked onto us now; even in the numbness of his grief he knew something was up with us.

'I have to go back one more time, then I'll tell,' Carpenter said. He was struggling into a sitting position. Without thinking he poked the sandwich in his mouth and forgot to chew.

'Why?'

Tears came into his eyes. He had to bend over for them to fall on the dry ground and vanish as fast as possible. Untouched food fell out of his mouth.

'My dad can't find the crowbar. He knows now, he's watching me.' He looked about desperately. Mitch was angling towards us across the playground and I hoped that his desperation was enough to get him up on his legs. I didn't think Carpenter would survive a police cross examination at this point.

I gestured to Kahu who came instantly, without a word, as if he had no feet. Together we made a show of getting Carpenter upright as Mitch arrived. For once I got the first word in.

'Home. Carpenter home.' I gave her my best ET look. I was wearing it out fast, but I wouldn't need it much longer. Just an hour or two would do it.

Mitch nodded, biting her lower lip. School was all but over before it had even got started. I could see a stream of disorganised kids dispersing from the gate like smoke from the chimney.

'He just lives around the corner,' Kahu said easily. 'We'll take him home, then I'll take Baby home.' He smiled and I saw for the first time what a wonderful open smile he had.

Mitch nodded with relief. Another tiny detail taken care of. She was getting tired of me; I was turning into a big nuisance.

Carpenter stared at Mitch in double agony. If he wanted to tell now was his moment. But he didn't. The crowbar held his tongue down.

Kahu and I escorted Carpenter home. He had a little more stealing to do, he didn't know that and I had no idea how to get him to do it, or how to get rid of Kahu, whose grief was starting to come back into his face. It filled his cheekbones like the veins of an old man.

I'd learned it with Adrian, there was no way of stopping love from becoming a curse.

Mrs Inna was in her rose garden, minus Softy. Her nose buried so fervently in a rose it looked like a bloodied handkerchief. She was sneezing blood into the rose.

I had that feeling again of being followed and had to remind myself that Rabbitt was dead; the thumb-sucker would no longer be on our trail, at least not alive. I wanted to laugh but it was the wrong thing to do; I was sailing too close to the edge to indulge a giggle. We put our heads down against the wind, which had gathered in force during the morning and had lost nothing in dry heat. The town was being scrubbed by sandpaper under an innocent blue sky. Kahu kept looking me over; he knew I was the leader of what was left of the gang and he didn't ask any questions. I appreciated that; with Kahu on board what had before seemed impossible now came within reach.

If Carpenter couldn't deliver the goods, Kahu might be able to do it. I might yet beat the odds.

Finding nobody home at Carpenter's place was our first piece of luck. Not surprising since both his parents worked, but catching his dad away from his workshop was an added bonus. Gratefully I took in the open double doors of his workshop-cum-garage, with all the promising bits and pieces lying around.

I deliberately steered us towards the garage.

'There's an awful smell around,' Kahu said.

Carpenter rolled his eyes. 'We need a control group. Y' can't draw any conclusions without a control group.'

I pointed to the garage.

Carpenter shook his head in terror. He had a dim idea of what I wanted. I made the idea a lot clearer by bending down and whispering a single word in his ear. When he took the word he stared fixedly at the garage. He dabbed the back of his hand against his face, for some of his sores had started to weep pus.

'Yous know where he is, don't y'?' Kahu said.

I nodded, not having to ask who. I was busy watching Carpenter. In particular his eyes. I thought he'd look straight at the thing I was wanting, but he didn't. He wasn't looking into the garage, he wasn't looking anywhere except the place where the crowbar should be, then he looked back at me.

'You can't do that.' His hands gripped thin air.

'Right thing the.' I said. To hell with the order of the words, he'd get the message. He knew it already.

'Don't have any,' he said, pulling free of us and walking on into his father's garage. 'Look for yourself.'

I didn't move. I knew it would be there somewhere, in some form. He did too. He was stalling, trying to figure it out.

The circle of chilled numbness in my head grew suddenly painful. Inside my skull, new pieces of bone fell away to nothingness.

'What the hell are you talking about?' Kahu said. He was getting that hectic look we all had by now, looking for somewhere else to breathe.

Kahu had to know, if he was to help me in the next stage. If he knew then the world would know. If I spoke the word aloud, it was in the air.

The hot dry air.

'Petrol.' I said.

HikitArua

Carpenter found it in the end because Kahu and I couldn't figure it out. We knew there had to be petrol there somewhere. Carpenter pointed to an old scooter lying under the dust and the nothingness.

It had a full tank of gas.

He knelt down beside the scooter and sucked the petrol out of a tube into his mouth, spat out what he could, and lowered the tube into a plastic mineral water bottle. His face screwed up as the gas hit his tongue and throat and he coughed from somewhere deep inside his body. Petrol poured into the mineral water bottle. It was only two litres but it was enough.

Once he knew what I was after, Carpenter grew quite enthusiastic, as if this were some great new scientific experiment. I'd need a lighter. He found one in a pair of his father's greasy overalls hanging from an upright nail. His father would probably never notice it. It was nothing compared to the crowbar. I could see that he had come up with a plan that made him more cheerful.

I didn't care about what he might be scheming. I had the bottle of gas, I was on my way, Kahu by my side like a second shadow.

We left Carpenter staring at us, his glasses opaque. I didn't stop to wonder why he hadn't come with us, I just wondered as I walked along, the bottle secured innocuously in my school bag.

'You know where he is, don't you?' Kahu said, repeating his earlier question.

I nodded. He thought for a long time. He thought about everything we'd just done. A thoughtful boy, was Kahu.

'You're going to kill him,' he said.

Thoughtful as he was, Kahu didn't understand death; I nodded nevertheless.

'Adrian is the arsehole of the universe,' Kahu said with great feeling. I agreed with him but he didn't have it quite right, he was just tuning into Adrian's image of himself.

I was plotting my route to the hospital, which I figured should be by the long way, around the back where I had witnessed Kahu's beating, when he grasped me by the arm. 'Here comes treachery,' he said, 'Get rid of him. I'll find you,' and he was gone, just like that. I trusted him although I could see no immediate threat.

I was walking alone through Hikitarua, but there was nothing quiet about the place; at long last our town had been roused from its ancient slumber. A helicopter scissored the air overhead. Cars hustled to and fro picking up kids as the shambles at the school spread into the town. Boss Hogg drove past but he wasn't looking my way. There were other police about too, but no one gave me a second glance. I knew this messy phase was the best cover I'd have, because afterwards people would hole up, the blinds would come down, the doors would lock and there wouldn't be a child in sight from one end of Hikitarua to the other. I had about an hour at the most.

Then I had to stop, right in the middle of the street, because I felt something happen inside my head. A tiny cave of darkness had opened at the back of my mind, a tiny trapdoor was lifted - and I knew what lay behind the inky darkness there.

I was seeing the hole in my forehead now, it had grown big enough to enter my inner world, the world of all my thoughts and feelings - the most private world that any human being can have.

And there it was, eating away at the core of my being; tiny wormy fingers probing at the back of my mind.

'Hey! Moron!'

I opened my eyes, which I hadn't realised had closed.

Brad. Adrian's old sidekick.

He laughed. 'That butt munch Kahu sure took off fast when he saw me coming.'

He seized me by the arm and thrust his face close to mine. 'You're not going anywhere,' he said in a low, triumphant voice. I stared at the ground and didn't say anything.

Adrian and Josie had sent him to kill me. Too cowardly to do it themselves last night, Adrian had somehow got to Brad. Promises had been made, I was sure.

I went to move on but he wasn't going to move out of my way, and he didn't let go of my arm.

'Adrian told me. He's got a secret place where he and Josie are hiding. He was shooting off his mouth about how cool he was and how he was screwing Josie...' He got a nasty look on his face, like someone who is missing out on all the action. I could see the Stench turning his mind into knots, tightening the knots that were already there.

I decided I'd push past him, but he wasn't going to leave it at that. He squeezed my arm a shade too tight.

'Is he? Is he fucking Josie?'

I nodded slowly, watching the information plunge him deeper into the torment of jealousy.

'He said you'd let me fuck you. He said you were just waiting for the chance.' He laughed as if the idea were just too absurd for words. Screwing Baby is not exactly something he'd want to be boasting about to his mates. Nevertheless he was looking me over, considering the idea - he wasn't too proud. Fucking the town idiot was better than missing out altogether. A fuck's a fuck.

'Ok,' I said, hearing my own voice flat and chill coming from my mouth. I took his hand off my arm.

For a moment he looked very surprised, flabbergasted even, then he recovered quickly and puffed himself up. 'And you'll take me to Adrian afterwards...he is hiding out with Josie isn't he?'

'Yes.'

'I didn't think he was lying.'

I kept walking and Brad swaggered along beside me. I didn't look at him. Not once did I look at him; I knew what I'd see in his face.

By the time we got to our street he started to get nervous. The reality of having to carry out his boast was starting to come home to him. He kept looking at me sideways, trying to make up his mind if he wanted to or not.

I didn't give him any help, I didn't even look at him except to notice a nasty, craven look as his fear got to him; all this was just wasting time as far I as I was concerned, taking me further and further away from my mission.

Everything was already shut down at the Rabbitt's as if it were night already; it had the air of a house in mourning.

Our place had the same feel. The big emptiness I'd heard when I had put my ear to the side of the hospital that first night.

Brad grabbed hold of my arm again. His face turned from craven to cruel. 'I want in on this,' he said in a low voice, 'Adrian promised he'd let me in on it.'

I led him through the kitchen and past Mum's room. I hadn't the time to stop and look in and besides, I was afraid of what I would find. I was sure she was no longer there, that she'd just wasted into a shadow and vanished from the bed as if she had never been.

'Where are we going?' Brad whispered uneasily.

I opened the door and let him through first. He made straight for Adrian's miniatures; he didn't want to face me.

He picked up Gorebag Ironclaw from his carefully calibrated place on the dusty battlefield. Behind him, out of the window, the clouds stacked up in a classic nor-west front; a dry storm full of lightning and dust.

'They reckon somebody must've been there to give Rachel a bit of a hand,' he said suddenly, gloating away to himself. He kept giving me sly looks, as if he knew more than he ever could tell. Gossip. That was what made Hikitarua go round.

He was delaying doing what he came here to do.

'You don't have t' believe me but I heard them talkin, Boss Hogg and my Dad. Boss Hogg was blastin his mouth off tryin to ask questions because Dad was the one who found Rachel not her parents. Dad went around in the morning to pick up Rachel's Dad for work and found her in the garage. Someone had given her a hand, that's what Boss Hogg said. They're lookin for a killer.' He wiped the sweat from his eyes with his sleeve. He had Adrian figured for the killer. It stood out like dog's balls in his mind.

I picked up Adrian's working knife and thought about it. I had taken Mitch at her word, and the official word was suicide, but what if either Josie or Adrian had followed her home after we all left? Adrian more likely.

It didn't matter much now, certainly not as much as he thought it did. When I reviewed events at the hospital I decided that Rachel had already died before we split that last time. She knew it too. She'd prophesied it. The rope and slip knot were a mere formality.

I pointed to Gorebag and to the battle field. I gave him the hard stare.

'Adrian,' I said warningly and he nodded in understanding. Adrian was pernickety about his miniatures.

'We better get on with it,' he said, licking his lips. As he stooped over the battle field, trying to see where to put Gorebag, his hand slipped and Gorebag's little bronze sword fell, landing on top of a dwarf. Brad leaned further over to get it and I swung the knife into the back of his neck three times before he woke up to what was happening.

By then he had nothing to remember. He gave a great loud groan as his body went down.

I shoved his body into my bed, pulled the duvet up around his shoulders and spread some of Adrian's paint around to make it look like some bottles had been accidentally tipped up, bottles of red, brown, bronze.

You wouldn't immediately think of blood.

⸱

I didn't feel a thing. I'd just killed someone, you'd think I'd be in a fever pitch of feelings but I was not.

I just did things. I operated my body as if by remote control, as if I were somewhere else entirely.

I went to the bathroom, calmly cleaned myself and changed my clothes. I replaced the plaster on my forehead too, for the skin was starting to pull at the adhesive.

I tried not to look at the hole, nor think of the stench creatures that had bored a hole in the back of my mind and were now spilling through. Slithering between thoughts. This was a trapdoor which, once opened, could not be closed. I erected barriers against them, walls of blankness, so that I could complete my mission.

No matter what kind of monstrosity I became, I would complete my mission.

The hole was almost too big for plasters now. I shoved a bandage in my pocket.

I passed Mum's door but I wasn't going to get past Mum. I came up behind her as she crawled from the hall into the kitchen. She kept going on one elbow; all the rest of her was dead, just one elbow kept her going, kept her in the world, scraping over the lino heading for the hospital.

'Baby,' she croaked, 'You're up late.' She was wearing a blue nightgown which, when she looked up at me, showed clearly her breasts which had gone dry and shrivelled; they were nothing more than a claw of skin around the nipples.

I understood something. The weak ones like her would go first. Soon, very soon, there would be others like her crawling through the streets towards the trapdoor. It was up to the strong ones like me to do something. So far there was only me, and maybe Kahu.

I stepped around her, my schoolbag still on my shoulders, and turned at the door to wave at her as if I were really going off to school. I got that foolish smile on my face I first got when I was five. It was supposed to disarm people.

But Mum cut through all that. She didn't believe for one minute that I was going off to school. She knew. Mothers always know.

'Take me with you,' she croaked, lifting up her good elbow to inch her body forward. The sweat had soaked her night dress into her body. 'I want to see Adrian.'

But I didn't have any heart strings left to play on.

◦

Kahu picked up my trail before I'd got to the end of the street. He didn't ask any questions about Brad although he must have seen us going inside. I didn't volunteer anything. I didn't want to think about Brad, lying in my bed making it look like I was there asleep. Just enough to fool a quick glance.

It was the knot of hatred that kept Kahu going, nothing more. He may not have believed, as Brad did, that Rachel was helped along, but he knew what had driven her to it and who lay behind it all.

He'd had Adrian's number right from the start.

I was glad to have him along, for if Mitch were to see me now, she'd wonder why I was going in the wrong direction, why I was heading away from home.

No sooner had I thought it than it happened. Mitch was driving this time, and she had another cop in the car, a detective who gave us a hard look. I saw Mitch saying something to him as they pulled over.

Kahu gave my arm a little squeeze and sauntered over to the car.

'I'm taking her t' my place,' he said to Mitch. 'There's nobody home at her place and she got scared.' Mitch nodded, a faint look of puzzlement on her face. She knew that mum was there sick in the morning. I could see her making a mental resolution to ring Dad and the Plant.

'Why have you still got your schoolbag?' The other cop asked me, his eyes very sharp.

I gave him a frightened look. 'Forgot!' I blurted out, and gave a loud laugh, more like a bray.

The detective looked at Mitch and Mitch nodded, confirming my idiot status.

'Where do you live?' the detective asked Kahu.

Mitch knew very well where he lived but Kahu was patient, treated the detective with great respect and gave his address and phone number. We should be at his place in half an hour, he said, because we might have a milk shake at the Galaxy.

'I'd skip the milk shake,' the detective said, as if Rush Jimmy's milk shakes were no good.

Mitch nodded. She'd lost her sense of self possession, her sense of control. Something had passed right by her which she hadn't seen and, because she was a brilliant person who knew things before being told them, she knew she'd missed something. Some clue. It was driving her crazy. She desperately wanted to solve this before the big shots from out of town took over completely.

This was her town, that's how she saw it. It was breaking her heart to see what was happening right now and she didn't even know the half of it.

We had to go to Kahu's place. The cop car virtually drove along behind us. I could see Mitch talking into the car phone. We passed the Galaxy and it was empty. Rush Jimmy sat behind the counter, cigarette in hand, staring up at his favourite James Dean poster.

Mitch waved to us as we turned into Kahu's place. Getting back to the hospital was going to be much harder than I thought. I noted a pair of bicycles by the back door as we went in.

'Don't worry,' Kahu said, 'there's no one home.'

But he was wrong.

Donna screamed when she saw me. 'What have you done to your head?' She reached out to touch the plaster and I brushed her hand away.

'But what is it?'

'Pimple.'

She looked at it curiously. It didn't bulge out the way a pimple would.

'What are you guys doing?' she said, trying to sound casual. In fact she was burning to know why I was here.

'Her mum's ill,' Kahu said. 'I told Mitch I'd bring her here.'

'What's wrong with your Mum, Baby?'

I shrugged. There was a far away, lonely feeling at the pit of my stomach. The truth was, Mum was dead; we'd all be dead soon if I didn't complete my mission.

Donna focused on me, eyes flicking back to the plaster. I knew she hadn't really swallowed my dumb act of the day before and she didn't look too happy to see me; at the same time she knew she had to be nice to me because Adrian was missing. Contempt mingled with pity was what she got out of that mix.

'Poor Baby,' she said, fiddling nervously with her hair, reminding me of Josie.

Kahu gave her a sharp look but didn't say anything. He was so quick. I'd never realised before. I wished I'd had someone like him for my big brother.

As she led us back inside, I could see her agitation growing; clearly my presence was annoying her. She walked up and down in front of the plate glass window that faced the street, fidgeting with her hands. She was blonde and skinny, like Josie, but she was not wiry and tough the way Josie was. More slender and frail.

'How about some sounds?' Kahu said, gripping hard on the edge of cool. He went over to the stereo and fumbled through some sounds. He kept looking through them and not finding anything; just as Mrs Manui had walked along the bookshelves in the library, her fingers leaping from book to book, Kahu discarded sound after sound until he was back at the beginning, going through them again only this time more slowly. The best thing for me to do, I thought, is to take one of the bicycles and make a run for the hospital; the passing hours were not going to make it any safer, or easier, to get there.

'Actually,' Donna said, 'I'd like to speak to Kahu. I mean alone.' She looked appealingly at Kahu to handle the problem of me being around. I thought maybe it was something personal. I didn't know they knew each other and didn't care; I didn't have time for these complications. All the while the Stench was gathering its power, pent up behind the walls of the hospital. I could see it coming out like a dark sooty smoke between the loose boards of the window, seeping through every crack.

Kahu, the music clutched forgotten in one hand, said, 'Can't it wait, Donna?'

'No it can't!' Her voice emerged as a stiff screech. 'It's something you have t' know.' She gave me a quick, scared look.

'We'll talk outside,' Kahu said. Apologising to me for this situation was beyond Kahu's social skills, but he managed to mumble something as they went outside.

I could see them through the window; Donna leaning forward talking urgently, Kahu, going pale, staggering where he stood as if she'd just punched him in the stomach. Then she saw me watching and pulled him out of my line of sight.

I wasn't going to waste any time. A quick search of the laundry rewarded me with a pair of blue overalls of the kind often worn by Plant workers or tradesmen in the town. They were in need of a wash but that wasn't going to worry me. The disguise wouldn't have to last me long. I also found a khaki green cap that would neatly hide my albino hair, a recognisable beacon for miles around.

I took off my school clothes, got into the overalls and stuffed the cap in my pocket, hesitating over whether or not to check the hole in my forehead. The trapdoor, as I thought of it now. I knew what I'd find, I didn't have to look; I could feel it well enough - the wheel of death inside my head. Turning, turning.

When I got back to the living room, I found Donna kneeling at my school-bag, where I'd left it lying on the floor, the bottle of petrol in her hand. She undid the lid and delicately sniffed at it.

When she looked up, her eyes were so blue you could see the sky behind them.

'You're going to burn down the hospital,' she said matter-of-factly.

I wasn't surprised that she knew. How she knew was anyone's guess. As I said, there were no secrets in Hikitarua; we were approaching a time when everybody would know and what I had to do would become impossible.

Kahu looked horribly pale and tense. It seemed to take him ages to recognise me dressed in his father's dungarees. He was trying to assimilate what Donna had told him outside, out of my hearing.

'But I'm not going to let you do it,' Donna said, reaching over and taking hold of Kahu's hand. 'I'm ringing Mitch now. She told me to.'

Kahu shook his head. 'Don't try it.' His voice was soft. It held all the warning she needed.

'But they're inside!' she shouted at him, as if he'd just said something totally outrageous. The sweats were starting up in her now; like Carpenter, her skin was starting to bleed all kinds of toxins. 'Josie and Adrian, and probably even Rabbitt. They're there! I didn't care while they were just hiding away. But we can't let her just... just... torch the place. They'll all die. The whole town will go up.'

She was on the verge of crying. She knew if she cried she'd lose it all.

I took hold of Donna's arm to make her look at me. She screamed and jumped away as if my touch were poison. 'Adrian, Josie,' I blurted, desperate to make my tongue work. 'Monsters are they! Dead! Dead!' My voice was all over the place, as if I had an unhinged jaw. My mouth was full of sliding vowels, and I couldn't find the consonants; the loudness came on all the wrong syllables. I sounded like a machine trying to learn how to talk.

Donna laughed. 'She's gone weird, Kahu.' She turned insistently to Kahu. 'She's loopy, can't you see that? Demented.' She gave me a cold, thoughtful look. 'She can't even make words properly any more.'

'Maybe,' Kahu said soberly. Whatever it was that Donna had told him, it was slowly tearing him apart inside. 'And maybe she's right. They're all dead.' He sounded like Rachel. As if Rachel had come back from the dead to shape his thoughts for a moment.

'Trapdoor,' I said to Donna. 'Hospital. Trapdoor under. Floor. Stench. You smell?' She had to listen to me.

Donna stared at me and laughed again. 'I smell it all right and it comes from you!' She turned helplessly to Kahu, 'That's where it's coming from. She stinks to high heaven.' She laughed again.

Kahu didn't laugh. He picked up an orange from the table and sniffed hard at the fresh, nose-prickly skin, as if to assure himself of its existence.

I moved away from Donna, backed away from her until I hit the kitchen bench. The knob of the cutlery drawer pressed against my leg. 'It's coming from. The hospital.' I said. I had to break it into two pieces to get it out right. But it didn't sound right. It sounded like a bunch of geese honking.

'I'm ringing Mitch,' Donna said, moving to the phone. 'Mitch gave me her cellphone number. I've got to tell her.' She didn't know she was thinking aloud. The words that came into her mind went straight to her lips, she wasn't fast enough to stop them.

She sat by the phone and stared at a piece of paper with some writing on it. A phone number. I could read the 021 from up-side down. I waited until she picked up the phone before I moved. I had the cutlery drawer open, a knife in my hand, and was on the move before Donna had finished dialling.

But Kahu was faster. I might have known he would be. He stepped in front of me and grabbed my hand before Donna had a chance to work out what was happening. His skinny fingers were as strong as wire. 'We don't have to do it that way,' he said in a hard whisper.

He was right, but then, he knew nothing about the Stench and how it worked. The trapdoor had opened in my mind now. I thought of brother Adrian, standing mighty tall, hurling the child Rabbitt through the shifting surface of the pit.

Sacrifice. Always the pit needed new victims.

But I had wanted to kill Brad, and I wanted to kill Donna too. It had nothing to do with my mission, or them getting in my way, or even the Stench itself. It had everything to do with betrayal.

We struggled for a moment in silence. Kahu pushed me away, turned, and slammed Donna out of her chair. She went over screaming and he was on her. He seized one arm and twisted it up her back. She was acting as if she were being murdered, but he was doing it to save her life.

I had no excuse for killing her now.

The phone fell on the table. We could hear Mitch's voice on the phone, a distant helpless scratching, before I grabbed it and punched the off button.

'She was goin t' to kill me,' Donna choked out. 'She's gone berserk, Kahu.'

Kahu sent me to the garage for some rope and it wasn't long before we had Donna well bound.

'You're making a serious mistake, Kahu,' Donna said, flexing her arms against the ropes. 'She's got some kind of power over you, hasn't she? I felt it when yous first came in. She's a killer, can't you see that?'

'It's because of what y' told me y'self,' Kahu said. 'That's why I believe her.'

'What?' I looked at Kahu.

'Rachel's body has gone missing,' Donna said coldly. 'It just wasn't there in the morning. It just wasn't there.' Her voice cracked wide open. 'Jesus, look out!'

I fell. It felt as if I was in the same position but the room had fallen. Fallen into the dark hole at the back of my mind.

I was taken immediately to the City of Gates, which shone with a remote purity, like the Southern Alps on a clear winter day when all the distances are shortened. But as I approached, I saw that the City itself was wounded. There was a huge gap eating its way into the walls, exposing the secret innards of the City and turning them to mush. The Stench poured out of the wound like a dark, rotting river. Unlike last time, when it had been teeming with creatures seeking their place in the vast library, it was empty, more like an endless tomb in which all the centuries of history were embalmed and awaiting their final destruction.

I perceived then how the Stench really worked, using whatever trapdoor it could find into whatever universe it could pollute. Even the pure realm of the City of Gates was not immune. Thought itself began to twist, torque out of line.

I thought of the Queen, the true Queen, still asleep perhaps in her stone and satin chamber. In her all purity resided and would do so until the end of time. Let death take her unknowing. Let her not have to witness what was happening to her kingdom.

I woke up with tears on my cheeks and the sun had turned the day around. Kahu was watching me as my eyes opened.

The first thing I knew was the plaster had gone from my forehead. I touched the edges of the wound. The flesh felt dead. A piece of bone came away in my fingers and crumbled into nothing.

Kahu came over and cradled my head gently in his arms. 'It's late. We have to move now while the Plant workers are going home.' He touched my cheek and there was tenderness in the feel of it.

'You believe me.' I said, still crying from the dream.

I couldn't credit the death of the City of Gates.

'I believe you,' he said. 'And so does Donna.' Hours, they'd had hours to turn me in, get hold of Mitch, do whatever they had to do. Instead, Kahu had sat here and watched over me.

Donna was still bound but she was not struggling. She couldn't look me in the eye. She couldn't help but stare at the dark star in my forehead; a vacant, revolted stare. She preferred to stay tied up.

I pulled myself to my feet. The hospital seemed a thousand miles away.

All I wanted to do was sleep, but I couldn't let the corridor grow too long, couldn't allow the memory of all that, and Rachel's death, to be buttered over by time.

'Are they all like you?' Donna asked.

'Worse.'

'Did they steal Rachel's body?' She was using a baby voice, a very small, frightened girl.

'Rachel walked.' I said, guessing. I couldn't see Adrian stalking through the streets carrying her over his shoulder. Rachel must have done it herself, put on a coat or something like we were doing, slipped between the streets, a shade among shades.

Death goes everywhere, unseen.

Leaving Kahu to find his own disguise, I went into the bathroom, found the bandage I'd put into my pocket earlier, in my clothes still lying on the floor, and bandaged the hole which was now as big as a fifty cent piece. I couldn't see through it any more, into the depths of my skull. It had formed a shivery, shiny skin. I couldn't see how deep because it was lost in blackness; trying to see in was like trying to look into the pit beneath the hospital. It had grown to the size of a cavern in the back of my mind, and my life was draining away through it.

The Stench was seeping from it.

I was now sustained solely by my purpose. The Stench could take everything from me but that; Rachel's last words to me.

Burn it up!

◦

The wind had dropped to nothing and the sun was low over the mountains. A gentleness had entered the air along with that yellow luminescence you sometimes get in late afternoon when all the colours go deep.

The lights had come on along highway 5, escorting the road out of town for a distance.

We biked in single file, trying to look casual, trying not to look as if we were peddling too furiously. The only cop we saw was Boss Hogg. He was coming out of the Milky Way with a hamburger dripping cheese. He was so busy trying to get his mouth around it he didn't give us a second glance.

Kahu had found a plastic orange jacket, the kind that showed up under headlights

Still I felt as if we were being followed. It reminded me of when Rabbitt was around. My mind flashed onto Maro, but I could see nothing around me but Hikitarua in its usual disguises.

I felt more vulnerable when we got to the back streets. Kahu must have felt the same because we both put on a burst of speed at the same time. The bottle of petrol, which I had transferred to my pocket, abandoning my schoolbag at Kahu's, bumped up and down against my side, where I'd stuffed it into the pocket of Kahu's Dad's overalls.

As soon as we got to the back of the hospital I saw the flaw in my grand plan. The bicycles were not easy to hide. They wouldn't fit through the back of the fence without trouble. Left lying where they were by the side of the road they would be like a marker, an arrow pointing to where we were.

Anybody following would be onto us in five minutes.

I might need longer than five minutes.

In the end Kahu did shove them through the fence but there was still nowhere to hide them once we were inside the hospital grounds . We left them propped up by the fence, out of the line of sight from the driveway, which was the best we could do.

The first thing I saw was the covering board hanging loose from the back window. As we stood staring at it, we could hear the sound of searchers on the river bed, hailing one another as they returned after the day. Now they had a missing corpse to add to the list. The first rich light of the full moon was in my face, as I stood there, Kahu beside me. I realised it had been growing for the last three or four days, slowly fattening itself. Slowly balancing the horizon.

At the last moment I hesitated. It was only fear. Kahu watched me. He didn't know what kind of hell was inside, but he could smell it, his nostrils had gone white with it.

I was just about to go through when a distant wailing started up. It began as a faint, unearthly sound and gathered strength, as if it were approaching us. It took both of us a long moment to realise what it was. Hikitarua was screaming. The whole town. A hysteria that was jumping from street to street as the news of some new horror struck, perhaps the discovery of Brad covered in miniature paint, perhaps something we didn't know about.

Hikitarua was coming alive to its pain.

Cliffs of bone inside my skull crumbled. The cold circle in my forehead tightened, like the rope around Rachel's neck must've done.

I went through with no more hesitation, coming in head first the way we always had to, a wriggly, ungainly exercise. Behind me I heard the sound of police sirens joining the collective scream, then it all faded.

The Stench was heavy around me, so heavy that it seemed to drip, as if I were in the hot, toxic belly of some great dark creature. There was no ambrosial camouflage now, no smell of fresh morning roses from Mrs Inna's garden.

I stopped and listened, for voices, an echo, a sound. Silence was not reassuring, not here; it usually meant nastiness and surprises. If Adrian and Josie were in the kitchen talking, I'd be able to hear them from the storeroom and I heard nothing. I saw nothing. The air around me was muffled, as if the Stench, at this strength, had the power to blot out the other senses.

I was just starting to wonder about Kahu when I saw his shoulders getting born through the window. He'd already stuck a handkerchief around his head to cover his nose. His eyes were as big as saucers. Welcome to the hospital, I wanted to say to him, would you like to sign the visitor's book? I remembered Josie's insane giggles and controlled my thoughts.

My eyes began to pick shapes out of the gloom - a door, a lintel, a light patch where a cabinet had stood like a ghost the cabinet had left behind, and a body lying by the door.

I didn't move and the body didn't move. We were like two strangers assessing one another. A dead body isn't a dangerous thing but it has a powerful presence. Kahu didn't see it because he didn't see anything; he kept turning his head from side to side as if he were having trouble with his neck.

I approached the corpse one foot slowly in front of the other. I thought I knew who it was going to turn out to be but I was wrong.

Carpenter was lying face up with his glasses on, looking quizzically towards the window, his mouth open a little as if about to speak. The skin of his face was bloated and covered in sores which, while he still lived, must have been weeping badly for in death they had become extinct craters, the area around them a crust of dried pus tears. Behind his glasses, his eyes were bits of black, shining jelly. They reminded me of the shot-out street lamp. He looked the way I'd drawn him in my doodle, a death's head with his eyes stuck out and a dark, swollen tongue coming out of his mouth.

I didn't think that the sores had killed him, however; something else had done that.

The crowbar lay in his hand as if he'd just picked it up. That's what he'd been thinking about as he came through the window, forgetting to replace the board behind him. The crowbar lay across his chest in the grip of his right hand. His left arm outstretched, fist clenched.

Kahu came up behind me. I didn't like the feel of it and moved to one side. The hospital was an arena in which nothing could be trusted and every motion hung in the balance. Kahu didn't stop until his feet hit the corpse, and even then he didn't look down but kept staring straight ahead into the kitchen.

Rachel lay propped up against the wall positioned in such a way that her stare was fixed like a curse on the doorway to the storeroom.

The cosmeticians or whoever dresses bodies had done a good job, Rachel was as pretty as she was ever going to look. Her dark curls had been combed cutely around her cheeks with a neat part down the middle. That neat part didn't look like her though, because her hair always got chaotic. Her perfectly pale face had been smoothed over with powder and her cheekbones had been darkened a touch. Her frozen beauty made her look more like a shop mannequin than a dead person. She was wearing a modest, full length frock but her white, alabaster arms were bare. It was a frock I'd never seen her wear before, except maybe at a school dance. Only her lips spoiled the effect, for they were thick and black as if covered in purple lipstick. And the purple marks around her neck where the rope had contrived its love bite. Mitch had told me the truth. There was no cosmetic to cover a wound like that.

When I looked harder I saw a line of ants trickling down her leg.

In front of her, two pillows with their kapok guts ripped out were strewn across the floor like the tattered remains of stuffed swans. A slashed mattress hung over the bench with its foam mouth open. Empty packets of cigarettes and butts were squashed into the floor. Carpenter's needles scattered and smashed. A whisky bottle with its neck broken.

Somehow little Luke's picture had survived, flanked on either side by the last of the candle wicks drowned in pools of wax.

Rachel stood up as soon as she saw us. Her movements weren't at all lumbering, the way you see corpses in the movies, and the way we'd played it just a few nights before. I don't know why people imagine that the dead stumble around with their arms outstretched like a bunch of mobile scarecrows; Rachel rose to her feet in one fluid motion that was at once graceful and horrible, horrible because live human knees don't work that smoothly. Suddenly she no longer looked like a mannequin but wonderfully, vitally alive; refreshingly there, as if she'd just stepped from a stimulating bath.

'Kahu,' she breathed, making it sound like a prayer.

Kahu would have gone forwards if his feet had found a way around Carpenter's body.

The petrol was tightly clutched in my hand. I had a sudden vision of my funeral, with all the good citizens of Hikitarua in attendance. Old Conk & Whiskers was there and he was crying. Not discretely, but weeping shamelessly as a grieving man should.

Would they hail me as a saviour or curse me as a destroyer? I doubted I would ever know.

I risked a trip across the room to rescue Luke's photo, hearing glass crunch under my feet. There was a faint greasiness on everything. It was like the skin of the Stench. With this flimsy film the Stench was growing itself a fungoid epidermis.

I put Luke's picture in my pocket, and fingering the lighter that sat in beside the picture, moved on alone into the corridor.

There were bits of Softy scattered from the door to the trapdoor hole. Something had shattered the Rottweiler into a thousand pieces; all I had to do was follow the bits to get there. There was no one around, no welcoming party from Josie and Adrian, no sounds from upstairs, just a huge cathedral silence. I couldn't even hear any sounds from the kitchen behind me, where I had left Kahu and Rachel facing each other.

I stepped into the silence and nothing happened, nobody leapt out at me from the shadows.

I followed the dog gore to the edge of the trapdoor hole and looked down, unscrewing the lid to the petrol at the same time. I saw nothing but the same fluid, absorbent surface, the same utter darkness.

There was no way I was going to take a peek down there now.

The Stench eased from the hole, the yellow puke-like gas reminding me of the pustules on Carpenter's dead face. A vomiting ectoplasm of muddy colours.

I proceeded to sprinkle the petrol around the hole like some pagan goddess sprinkling a sacred blessing, murmuring an incantation of words to purify the world; all that was needed was the flame to ignite the wind.

Up out of the hole in the floor, emerging like a reflection through glass, came Adrian, with Josie riding piggyback like a Siamese twin. Their bodies were half in death and half out of it as if they were wading waist deep in a shadowy pool. Her fingernails were raking Adrian's shoulders but making no impression, just a momentary phosphorescent flare. They were both somehow slicked down, smooth and hairless, breathing through their blood like babies in the womb.

Adrian lifted up his head like a cat that's been slurping cream.

'Baaaby!' he said, sliding like an otter out of that cube of darkness to sit up bedside me on the floor. 'It's Baby,' he said again to Josie as if she didn't have eyes. He made it sound as if he'd been waiting a lifetime for me to arrive. The darkness below threw a mercury reflection across his face. Grey blood dripped down from his shoulders where Josie had scratched them and fell through the open trapdoor in slow, dirty tears.

I sprinkled more petrol around and said nothing. All I had to do was compete the task; that's all I had to do, all I had to think about. I didn't have to think about the death that was stalking me now through my head, or the now pulsing hole in my brain. I didn't have to think about how long it would be before I tipped myself down the trapdoor forever in final surrender.

'Have you brought me anything, Baby, some hot fish & chips?' Josie asked, bobbing up and down in it as if the great darkness was nothing more sinister than her home sauna. Her voice was rich with an old heartbreak, 'Or at least still warm.'

But Adrian wasn't fooled. He saw the lighter in my hand. He made a cautionary signal to Josie.

'Baby,' he said in his most wheedling voice. 'It's just a game. You've got carried away with it, the way you always do. You've got the wrong end of the stick. We're just having some fun. Just playing ghosts and dead people.'

'That's all,' Josie said, her voice like a sponge cake with too much icing sugar. 'You've gone apeshit, Baby. You're on a rampage. What fun.'

Adrian grabbed her hand and squeezed it into a painful fist. He knew how to handle his crazy sister, how to talk me around, Josie was only a nuisance. Josie could fuck everything up if she were not careful. At the same time he made all the appearance of settling into a brotherly talk with me, prepared to discuss until doomsday how wrong I was, how badly off the mark, what a big little moron I turned out to be after all.

Most of the petrol was used up. I had the lighter ready, my thumb fumbling for the position.

'I'm sorry for everything we've done, the way we've mocked you, and haven't treated you like a real person. I'm sorry. I'm sorry. I'm sorry for all those years I stood on your voice and didn't let you speak. I'm sorry because I was a bully and I was wrong.' His gaze was full of concern. 'I've been a real bastard.'

'I'm sorry too,' Josie said in a contrite voice, sliding her body in behind Adrian's. 'I've been a real bitch.'

'We'll never bully you again,' they said together. They were like brother and sister, they spoke through each other's mouths. Breathed each other's snot through their nostrils. At the same time they both looked down into the mouth of the trapdoor, hinged to the darkness of the square mouth below.

Adrian held his hands out towards me, and smiled, just like my brother. 'I'd better have the lighter,' he said regretfully.

Behind him, still in the sickly caress of thick shadows, Josie screeched, not so much a throat sound but a noise like glass on glass. It woke me up or nearly did, enough to remind my thumb that it had to move on the lighter, to turn the flint and grate the spark.

There was petrol vaporising the air like lemonade bubbles in a freshly opened bottle but my body had grown enormous, all my limbs were inflated and my thumb was stuck on the flint like a great sausage.

'She's flipped her lid,' Josie said in an undertone to Adrian. Her face had been sucked out to the point where nothing was left of it but stretched skin and eyes.

As Adrian stood up he changed from the sleek hairless demon of the Stench into something resembling my brother. His clothes were looking somewhat worse for wear and his hair stood out on end as if he'd had an electric shock. He was wearing his old, roguish, Huck Finn grin with a touch of Gorebag Ironclaw.

'C'on Baby. You know how you imagine things, y' know, build things up out of whack, makin a big fantasy out of everything.'

I had enough control over my huge rubbery limbs to retreat a few steps, allowing more petrol to dribble out.

Adrian took a few paces forward. 'Remember that time you thought that

Brad was in love with you.' He was struggling to keep his grin under control. 'You thought everything he did was because of you. Y' made a great big thing out of it, remember? Y' went right out of kilter.'

I remembered.

Behind him, Josie too transformed herself back into a skinny waif teenager with straggly blonde rats' tails and an inane giggle.

But she wasn't giggling now. Neither of them were. They were just two frightened young people out of their depth, not knowing how to handle the situation, the loony sister run amok. Just two ordinary kids.

'You can stay here with us,' Josie said as if some obscure domestic arrangements were all settled. 'I won't mind. Truly.'

'Me neither,' Adrian said, snapping up her lead. 'There's lots of beds.'

His eyes lit up as he laughed, wanting me to laugh along. Josie did a bit of a giggle. I was expected to honk back and everything would be all right.

'Really, Baby,' he said, trying to look relaxed, trying not to look at the lighter and my thumb resting on the flint. 'We've got to talk about this, talk it over, please.'

That did make me want to laugh. When had he ever allowed anything I said to make any sense? What patience had he ever had with my stumbling tongue?

Josie was shifting around behind him getting ready to make a spring, all coiled up like a tight wire. He was covering for her, trying to keep me listening, pouring out his insidious talk.

'Baby,' he said in alarm, 'Don't!' He lifted up his arm in terror as I showered both of them with the remaining petrol.

'I told you...' Josie said. She couldn't make her spring because she had petrol in her eyes and was busy clawing her face.

My sausage thumb came to life and sprang the lever. Nothing happened.

There was a bit of lint stuck in the jet.

I was pulling it away with elephant fingernails when an enormous sound descended from the roof, an earsplitting clattering and whistling that made the timbers of the old hospital shake.

A shaft pierced the coloured glass above us, sending a crazy red eye skidding across the floor hot with light.

A helicopter.

I was shrinking to human proportions and could move my body; my thumb found the lever again and snapped it down.

A thin flame sprang up. And held steady.

Adrian was clawing his way towards me as I held the lighter under the empty plastic bottle.

It sucked itself eagerly into flame. Plastic and petrol dripped onto the floor.

Adrian desperately tried to back pedal, falling over Josie who was clinging like a child onto his back again. She was screeching at me like a parrot.

I dropped the bottle to the floor and the flame licked along the path I'd made to the trapdoor, hit the petrol-sodden timbers and gushed upwards.

Adrian and Josie screamed together as the fire rippled over their bodies. I watched them melt into bone as they scrabbled for the trapdoor. Briefly, Adrian emerged on his hands and knees, his eyeballs on fire, his tongue turned to charcoal.

There was a scream behind me and I turned to see Rachel and Kahu, with Mitch and Maro following behind, racing towards us. Rachel moved with firm steady steps. She walked across the floor of fire and did not get burned. I suddenly understood the miracle that was keeping her upright. She was reaching out towards me the way you reach out to the dying. She was calling out to me in her own language, giving me another name. She was trying to tell me something desperately important.

She said she'd be there for me at the end, and she was. I reached out to Rachel. I wanted to live. I would live in the City of Gates, which would be healed, with Rachel forever.

Suddenly all around us timbers exploded into flame and the windows blew out. A piece of red glass from the alcove window was hurled up into the open sky, bright, like a piece of transparent flesh.

I took one last look at the trapdoor. The hole was gouting flame the way a fresh wound gouts blood. A black fire rose like a slug coming out of its hole; it was the Stench going up in a great ugly roar. I saw Mitch and Kahu go down overpowered as the flames ate into the heart of it, but Maro wasn't daunted. He was still in his rugby shorts and striped top and he ran for Josie like a player running for touchdown. He got as far as pulling a flaming mess from the lip of the trapdoor but that's as far as he got. The black fire sucked him and Josie in together, lifting them up in the air in its ferocity where they hung in the vortex like burning torches.

Mitch had come to a little and was trying to drag the scorched Kahu back, but her eyes were fixed on Rachel who was unconcerned by the heat or the Stench; the boards beneath her feet were bloodied with flame but she walked calmly through the conflagration in her funeral dress as if nothing could touch her, so strong was her love even in death.

She was coming to save me.

◽

There was a tremendous roaring in my ears as I opened my eyes. I saw the sound passing in windmill rushes across the window of the helicopter.

There was Hikitarua, vanishing away below. The hospital, a fountain of flame beneath a black claw of smoke, was followed by the rest of the town, with spots of fire breaking out everywhere like a rash. The norwester had got up again and the flames were leaping from house to house in random jumps. People were streaming like ants onto the streets. Highway 5 was lighting up.

Hikitarua was burning.

I caught a brief glimpse of hurried activity which somehow looked dreamlike and slow, of police cars and fire engines. I struggled to try and see more but the view was whirled away from me as the helicopter banked.

A soft hand restrained me. Light, delicate fingers were encased in a see-through rubber glove.

'You're going to be all right,' a reassuring voice said. Beside me there was a nurse. She was wearing a surgical mask, the same as Carpenter. Above it her forehead was smooth, her eyes kind. Those kind eyes found mine. They were filled with compassion.

She began to unwind the singed bandage on my forehead.

She said, 'Don't worry, we're taking you to hospital.'

End

Also by Mike Johnson

Novels
Driftdead
Lethal Dose
Zombie in a Spacesuit
Hold My Teeth While I Teach You to Dance
Travesty
Counterpart
Dumbshow
Antibody Positive
Lear: The Shakespeare Company Plays Lear at Babylon

Shorter Fiction
Confessions of a Cockroach/Headstone
Back in the Day: Tales of NZ's Own Paradise Island
Foreigners

Poetry
The Raising Light Trilogy
Ladder With No Rungs, Illustrated by Leila Lees
Two Lines and a Garden, Illustrated by Leila Lees
To Beatrice: Where We Crossed the Line
Vertical Harp: The Selected Poems of Li He
Treasure Hunt
Standing Wave
From a Woman in Mt Eden Prison & Drawing Lessons
The Palanquin Ropes

Non-Fiction
Angel of Compassion

Children's Books
Flippity Fluppity Flop, Illustrated by Daniela Gast
A House With No Windows, Illustrated by Ingrid Berzins
Kenni and the Roof Slide, Illustrated by Jennifer Rackham
Taniwha. Illustrated by Jennifer Rackham

Lightning Source UK Ltd.
Milton Keynes UK
UKHW041422081221
395308UK00002B/342